**"OH!" IT CAME OUT LIKE A SMALL GASP,
A TINY PUFF OF AIR.
SHE FELT HER KNEES WEAKEN
AS HIS DARK EYES MET HERS.
"IT'S YOU."**

She thought she saw the corner of his mouth twitch, and, for the briefest of seconds, his eyes narrowed.

"*Ja*, it's me," he muttered in a low voice. As he stood on the other side of the counter, he placed his hands on the edge. "And I take it that's you."

Was he teasing her? Myrna blinked, trying to determine whether he was being sarcastic or playful. Nothing about his expression indicated either. "May . . . may I help you with something then?"

"I've come for some supplies, *ja*," he said at last, reaching into his pocket for a folded piece of paper. "But before you help me with those, I have something I need to say."

She swallowed.

He leveled his gaze at her. "It's kind of you to step in to help me with my *kinner*. It's an unfortunate situation for all of us."

Unfortunate situation. What a strange choice of words, she thought. She wondered what he meant by that. Was he referring to his sister-in-law leaving, she herself helping out, or the matter of his wife dying in the first place? Perhaps a bit of all three, she decided.

"The *kinner* have been through a lot," he continued, his voice softening. "Some of it preventable. But painful. Grief no parent wants their little ones to experience."

~~The~~ ~~expression~~ ~~on~~ ~~his~~ ~~face~~ ~~sh~~owed evidence of his enc~~~~ ~~~~~~~~ ~~~~~~~~ Myrna felt her heart bre~~~~ ~~~~~~~~ ~~~~~~~~ ~~be~~tter plans for him, she~~~~ ~~~~~~~~ ~~~~~~s~~ life.

Also by Sarah Price

Belle: An Amish Retelling of Beauty and the Beast

Ella: An Amish Retelling of Cinderella

Sadie: An Amish Retelling of Snow White

Published by Kensington Publishing Corporation

The Amish
Cookie Club

SARAH
PRICE

ZEBRA BOOKS
KENSINGTON PUBLISHING CORP.
www.kensingtonbooks.com

ZEBRA BOOKS are published by

Kensington Publishing Corp.
119 West 40th Street
New York, NY 10018

Copyright © 2019 by Price Productions, LLC

All rights reserved. No part of this book may be reproduced in any form or by any means without the prior written consent of the Publisher, excepting brief quotes used in reviews.

To the extent that the image or images on the cover of this book depict a person or persons, such person or persons are merely models, and are not intended to portray any character or characters featured in the book.

If you purchased this book without a cover you should be aware that this book is stolen property. It was reported as "unsold and destroyed" to the Publisher and neither the Author nor the Publisher has received any payment for this "stripped book."

All Kensington titles, imprints, and distributed lines are available at special quantity discounts for bulk purchases for sales promotion, premiums, fund-raising, educational, or institutional use.

Special book excerpts or customized printings can also be created to fit specific needs. For details, write or phone the office of the Kensington Sales Manager: Attn.: Sales Department. Kensington Publishing Corp., 119 West 40th Street, New York, NY 10018. Phone: 1-800-221-2647.

Zebra and the Z logo Reg. U.S. Pat. & TM Off.

First Printing: June 2019
ISBN-13: 978-1-4201-4917-3
ISBN-10: 1-4201-4917-2

ISBN-13: 978-1-4201-4920-3 (eBook)
ISBN-10: 1-4201-4920-2 (eBook)

10 9 8 7 6 5 4 3 2 1

Printed in the United States of America

Chapter One

The smell of freshly baked cinnamon rolls always reminded Edna Esh of her mother.

Lifting the pan toward her face, Edna shut her eyes and inhaled deeply, enjoying the warm steam that brushed against her cheeks as she savored the scent of freshly ground cinnamon.

In the silence of the moment, she thought back to the days of her youth. Saturdays. Those were the mornings her mother baked cinnamon rolls at her father's farm outside of Seyberts, Indiana. Farm life was always busy, but, even though all the children were home for the day, Saturday mornings were less chaotic for her mother. No school lunches to prepare, no faces to wash, no children to hurry off to school. With her brood filling the house with laughter, Edna's mother was always in her glory. Back then, her gift to her children was those gloriously wonderful cinnamon rolls which began every weekend like a tasty note of love.

"I'll never understand you." The teasing voice of her husband interrupted the moment. "Baking sweets before your friends visit so you can bake more sweets!"

Opening her eyes, Edna smiled at Elmer. For almost

thirty years, he'd been her husband, partner, and—most importantly—her best friend. She watched as he stood in the doorway, kicking off his work boots—one, two . . . each landing with a loud clomp on the mudroom floor— before entering the kitchen. He didn't seem to notice the clumps of dirt which fell from the soles. Sighing, Edna made a mental note to sweep the floor before her friends arrived.

He had already removed his hat, which had left his salt-and-pepper hair pressed flat against his head. "Seems you have those gals over more for visiting than for baking!" he teased.

"Oh now, Elmer!" Despite the truth to his statement, Edna protested. "You know I like to welcome the girls with something special to nibble on during their visit."

Elmer shuffled his stockinged feet across the floor and peered into the pan, careful to keep his long beard from touching the baked goods. Like his wife, he, too, breathed in the aroma. "Mmm!" Teasingly, he reached a finger toward the pan. "How about I sample one?"

But Edna was quicker than he was. After twenty-nine years of marriage, she'd anticipated his attempt to taste the frosting on one of the rolls. She swooped in and shifted the pan from his grasp. "I do believe we were both standing in the same room when the doctor told you no sweets, Elmer Esh!" she said as she set it onto a rack near the stove to cool.

"Oh, pssh!" He waved his hand dismissively at her. "What do doctors know about anything anyway?"

Edna laughed, her dark, almond-shaped eyes crinkling into half-moons. She couldn't help but look at her husband with tenderness. How hard it must be for him to give up sweets! But the doctor's orders were quite clear: avoid sugar. Perhaps even worse than giving up desserts and treats was that Elmer had been forced to give up sugar in his coffee. While Edna didn't mind drinking her coffee black, Elmer fussed about that almost as much as he fussed about giving up cookies and pies.

"Well, I sure do think Dr. Graham knows a spell more than you do about your heart!"

Elmer scowled. "Bah!"

"Now don't you 'bah' me," she scolded playfully.

He turned to the sink and began to wash his hands. "So what're you girls making today anyway?"

She was surprised that he asked that question. Whenever her friends Mary Ropp, Wilma Schwartz, and Verna Bontrager came over, they always baked the same thing. "Why, cookies, of course!"

Twice a month, the four women gathered to bake different types of cookies for the fellowship meal that followed the Sunday worship service. They had started the tradition when Wilma's twins, Rachel and Ella Mae, turned sixteen and began their *rumschpringe*. Wilma had taken quite a turn, falling into a blue mood without her youngest daughters spending their free time at home. An empty house began evolving into an empty heart.

The truth was that *none* of them had little ones at home anymore. The realization that this phase of motherhood had ended and a new one had begun distressed all of them, but none more so than Wilma.

It was Edna who came up with the idea to meet on the Fridays before church Sundays. She'd sat down, written each of her three best friends a letter and detailed her idea for gathering twice a month to bake cookies. After all, she had written, they needed each other for support, and what better way to provide that than meeting on a regular basis? Besides, who didn't love cookies?

And there was no better way to give each other support

than to bake together. They would fill cookie sheet after cookie sheet with freshly made dough—usually sugar or oatmeal cookies but sometimes they'd choose another equally delicious recipe—and bundle them up in storage containers to bring to their respective worship services.

All three of the women readily agreed with Edna's plan. After all, it was a great reason not only to spend time together, but to support each other as well.

Elmer and Edna lived on an old farm that was farther from town, while the other three women lived closer to Shipshewana. Only Verna and Mary lived in the same church district, so the four of them rarely saw one another except for these two precious Fridays each month.

"No sense in trying to talk you into making those oatmeal cookies, I reckon?"

Edna laughed at her husband. "*Nee*, Elmer. You know that the little ones always ask for sugar cookies. It's expected, I suppose."

"Woe to the *kinner* who prefer oatmeal cookies to sugar cookies!" Elmer groaned. "Well then, I best be making myself scarce then. Wouldn't want to get in the way of you womenfolk." He dried his hands on a dish towel, then draped it over the sink. "You need anything from town?"

"*Ja*, I do!" Edna scurried over to the breakfront and opened a drawer. "Annie's supposed to be finished with that quilt back she's piecing for me."

Elmer raised an eyebrow. "Another quilt? Land's sake, Edna. You have the energy of ten men."

She ignored the compliment. "I'm making this one for Jacob and Mary's baby. Might you stop by Jennifer's shop and see if Annie dropped it off? If so, give Jennifer this envelope and bring home the package." She didn't wait for his response as she handed him a plain white envelope. "And don't lose that! It's cash."

Elmer frowned. "One time, Edna. Just one time. Will you ever let me live that down?"

She smiled and leaned over, placing a soft kiss on his cheek. "Never."

"That's what I thought." He slid the envelope into his back pocket and then patted it as if to reassure his wife that it was secure. "Safe and sound."

Edna watched as he crossed the room and disappeared into the bedroom. She suspected he was going to change his shirt, which was dirty from tending to the livestock that morning.

She worried about him. He was looking older and more tired as of late. Edna knew that he worked far too hard for far too little. It was increasingly difficult to make ends meet on the farm. Why, her cousin Norma's husband had recently given up his dairy herd because there just wasn't any money in it anymore. But Elmer insisted on continuing to raise cows, just like his father and grandfather and great-grandfather before him.

To make ends meet, Edna cooked for *Englische* tourists during the busy seasons—usually from May until October. Over the winter, she took a break and focused on making quilts. After all, when the weather changed, the tourists weren't as plentiful as during the warmer months.

Still, the lack of that extra income in the wintertime meant Elmer had to work even harder. Despite enjoying her winter reprieve, Edna was glad that springtime had returned and, beginning in mid-May, she'd start hosting *Englische* meals again in her farmhouse on Thursdays, Fridays, and Saturdays.

Living on a farm was always a struggle.

While Edna knew that they would be all right, she wasn't quite so certain that their eldest son, John, would fare the same.

With three sons, and no daughters, the farm was destined to pass down to a fifth generation of Esh boys. However, only John expressed any interest in farming, even though he worked part-time at the auction house in Shipshewana. The two younger boys, Jonas and Jeremiah, weren't settled into careers yet, although Jonas appeared to favor construction. They much preferred hanging out with their friends and traveling to different places—camping or hunting being their favorite things to do. Neither of them had yet to take his kneeling vow, either.

It was a great cause of concern for both Edna and Elmer.

The bedroom door opened, and Elmer stepped out. He wore a clean light blue shirt, and his hair was freshly combed.

"Still got my envelope?" she asked, half joking.

Elmer patted his back pocket for a second time. "Sure do."

"Send my best to Jennifer, and if you see John in town, remind him that he's to stop at Yoders' for some cheese. I need it for Sunday. I promised to make my cup cheese for the fellowship meal."

"Quilt. Cheese. Got it." He slipped on his boots, not bothering to tie them, and grabbed his hat. "Reckon I'll be home about four, so you've plenty of time to enjoy your visit with the girls."

She gave him a warm smile. Some husbands might grumble about having women take over the kitchen twice a month to meet with friends, but not Elmer. He'd always been kind and considerate like that. Perhaps it was because he grew up with five sisters. It was the only regret that Edna ever had: not having a daughter. But God had chosen for her to be a mother of sons, and she wasn't about to question His plan.

A few minutes later, she heard the horse and buggy as it rolled down the gravel driveway toward the main road. With the house empty again and the cinnamon rolls cooling, Edna took a quick look around to make certain everything was just so. It wouldn't do to have even one thing out of place. The last thing she wanted was for anyone to think her house was unkempt.

It was just after twelve thirty when the black buggy rolled into the driveway. Hearing the wheels rumbling on the gravel, Edna felt that familiar surge of joy. She hurried to the window and peered outside, smiling when she saw the horse stop by the barn.

As usual, Verna had driven, stopping to pick up Mary first and then Wilma. And, as usual, the first woman to emerge from the buggy was Wilma. Her dark green dress still had flour marks on the sides, probably from baking fresh bread for her family that morning. Her white prayer *kapp* covered her graying hair, but a few strands had sprung free and poked out from the back of the stiff white head covering.

Quickly, Edna hurried through the kitchen door and onto the porch, eagerly waiting to greet her friends.

"*Wilkum!* And hurry! The cinnamon rolls are still warm from this morning!"

Wilma didn't wait for Verna or Mary. She hurried up the walkway toward Edna. "Cinnamon buns? Why, I should've known better than to have a slice of pie after my noon meal!" With the other two ladies out of earshot, she leaned over and whispered, "Prepare yourself. It's going to be another one of *those* afternoons."

Edna's eyes widened and she immediately looked over Wilma's shoulders. "Verna?"

"*Ja*," was the whispered answer.

"Oh help."

"And this time it's a doozy."

Edna took a deep breath. If she had started the regular baking gatherings for support when Wilma was going through her blue spell, they had all maintained it for Verna's sanity.

There was no more time for whispered exchanges as both Verna and Mary headed up the walkway, too close for Edna and Wilma to risk further discussion of the matter.

It always struck Edna how similar Verna and Mary looked. Today was no exception. If ever there were two long-lost twins, Verna and Mary were surely they. Of course, Mary was a year younger than Verna and was a second cousin to her rather than a sister. But they shared a similar petite stature and dark brown hair that seemed to defy aging, for neither one had any gray hairs yet.

As she neared the porch, Mary pushed her glasses back onto the bridge of her nose. "Not a day too soon, let me tell you. I was counting the hours until Friday," she said, "starting on Tuesday!"

Edna glanced at Wilma, who merely shrugged.

Verna caught her breath, a little noise escaping her pursed lips. "Oh, Mary, I never even thought to ask how Bethany's doing. Why! I was so wrapped up in my Myrna's latest troubles that I neglected to inquire about yours!"

"Well, I reckon you've got your hands full with that fiery redheaded *dochder* of yours," Mary replied. "Can't say I blame you for fretting over her."

The downcast expression on Verna's face spoke of her disappointment in her daughter. "That's no excuse."

Edna knew that she needed to take swift control of the situation or they'd have Verna or Mary—or mayhaps even both!—in tears. Between Verna's constant need for approval and Mary's worrying, it wasn't unusual for someone to wind up crying.

"*Kum* now. Let's sit inside. I've a fresh pot of coffee brewing. We can discuss what's happened once we've a hot cup to dunk our cinnamon buns in!"

She guided them inside, catching Wilma's woeful gaze. Usually during their gatherings, the four women laughed and talked, sharing stories about their families. Occasionally there were a few tears over little disagreements or worries. As of late, it seemed that Verna was having the worst of it with her daughter, Myrna. But today, clearly Mary needed to vent as well.

Edna prayed she'd made enough cinnamon rolls to get them through *both* women's complaints.

By the time everyone had settled in and begun mixing the batches of sugar, flour, and other ingredients, both Mary and Verna had relaxed a bit. For this, Edna thanked the good Lord. She had been looking forward to a fun afternoon with her friends. Since it had started out with a litany of complaints, though, it was apt to be anything but.

"Your *haus* sure is quiet," Wilma said as she mixed the sugar cookie dough with her hands. "Can't remember the last time I had such a luxury."

Edna laughed. "Your twins still at it?"

"Oh, wouldn't you know it!" Wilma squished the dough between her fingers, then began forming a ball. "Rachel and Ella Mae just about wear me out with their constant bickering." She patted the dough ball and left it in the bowl to rest. "Can't wait for them to get married and move on out!"

"Oh now, Wilma!" Edna clicked her tongue. "You say that now, but we all know you'll be feeling the blues when that time comes."

"Hmph. Don't be so sure of that." Wilma wagged a plump finger in Edna's direction. "When your boys finally settle down—"

"Finally," Edna repeated good-naturedly.

"—you'll be wondering why you were in such a hurry for them to get married!"

Edna rolled her eyes. "What. Ever." But there was a teasing tone to her enunciated words.

"I'd take the bickering of your two girls over the deafening silence from my Bethany," Mary offered in a soft voice. "Why, I've never seen such a deathly shy girl in my life. Just the other day, I asked her to run into town to fetch me some cheese from Yoders' Store and she nigh 'bout fainted!"

Edna clucked her tongue again. It was such a shame that Bethany wasn't more outgoing. Not only was she a pretty girl, but she was also a hard worker. She'd make someone a right good wife, if only a man could break through the wall of silence that surrounded her. But she'd always been a quiet child, and her shyness hadn't changed now that she was nineteen.

"I don't know what to do with her," Mary continued, her voice full of concern. "It's just not natural to be so introverted."

"Be glad *your dochder* is not extroverted," Verna countered. "Like mine."

Immediately, the energy in the room shifted from Mary

to Verna. Edna braced herself for what she knew was undoubtedly coming: another Myrna story.

"That girl," Verna began, shaking her head. "She's never going to change."

Taking a deep breath, Edna pinched a piece of the dough ball and began rolling it between her palms. "What did Myrna do this time?"

A scowl crossed Verna's face. "She went and got fired. Again."

"Again?"

"*Ja*, that's right. Again!"

Edna shut her eyes. "Oh help."

Tossing her hands in the air, Verna's eyes widened. "She's been hired and fired from every shop in Shipshewana!"

Despite the seriousness of the conversation, Edna couldn't help but chuckle. "That's a bit of an exaggeration, don't you think?"

Verna began counting on her fingers. "The auction *haus*. Yoders' Store. The tea shop in the Red Barn. The theater. The quilt shop. And now the grocery store!" She made a face. "No one gets fired from the grocery store!"

Wilma rolled her eyes. "No one except your *dochder*."

"Exactly!"

Edna placed the ball of dough onto the cookie sheet so that Mary could press it down with the bottom of a canning jar. "What happened this time?"

"She scolded an overweight man for buying chocolate and soda. Said it was unhealthy for him. She refused to ring up his order!" Verna sighed. "Who does such a thing?"

Edna swallowed the laugh that threatened to escape from her lips. She could only imagine Myrna shaking her finger at the man as she gave him a tongue-lashing. "Oh my," she managed to say with a straight face.

Wilma made a noise of disapproval. "Certainly has her opinions, don't she now? Comes from being so spoiled, I reckon."

Edna shot Wilma a stern look.

"Well, you must admit that Myrna *had* good intentions," Mary offered in defense of the girl.

"Those good intentions just cost her another job!" Verna grabbed some more dough from the bowl and began rolling it in the palms of her hands. "Who will hire her now? Her reputation is downright awful. I'm sure all the store owners in town have heard about her by this time." She sighed. "I told her she's going to have to start doing childcare or cleaning *haus* for the *Englischers*. But I'm not certain that would be such a good idea, either. I can't imagine what she'd do if the *kinner* talked back to her or the *Englische* tried telling her how they wanted their *haus* cleaned."

Edna knew what would happen: Myrna would certainly explode. At twenty-one years of age, Myrna wasn't about to let *anyone* tell her what to do or how to do it. "Whatever are you going to do with that child?"

The expression on Verna's face shifted from distress to exasperation. "Short of putting duct tape over her mouth, I'm not sure what can be done."

Mary clicked her tongue and shook her head. "Yours talks too much and mine doesn't talk at all!"

"If only we could find her a right *gut* job," Edna said with a sigh. "One that would embrace her"—she paused, searching for the right word that wouldn't offend—"peculiarities. That would just solve all your problems, Verna."

"From your lips to God's ears," Verna quipped. "I'll just keep praying for something to calm her tongue a bit. Otherwise, she'll never settle down and get married."

Even though Edna believed in miracles, she suspected that God would have to work overtime on this one.

A few minutes later, after the cookie dough was placed on the baking sheets and into the oven, the women moved over to the sitting area near the back window that overlooked the pastures and fields. As they settled into the chairs and sofa, silence engulfed the room. Shortly, the only noise was the gentle clicking of knitting needles and the soft sound of yarn being pulled from skeins. With MayFest only a few weeks away, Edna knew they had their work cut out for them. Not only were they each donating ten baby blankets to raise money for Amish Aid; the four women had agreed to work the table, selling their goods throughout the day of the event. Anything Amish always sold better when an Amish woman was there to sell it.

As she crocheted, Edna's thoughts drifted to each of the women seated in her sitting room. Years of friendship had not been dimmed by marriages, new homes in new church districts, or the raising of many children. *Very different children*, she reminded herself. Throughout the years, they'd kept in touch, helping each other through the good times and the bad.

They'd always been there for each other.

"Why should that stop now?"

Mary looked up, her fingers stopping in mid-chain. "What did you say, Edna?"

Surprised, Edna's eyes widened. Had she said that out loud? Feeling a bit foolish, she gave a slight shake of her head as if to remove the cobwebs that clearly had gathered in her mind. "I was just thinking," she began, trying to hide her embarrassment at having spoken her thoughts, "that we've been through a lot over the years. We've helped each other in times of trouble, haven't we?"

Wilma, always the boisterous one, slapped her hand on

her knee as she loudly proclaimed, "That's what friends do, *ja*?"

"Well, seems to me that the three of you have some worries right now," Edna continued, carefully choosing her words. "Your *dochders* all have their own little quirks, wouldn't you say?"

Mary pressed her lips together and reached up to push her round reader glasses, which she always wore when she crocheted, farther up the bridge of her nose. "I much prefer to think of Bethany as unique." She looked up, peering over the rim of her glasses. "An individual."

Wilma gave her a mocking frown. "She has her quirks, as do my two, that's for sure and certain. Only *yours* won't open her mouth, while Verna's and mine won't shut theirs!"

Swallowing the laugh that threatened to slip through her lips, Edna nodded. "Whatever you want to call them, your *dochders* do present some interesting challenges when it comes to finding a suitor, wouldn't you say? Mayhaps it's time we came up with a plan and helped each other out a bit."

When she surveyed their reactions, Edna found the other women staring back at her, blank expressions on their faces. She remained silent, letting her words sink in and waiting for one of them to speak first.

After a few drawn-out seconds, it was Verna who cleared her throat and leaned forward. "You mean as in matchmaking?"

Mary's expression changed to horror.

"Oh, I couldn't!" she exclaimed.

Wilma laughed. "You can, and you will if you ever want a *boppli* from Bethany!"

Mary looked away.

Edna tried to explain. "Mayhaps we start with Myrna. After all, she's the most pressing problem at the moment—"

"Not if you lived in my *haus*!" Wilma interrupted.

"—so I say we find her a job. A *new* type of job. Perhaps as a mother's helper or something of that sort."

Verna moistened her lips as if tasting the words. "Mother's helper."

"Surely among the three of us"—Edna gestured to Mary and Wilma—"we can find a young mother who might need some help."

"Or mayhaps an elderly woman," Mary offered. "They often seek help with tending to the *haus* and cooking."

Verna made a face. "I don't see Myrna being one to put herself in either of those positions."

Wilma rolled her eyes. "Oh, Verna! That girl's been coddled too much. Time for her to learn how to be a caregiver," she declared. "Mayhaps then a young man will take notice of her."

Edna shot Wilma a warning look. "We all have our imperfections," Edna said softly. "'And why beholdest thou the mote that is in thy brother's eye, but perceivest not the beam that is in thine own eye?'"

"Hmph."

Verna turned her shoulders, just enough so that she faced Edna but blocked Wilma from view. "Do you think this might work?" She glanced at Mary. "I mean, a job in an Amish *haus* might be just what Myrna needs. Less interaction with *Englischers*—"

"They always ask such silly questions!" Wilma quipped.

"—or dealing with business things. And she can develop some other useful skills that might, indeed, improve her temperament."

Edna lifted her chin, feeling just a little pride at having

thought of the idea. "It'll work, for sure and certain. No one knows these young women better than we do. And if they can't find their way on their own, then surely we have to lead them. Now, let's keep our eyes and ears open and see if we hear of any opportunities. If we can get Myrna a job where she can foster her maternal skills, maybe then she will settle down a bit and start courting someone!"

Chapter Two

Verna ran the hard brush along the flank of the horse, barely noticing the dirt and dust that rose to the top of the mare's brown coat. Her mind was elsewhere and certainly not on grooming the animal. Instead, she was thinking about the conversation at Edna's house that afternoon.

It was embarrassing enough that Myrna kept losing jobs. But to take advice from Wilma, of all people? Why, *her* daughters were almost as incorrigible as Myrna! At least Myrna had good intentions, unlike Rachel and Ella Mae, who just bickered all the time. She should have known better than to say one word about Myrna. In hindsight, she knew that she should've kept her mouth shut and remained mute on the topic. At least around Wilma.

So opinionated, that Wilma. If she ever wondered why her two daughters were so competitive, she had only to look in the mirror!

"Easy there, Verna."

Startled, she glanced over her shoulder and, when she saw her husband, frowned. "Easy there what, Simon?"

He gestured toward the horse. "Gonna groom that mare bald, you keep up that pace."

Verna dropped the hand that held the brush and with her other one touched the horse's back. "Sorry, ole girl."

Simon stepped forward and took the brush from her. He reached out and began to gently run it over the horse, who responded with a soft nicker. "Everything okay today at Edna's?"

For the briefest of seconds, she debated not telling Simon. Surely she would sound petty and childish, complaining about Wilma's thoughtless comments. Knowing her friend the way that she did, Verna realized that Wilma meant no harm. She sighed. Why share her aggravation with her husband?

But after mulling it over, Verna decided that she couldn't keep her bruised feelings—or the event that had caused them—from him.

"*Nee*, not entirely," she answered slowly.

"Oh?" Simon's expression changed, his face etched with concern. "That's unusual. You usually have such a right *gut* time with your women friends."

"Not today," Verna admitted.

"So, what happened?"

Verna took a deep breath and exhaled slowly. She knew that he'd be unhappy when she confided in him. But would he be unhappy with Wilma or with the fact that Verna had shared their daughter's woes with her friends? "I told them about Myrna losing her job," she admitted, her voice soft and full of remorse. "I know I shouldn't have, Simon, but I needed to talk with someone about it."

He pursed his lips in a thoughtful way. "I reckon that's understandable."

Leave it to Simon to be so tolerant, she thought. Other husbands might reprimand their wives for sharing such personal matters with others. Most Amish people liked to keep family problems close to the heart and far from the mouth. She was already disappointed in herself. It helped that Simon didn't see reason to add to her burden.

Reaching up to scratch the back of his neck, Simon cocked his head and looked at her. "Still, I'm not sure how sharing that would ruin your gathering. Seems a bit extreme, unless something else happened."

"*Ja*, you're right." Her shoulders drooped, and she stared at the ground. "Wilma made a comment about Myrna and it just didn't sit well with me."

"Ah, Wilma." He made a noise and shook his head. "Leave it to Wilma to have something to say. And now I'm curious, Verna. What, exactly, was that comment?"

Taking a deep breath, Verna forced herself to speak. "She said that's what happens when a *dochder* is spoiled."

For a moment, Simon didn't say anything. His silence caused Verna to look up and she noticed that his right eyelid twitched, just a little. Surely he was as bothered as she had been by Wilma's comment. Yes, Myrna might be treated a bit differently from their other children, but to call her spoiled? That statement just wasn't true. Verna couldn't help but wonder why Wilma would think so. Even worse, she wondered if other people thought Myrna was spoiled as well.

"Is that right?" Simon said at last.

Verna pressed her lips together. "You don't think others believe that, do you?"

He reached up, removed his hat, and wiped his forehead with the back of his arm. "Seems to me that Wilma sure has an awful lot to say regarding something she knows little about. It also seems to me that she should be focusing on her own two *dochders*, who, if I know one thing at all about them, are rather spirited and quarrelsome young women, aren't they now?"

Despite the truth in Simon's words, Verna could only focus on one thing. She gave him a pleading look as she asked, "But Myrna! She's not spoiled, is she?"

Simon frowned. "Now, why would you even ask such a question, Verna?"

"Well, she *does* get away with a lot." Verna wrung her hands. "Have we been too lenient with her? Coddled her?"

"Spoiled? Coddled?" His expression sobered as he returned his hat to his head and, with his other hand, pointed the horse brush at his wife. "We've treated her no different from our other *kinner* and not one of them has turned out poorly. Myrna's just a bit more forthcoming with her opinions and it gets her in trouble, that's all. She'd be spoiled if she were pampered and catered to, Verna. But she ain't. Whenever she gets herself into a tight spot, we don't bail her out. And when she loses a job, we don't let her sit home, now do we?"

Verna felt the tightness in her chest slowly dissipate.

"Rewarding bad behavior would be spoiling her, Verna. But we don't do that." Simon rested his arm on the backside of the horse. "Now, you just leave our *dochder* to me, Verna. She won't be sitting around tomorrow. I've told her she needs to come to the hardware store and help out there until she finds something else."

"Oh help!" Verna shut her eyes. "Just keep her away from your customers, Simon."

"She can stock shelves or clean the inventory room." Simon gave a little chuckle. "She wasn't happy about it, but I laid down the rules. I reckon she'll be fine."

"Well, God *does* perform miracles."

This time, Simon outright laughed. He reached over and

placed his hand on his wife's shoulder before drawing her into his chest for a brief embrace. "Now, Verna, we both know God has more important things to do than waste a perfectly *gut* miracle on Myrna."

His joke lightened Verna's mood, and she found herself enjoying the moment with her husband.

Not quite thirty years ago, she had fallen in love with Simon Bontrager, and when, after a one-year courtship, they wed, Verna had never looked back. For the first few years, she'd worked alongside him at the small hardware shop he'd opened just outside Shipshewana. Together, they turned it into a thriving business. Even after their first son, Peter, was born, she'd managed to keep helping Simon at the store. But after Luke was born, Simon insisted that she stay home. It was one thing to bring Peter to the store when he was just a baby, but it was quite another to have a toddler ambling around while a newborn fussed in the back office. Of course, it hadn't taken long for Myrna, Samuel, and Timothy to arrive and, by that time, there was no question of Verna being able to help her husband.

Now that the children were older—both Luke and Peter had their own families now—Verna wished she could go back to helping at the store. But Simon liked knowing she was home tending the garden and taking care of the household chores. Besides, he had plenty of help from their two youngest sons.

When Timothy and Samuel worked at the store, Simon would often come home an hour early so he could tackle some chores of his own. Those were the best days for Verna. She loved having her husband around without the children present. She often helped him, too, whether it be cleaning the stable or tending to the yard. It was their private time together.

Of course, today, Verna had been at Edna's, and now the usual blissful mood was lacking.

Nothing was ever happy when Myrna was the topic of discussion.

"So, tell me now," Simon continued once their conversation took on a lighter tone, "what else went on at your cookie club?"

Cookie club. Oh, how Verna disliked it when people called their gathering that. She knew Simon meant it in jest, a teasing term he used when they were alone together—unlike some other people. "Besides the fact that it's not a *club*—"

He laughed.

"—things were rather interesting today."

Simon raised an eyebrow. "Oh *ja?*"

She nodded. "Edna came up with an idea."

"She usually does," he said, not unkindly.

"We're going to try to find a job for Myrna, one that will refine her rough edges, mayhaps make her a little more skilled in housekeeping and possibly better suited so a young man might consider courting her." Verna smiled at him, hoping her husband would agree that Edna had come up with a brilliant idea. "We're going to see if any Amish mothers need helpers or if any elderly women need care."

For a long moment, Simon stared at her, his eyes unblinking and his mouth hanging open a little, just enough to give him a dumbfounded appearance. Her heart felt as if it had fallen. He hated the idea. She could just tell by looking at his expression. And if Simon hated the idea, she'd have no choice but to tell Edna so. He was, after all, her husband and Myrna's father. But when the shock dissipated from his eyes, the corners of his mouth turned up, and the hint of a smile slowly spread across his face, she realized she had misread him.

"Land's sake, Verna." Now he was full-on grinning. "That's just about the most *wunderbarr gut* idea I've ever heard! That's exactly what Myrna needs: a job in an Amish household!"

Silently, Verna rejoiced. She'd never go against her husband's wishes, so having his support was a relief. "I thought so, too." She leaned over and lowered her voice. "And it would keep her away from the *Englische*."

"Well, that, too," he laughed again. "My customers will thank you, that's for sure and certain." He stared into Verna's face before turning his attention back to the horse. "Now, why don't you let me finish with the grooming and you go start supper?"

"I'm perfectly capable of tending to the horse," she protested.

"Now, now, Verna, you do as I say." His tone was firm but gentle. "Don't want to have a bald horse when I hitch her up to my buggy for worship on Sunday."

She smiled at his jest and leaned up to place a soft kiss on his cheek. "You're a right *gut* man, Simon Bontrager."

That evening, at the kitchen table, with the green and white checkered cloth covered with platters of fried ham, baked chicken, and steamed vegetables, Simon broached the subject of Myrna working at the store.

Verna had just lifted her head after having bowed it during the silent prayer when she heard Simon clear his throat. He reached for the boiled potatoes as he did so.

After all these years of marriage, Verna knew that, when Simon cleared his throat, he was about to make an important statement. And so did the rest of the family. The only difference was that, this time, Verna already knew what her husband was about to say.

"Myrna, I've something to discuss with you," Simon began in a deliberate manner. Verna braced herself. His tone reflected the nature of the upcoming discussion: unpleasant. Timothy and Samuel looked up, glancing at each other before turning their heads to stare at their sister.

Myrna had just scooped some applesauce onto her plate, and at her father's words, her hand hung in midair. "Oh *ja*, Daed? What are we to discuss?"

Her tone was flat, and Verna hoped she was the only one to notice the way Myrna had emphasized the word *discuss*. She glanced at her husband and saw the muscles tighten along his jawline. Surely he, too, had noticed.

"There's been quite a pattern here, Dochder." His voice was stern and commanded Myrna's attention. "For the past year or so, you've been working countless jobs, and you've been let go from just about every one of them!"

Inwardly, Verna groaned. She'd have used a different strategy if she were broaching this topic with Myrna, but Verna knew better than to criticize her husband in front of the children. She said a quick prayer that God would help guide Simon's tongue.

Myrna, however, raised a delicate eyebrow. "It's not as if I'm getting *fired* on purpose."

That was the way Myrna always responded, finding an excuse and laying blame on anyone but herself but in a way that sounded perfectly logical. Sometimes Verna thought she was just a little too smart for her own good. Other times, Verna felt enormously proud of her daughter for standing up for herself. She knew many Amish women didn't possess that trait. Unfortunately, it wasn't always becoming.

"Nor is it for lack of responsibility or laziness, Daed."

Myrna laid her hands in her lap and met her father's gaze without wavering. "I work hard. I learned that from you."

Verna pressed her lips together, hoping she didn't look as amused as she felt by her daughter's flattery. Leave it to Myrna to try to soften her father's frustration with a compliment.

Clearly, however, Simon was not charmed. "Now, Myrna—"

"You always told me to do what's right and to stand up against what's wrong," Myrna continued, her green eyes flashing and her voice becoming animated. "And sometimes, in order to do that, I have to make unpopular choices. Choices that might seem irresponsible, but I can assure you are necessary."

Verna avoided eye contact with her daughter, because if she didn't, she knew Myrna would ask her mother's opinion on the matter. Being of a gentler spirit than Simon, Verna would certainly try to take the edge off the discussion. And surely Simon would become frustrated and impatient with her, especially after their earlier conversation. No. The last thing Verna needed was for Myrna to start pitting her against Simon. That, too, had been a pattern she hoped to break now that her friends had admitted they thought her daughter to be spoiled.

"That's no reason for—"

"I'm sure you can see that each time I had a valid reason for being let go," Myrna interrupted, placing emphasis on the words "let go" as if they were more appropriate than the word "fired." "This last time, I was merely trying to look out for that overweight man at the grocery store. His choices were unhealthy, especially given his large girth." She glanced at her mother. "Surely you can see that my intentions were not malicious but based on concern."

Verna felt Myrna's gaze bear down on her but refused

to give in. *Do not look at her. Do* not *look at her.* In her mind, she recited those five words over and over again.

"Why, the store manager should've rewarded me for being so concerned!" Myrna exclaimed, a growing sense of urgency in her voice. "It's not every day that a mere cashier cares so much about the customers. And that manager didn't even thank me when I spent my own time, not even on the clock, organizing the shelves. Why, they had oatmeal in the middle of cereal boxes! How ridiculous is that? And granola bars alongside junk food. There's no rhyme or reason to the way they have that store set up at all!"

Timothy made a noise that sounded like a laugh and immediately tried to hide it by coughing into his hand.

"What?" Myrna glared at him. "You know that being organized is the only way to run a business efficiently!"

Samuel rolled his eyes. "As if you've ever run a business."

Her eyes narrowed. "I reckon I could run Daed's business much better than *you* can. Why, his inventory shelves are just as unorganized as that grocery store!"

"Enough!" Simon dropped his hand onto the table, the utensils clattering against plates and bowls. Samuel and Timothy stared, wide-eyed, at their father. "I'll not be listening to this ridiculous bickering at my table. Nor will I be subjected to your silly excuses, Myrna Bontrager. What I will be having is you working at the hardware store—"

She groaned.

"—and doing so without interfering in the way we run our business. There will be no fussing with the stock, either. And I don't want to hear so much as a peep to our customers! You are to keep your opinions to yourself."

Myrna pressed her lips together. "I told you I was sorry about the construction man—"

"We nearly lost his account because of you," Simon blasted, the discussion heating up even more.

"Now, now," Verna put in, trying to bring the discussion down a notch. "This is the supper table." Her eyes met her husband's. "The family supper table. There's no need for harsh words or arguments here."

"Sorry, Maem," Myrna muttered.

Simon bristled at his wife's reprimand. For a few long moments, he remained silent, pushing mashed potatoes around his plate, a scowl etched upon his face.

"Besides," Verna said, "that was well over a year ago." *A long year ago*, she did not add. "And you *didn't* lose the account, Simon." She forced a soft, motherly smile to her face, looking at her husband first before turning her attention to Myrna. "Are we not supposed to forgive, as Jesus taught us to do?"

An awkward silence fell upon the table. Samuel and Timothy sat stiffly in their ladder-back chairs, staring down at their plates as they shuffled food into their mouths. As it was a Friday, she suspected they both wanted to hurry and finish their meals so they could head out, surely intending to meet up with their friends. The longer the bickering went on, the longer they'd have to wait for the after-prayer.

But Verna knew that some things couldn't be rushed.

It was Myrna who finally broke the silence. "How long, *exactly*, must I work there, Daed?"

Fearing that the condescending sound of their daughter's voice might set off her husband further, Verna reached out and placed her hand over her daughter's. "Until you find something more suitable." Her eyes held Simon's. "Right, Simon?"

"Suitable. *Ja*." He pushed his plate away, clearly uninterested in finishing his meal. "Mayhaps that suitable job will be settling down with some nice young Amish man come next autumn."

Immediately, Myrna shot to her feet, her chair scraping the floor as she pushed backward. The motion was so abrupt, her supper plate clattered to the floor and broke in half.

"Myrna!"

Verna got up and hurried over to the sink to fetch a rag. Inwardly, she groaned, hoping Simon didn't disclose the plans she'd made with Edna, Wilma, and Mary. That was the last thing Myrna needed to hear. If Myrna had any idea that her own mother was teaming up with her baking buddies to find her a more suitable job—a job that would prepare her for marriage—Myrna would refuse to cooperate.

"So, you'd have me married off to get me out of your hair, *ja*?" She placed her clenched fists on her hips and gave her father a dark look. "*Nee*, Daed. This is the twenty-first century and I'll not marry the first man who comes courting just to satisfy *you*."

Before Simon could respond, Verna shot him a warning look. How many nights had they whispered in the faint glow of the kerosene lantern, wondering if Myrna would ever court *anyone*, never mind settle down? It wasn't that she was difficult. No, that wasn't it. But she behaved in a way that was not harmonious with Amish ideals. Her outspokenness and tendency to voice her opinion when she should remain silent, and her refusal to heed the norms of the Amish community, did not make her a very popular girl, at least not among the Amish men in their church district. Too many people were aware of Myrna's spirited nature.

"Now, Myrna," Verna began softly, hoping that her tone would placate her daughter, "your *daed* didn't mean that, I'm sure." She gestured toward the empty chair. "Get yourself another plate and sit, Dochder. There's no sense going to bed with an empty belly."

Reluctantly, Myrna grabbed a clean dish from the drain board, then took her place at the table and, without another word, finished eating. Verna waited for the tension to evaporate from the room. She certainly didn't want the strain to remain between her husband and daughter, but wasn't sure how to quell it. Finally, an idea popped into her mind.

"Myrna," she began slowly, "I think what your *daed* means"—her eyes flickered in her husband's direction, hoping he would remain silent—"is that you've been working among the *Englische*, and mayhaps that's not suited to you. But if you found something that wasn't so . . ." Quickly, she tried to find the right word. ". . . worldly, you might fare better."

Myrna's eyebrows knit together and a frown formed on her lips. "'Worldly'?"

"*Ja*, worldly." Verna kept her gaze on her daughter. The last thing she wanted was to exacerbate her daughter's sensitivities. She knew how hard her daughter tried, often with a passion that came from deep within. But Verna also knew that not everyone appreciated her outspoken ways. "Working in a shop or store, I mean. Among strangers and *Englischers*. You know, people who don't know you, aren't used to your"—another pause—"spirited nature."

She watched as Myrna pursed her lips, her expression changing as if she was in deep thought. Without doubt, of all Verna's children, Myrna was certainly the wisest, a trait that often came with being reflective.

Across the table, Samuel shifted his weight, catching Verna's gaze. He winked at her, a slight hint of a smile on his lips. As his mother, Verna didn't need a translator to know that her son, while only nineteen years old, was smart enough to understand what she had just implied. And he clearly approved of her discreet choice of words.

"I think I understand," Myrna said at last. "Mayhaps you're right."

With a long, drawn-out sigh, Verna relaxed. "I'm glad you agree. Something will come up, Myrna, but in the meantime, you can help your *daed* at the store."

Simon cleared his throat.

"But under his rules, *ja*?" Verna quickly added. "Let's not cause any waves there."

With that, the matter was put to rest and supper became everyone's main focus.

Verna tried to enjoy the rest of her meal, but the lingering—and deafening—silence that surrounded her family made every bite tasteless and unpalatable to her.

Chapter Three

On Saturday, Myrna knelt on the floor in the stockroom of her father's hardware store, her dark green dress blanketed in dust. To keep her from getting in trouble, her father had instructed Myrna to remove all the items from the shelves, wipe them down, and inventory them before placing them back where they belonged.

It was busywork and she knew it. Perhaps a bit useful, but not necessary when there were so many other things she felt could use her attention.

The last thing she wanted was to work at her father's store. Again. Timothy and Samuel always gave her a hard time, teasing her in the way that younger brothers could do.

And, to make matters worse, her father watched her like a hawk. If she tried to move even one item to another spot, he seemed to magically appear, hands on his hips and a scowl on his face. If she didn't know better, she'd have suspected he had secret cameras watching her. But the bishop would *never* allow those, and her father was far too conservative to even *think* about such a thing.

Still, her father seemed to know.

Oh, how she hated working in the back room! It wouldn't be half as bad if her father let her organize everything. She would have enjoyed *that*. Reworking things and improving efficiency were definitely her two favorite things to do. But her father was adamantly opposed to any of her suggestions. And she couldn't understand why. His shelves were a complete mess! Nails were stocked with boxes of screws instead of with the hammers and compressors! That made no sense at all to Myrna. And hoses were in the plumbing section, not on the garden shelves.

But her father wouldn't hear one word about efficiency.

"It works for me," he had told her earlier that morning when she complained about the disarray in the stockroom. There was a familiar tone in his voice, the one that said he wasn't going to listen to reason. But that had never stopped Myrna before, and she continued to plead her case.

"It's just not logical!"

Simon raised an eyebrow. "Mayhaps not to you, but that's not your concern, Myrna." He sounded exasperated. Again. "Now just do your job and don't try to fix something that ain't broke!" And, with that, he walked away, leaving her alone to pout in the stockroom.

No matter what she did, she always displeased someone!

She didn't understand why, though. All she wanted to do was to help. It was obvious that the shelves needed help, and so had that man at the grocery store! He was eating all the wrong things and needed her guidance. All those processed foods with high sodium and lots of preservatives— not to mention saturated fats!—would surely cause high blood pressure or heart disease. And, when she worked at the tea store before she was fired from the grocery store, she'd had to speak up when the woman tried to buy a teapot that was all wrong for an elderly relative. Ceramic was far too heavy for an old woman to lift when filled with water. She couldn't help it if the woman had her mind set on that one, all because of the horse and buggy painted on the side.

No. Everyone seemed to think she was trouble simply because she always spoke the truth, even if it caused problems. Honesty was important, and practicality should have won out over a pretty painting of a horse and buggy. But, in the end, the store manager thought she was being difficult and causing trouble and losing a sale, which was bad for business.

To Myrna, nothing could be further from the truth. She just wanted to help people make good choices, and if that meant eating healthier or buying a lighter teapot, then so be it!

Sitting back on her heels, she raised her hand and brushed a lock of her red hair from her face. Somehow it had fallen free from her prayer *kapp*. And she liked to be neat and tidy, that was for sure and certain. Not that it mattered. She wasn't going to see anyone, since her father had banished her to the stockroom all day.

With a tired sigh, Myrna got to her feet. Her knees cracked, and she paused to place her hands on the small of her back while stretching. She needed a break. Her shoulders hurt and her eyes ached, for the lighting in the room was poor. The gas lantern wasn't working properly, so she had to use two smaller kerosene lanterns instead. She had told her parents that light eyes required better lighting— she wasn't entirely sure if that was true, but being the sole green-eyed Bontrager, she had thought it was worth a try. Unfortunately, neither her mother nor her father listened to her complaints, regardless of whether she was home or at the hardware store.

And, of course, it was damp and chilly in the stockroom as well. Despite the beautiful spring weather, the stone foundation seemed to retain moisture, especially since the building backed up to a hill. It always felt fifteen degrees colder in the back of the building. She should've thought about that before coming to work that morning. Her father *always* kept the heat down, even in the winter, so he certainly wasn't going to turn it on in April.

His frugality sometimes bordered on miserly, at least in Myrna's opinion.

Still, even knowing this, she hadn't remembered to bring a sweater with her, and she certainly wasn't going to wear her black shawl draped over her shoulders all day. It would be too cumbersome and get in the way of her work. So she was left shivering as she worked, her hands chilled to the bone from handling the damp rag as she wiped down the shelves. On a positive note, the more she cleaned, the more the room smelled like the fresh, oaky scent of Murphy's Oil, and *that* was something she'd never complain about.

She wandered over to the door that separated the stockroom from the sales floor. Slowly, she opened it and peeked out. The store was practically empty. She knew her father had stepped out to deliver some packages to the post office, but where was Samuel? Her eyes traveled to the wall where the clock hung. It was almost time for lunch. Her brother was probably sitting outside eating his noon meal.

Feeling emboldened, she left the stockroom and stood near the register. She ran her fingers across the buttons. How long had it been since her father had permitted her to work behind the counter? Certainly a year or more. She had started working for her father when she turned seventeen. Just a few days each week. He'd let her interact with the customers during busy times if he was short staffed, but she was mostly charged with straightening up the shelves and managing the books—two tasks that kept her well hidden away.

But that had ended when she got into an argument with the *Englische* man from R.B. Construction.

Standing behind the counter, she tried to remember what had caused the heated exchange. Something about him having forgotten to pay his bill the previous month. When he arrived and wanted to make a big purchase for a new construction job, Myrna had stuck to her guns. Delinquent accounts meant no more credit.

Tapping her finger on the counter's edge, she felt her pulse quicken as she recalled the argument. Her father had returned to the store in the middle of it and had refused to back her, extending more credit even though she knew it was a mistake.

He also let Myrna know that it was time for her to find another job.

She sighed, shaking her head at the memory. The man threatened to take his business elsewhere and her father blamed her for the soured relationship, but Myrna knew the truth: the man had taken advantage of her father and his belief in the universal goodness of human nature. It was too often that Simon's trust was abused by certain of his *Englische* customers. And, as she could've predicted, her father had extended the man's credit even further to appease him.

The bell over the door jingled, interrupting her thoughts. Myrna turned her attention to the noise. To her surprise, it wasn't Samuel returning from wherever he had gone, but a customer, and he was walking directly toward her.

A tall man with broad shoulders and the familiar mustache-less beard worn by married Amish men stood in front of her. His dark hair poked out from the sides of his battered straw hat, perfect ringlets covering the tips of his ears. She'd never seen the man before, which wasn't surprising, since many Amish men patronized her father's store from surrounding areas. And he was older, probably in his early thirties. While she might have considered him a pleasant-looking man, the sober expression on his face made her wonder if something was amiss.

"May I help you?"

Upon hearing her voice, he paused and studied her for a long moment, his dark eyes flashing. He seemed transfixed when he gazed at her red hair, which was peeking out from the front of her *kapp*.

Myrna straightened her shoulders and tucked a loose strand behind her ear. It wasn't unusual, his reaction. Many times, people seemed taken aback by her appearance. During her younger years, her mother always told her that people were curious because there weren't many redheaded Amish children. But as she grew older, one of her friends commented that it was Myrna's unusual beauty that attracted so much attention.

Myrna didn't know about *that*. She often suspected it was her reputation, more than anything else, that made people stop and stare. But as she didn't know this man who stood before her—a *married* man from the looks of his beard—she doubted that held true in this situation.

Still, the way he was looking at her was, indeed, puzzling. It was almost as if he had known her before. At first, anyway. And then his eyes changed, as if he had recalled something. Perhaps, she thought, he had heard about Simon Bontrager's redheaded daughter.

Finally, the man cleared his throat. "You're not Simon."

She almost laughed. *What a silly statement*, she thought. "Obviously."

The man's cheeks turned pink. He shifted his weight as if uncomfortable. "Stupid comment, that," he acknowledged. "I suppose I meant, where's Simon?"

There was something endearing about the fellow's

awkwardness. She felt a quickening inside her chest and wondered who, exactly, he was. "I'm afraid I don't know." She tried to smile, hoping to put him more at ease. "I was working in the back, you see." She gestured toward the door. "He must've stepped out for a moment. Not like him to up and leave that way without first telling me."

"Hm." It was a curiously soft noise that came from his throat, both guttural and husky. An acknowledgment without saying a word.

"So"—she widened her smile—"how may I help you?"

He gave her another long, uncomfortable look. "I don't know you."

Immediately, she felt her heart race. What was *that* supposed to mean? "*Nee*, you don't." She had to swallow to try to keep her temper in check. "But I'm behind this counter and can assist you, if you'd let me know what it is you need."

For a moment, he chewed on the inside of his lower lip, his mouth pursing just a bit as if considering her. He frowned, his tanned brow wrinkling. Something about this man was different—his strange reaction, the way he didn't speak much . . . and, of course, the dark expression on his face as he continued to study her.

She wondered at his delayed response. And yet, as his eyes met hers, Myrna realized that she was holding her breath, so she focused on her breathing, even more curious about the impact this stranger—this *married* stranger, she reminded herself again—was having on her. Swallowing, she averted her eyes, ashamed of herself for having such a strange reaction.

The front door opened once again, and her father entered. He paused when he noticed his daughter standing behind the counter facing a customer. But then, recognizing the man, he stepped forward to greet him.

"Zeke!" A smile crossed Simon's face and he patted the man on his shoulder. "Long time since I've seen you," he said, while giving Myrna a sharp look. "How're things going?"

She knew what that look meant. Her father had repeatedly told her that she wasn't to interact with customers. So, quietly, Myrna stepped back, then slipped into the shadows.

With her father engaged in conversation with this Zeke fellow, she stood in the doorway of the stockroom and watched, curious to witness the change in the man's demeanor. Clearly he was more relaxed around Simon, and she was all but forgotten. She took advantage of the shadows to observe him as he spoke freely with her father, no longer awkward in his manner.

His expression changed while he talked with Simon. Although he still seemed serious, and there was something resigned about his appearance, he seemed much more comfortable than he had been a few moments earlier. But despite his broad shoulders and refined features, he had a stoic look about him. It was clear something was wrong. His smile was masked by a sorrowful look in his eyes. While curiosity made her want to learn more, she knew she was already facing a tongue-lashing from her father for having left the stockroom in the first place.

Sighing, she retreated into the darkness of the damp stockroom rather than risk upsetting her father even more.

Myrna sat at the kitchen table, drumming her fingers against the tablecloth. Outside, she could hear the cars passing by their house on North 700 West Street. It wasn't quite rush hour yet, but it soon would be. The increasing traffic indicated as much. Over the years, an increasing

number of cars cut through their rural street to bypass the
heavier traffic on Highway 20. It was problematic, living
just a mile from town, but something Myrna had learned
to live with.

Until today.

With each car that passed, Myrna felt a rising pressure
tighten her chest. Impatiently, she stood up and began to
pace the room, her mind racing and her pulse quickening.
She wasn't certain how much longer she could work in her
father's store! It was depressing being stuck in the stockroom all day. She felt like a little mushroom kept in the
dark. While she longed to be on the sales floor, working
with customers, it was clear her father felt otherwise.

"Remember what happened the last time, Myrna?" was
all he had replied when she had complained that morning.

Why, oh why, couldn't she keep her opinions to herself?

But she always found it impossible to stop herself. Whenever she saw a person doing or saying something foolish,
Myrna *had* to speak up. She cringed, remembering the exchange she'd had with one particular customer last year,
just before the R.B. Construction incident. The man's lack
of knowledge about tools and the silly questions he'd asked
had put her in rare form, and her patience had been tried.

If only her father hadn't been nearby, overhearing her tell
the man that the best thing he could do was hire a plumber!
She was still paying the price for that exchange and for the
extended credit argument, almost a year later.

Frustrated, mostly with herself but also with her mother
because she was late returning home—where *was* she,
anyway?—Myrna plopped back down in the kitchen chair
and picked at her cuticles.

Finally, she heard the buggy pulling into the driveway.
Myrna shut her eyes, saying a quick prayer, begging God
for her mother to be in a good mood.

"What are you doing, Myrna, sitting here all alone like this?" Verna asked when she walked into the kitchen and set her purse down on the counter. As usual, her mother's maternal concern kicked in, and she hurried over to where Myrna sat.

"You feeling poorly?" she asked as she pressed her hand to her daughter's forehead. "Mayhaps you need something? Pain reliever?"

Myrna shook her head. "*Nee*, Maem," she replied slowly, her words drawn out and deliberate. "I'm just cold, but I feel fine."

"Cold?" Her mother slid into the chair next to her.

"Trying to thaw out a bit."

Verna made a face. "What on earth?"

"It's freezing at the store, Maem. Or, at least, in the stockroom."

Upon hearing this, her mother relaxed. "Oh. That."

"*Ja*, that," Myrna said, her tone a bit sharper than she intended. "I might not be ill now, but I'll surely catch my death of the cold if I have to spend my days cooped up in that dungeon!"

Verna chuckled.

"It's not funny!"

She watched as her mother sobered. "Oh, Myrna, you've always loved it warmer than most. Mayhaps if you had a little fat on your body, you'd enjoy the cool air."

At this comment, Myrna groaned. "Even old Miriam Schrock would freeze back there!"

"Myrna!"

"You know it's true. Why, if Daed doesn't turn on the heat, I'll be in bed with pneumonia by Wednesday of next week." She reached out and took her mother's hands. "Please, Maem. Speak to him. Mayhaps he might let me work a bit out front—"

"Myrna," her mother interrupted. "You know he can't do that."

"Why ever not?" she cried out. "I promise I won't talk to the customers."

The way her mother looked at her spoke volumes. It was clear she didn't believe that was possible.

"Well, I'll try not to, anyway," Myrna added. "Why, I could be a great asset to him! Really, I could! I'm great with organizing, and trust me, Daed can surely use my help in that department. And I'm quick to learn about new products, so I can help the customers find what they need but also upsell them!"

Myrna watched her mother's reaction, pleased to see her sigh in defeat.

"I can speak to him," Verna said at last. "But I wouldn't expect much from it, Myrna. He can't afford to have you driving away clients with your stubborn opinions."

Myrna smiled to herself. If anyone could get through to her father, it was her mother. "I won't upset anyone, I promise." She stretched out her fingers and wiggled them. "Remind me to bring gloves with me on Monday, Maem. You have no idea how cold it gets in there."

"I don't understand that. It's been a beautiful April!"

Myrna made a noise, scoffing at her mother's comment. "Well, you'd never know it in that stockroom, that's for sure and certain."

"Well, I can only promise to speak to your *daed* about working out front, Myrna. But I will certainly insist that he heat up that room a bit. No sense in you complaining every day about it," Verna said.

"*Danke*, Maem."

Her mother patted her hand in a motherly way. "Now, let's get some supper started. Surely Daed and the boys will be home shortly, and knowing their appetites, they'll be eager for a hot meal before Samuel and Timothy go out with their friends." As her mother stood up, she glanced at Myrna. "You can start the stove, boil water for egg noodles, *ja*? It'll warm you up some," she teased.

"Doubtful," Myrna shot back.

"Oh, Myrna," her mother chuckled. "Come summer you'll be pining to get to the stockroom each morning so you can enjoy the cool air."

If I'm still there, Myrna thought.

She had no intention of spending her summer at her father's store. As soon as she could, she was going to start looking for another job where they appreciated her skills, just as her mother had suggested. A job where she could use her organizational skills and one where she could take charge.

Now, if only she had an inkling of what kind of job that might be . . .

Chapter Four

After worship on Sunday, Edna stood at the sink, washing cups and serving platters. Usually, the younger women helped the hostess, but Edna often volunteered, too. She enjoyed the camaraderie among the women who washed the dishes. And, today, it was as good a place as any to learn of possible new job opportunities for Myrna.

Susan Schwartz walked into the kitchen, her hands holding a tray laden with dirty platters. With a heavy "oomph," she set it on the counter next to the sink and rubbed her upper arm. "Don't know when empty platters got so heavy," she complained good-naturedly.

Edna laughed. "Mayhaps when we got older."

With a loud guffaw, Susan pretended to scowl. "Speak for yourself, Edna. I'm still only thirty-five."

"Ha!" Edna reached for an oval platter and began washing it in the sudsy water. "Plus thirty, I suspect."

This time, it was Susan who laughed, her eyes narrowing as she did. "But you'll never know for sure, will you, now?"

As Edna washed the platter, she recognized it as her own, the one she'd used to set out the cookies. She wasn't surprised they'd gone so quickly.

As if reading her mind, Susan leaned her hip against the counter, still rubbing her arm. "Seems those young ones never get tired of your sugar cookies, Edna!" She gestured toward Edna's hand, covered in suds as she ran a rag over the surface. "Empty again, I see. I think half of them were eaten by my own *gross-sohn*." She laughed, her eyes full of warmth. "Even if I had the time to make sugar cookies at home, that little one would still tell me they weren't as buttery and light as yours."

Edna smiled, secretly delighted. She didn't know what she would do if the children didn't enjoy her cookies so much.

"It sure is nice that you and your friends bake the sweets for worship," Susan said, reaching for a towel to help dry the freshly washed items Edna set on the counter. "Your cookie club sure is popular with *die gleeni kinner*."

"After church, the little ones deserve a treat," Edna agreed.

"And *die grossmammis*, too!" Susan teased. "Mayhaps your cookie club might *machscht meh*!"

"Make more? Why, with all the cakes and pies, there's plenty of choices for all," Edna replied lightheartedly. "But I can certainly suggest as much. We'll be meeting again on Wednesday. We're making baby blankets to sell at MayFest."

"Oh, to be young again." Susan sighed.

Edna laughed. She would be fifty the following year, not that much younger than Susan. Still, it pleased her that Susan thought of her as being "young."

"Why! You and your three friends have so much energy, Edna Esh," Susan continued. "I often think I should do the same thing with my friends, but I never seem to get to it. Puts us to shame."

Immediately Edna regretted having brought up making the blankets for MayFest, fearing that her mention of the charitable act sounded as if she were boasting. The last thing she wanted was to sound prideful. "No more than any other woman with grown *kinner*," she said hastily. "And, truth be told, our gatherings are as much for the fellowship as for the charity, if I'm perfectly honest."

This time, Susan nodded her head, understanding the implication of Edna's words. "Fellowship with friends is *wunderbarr*. I wish I'd made more of an effort to keep in touch with my childhood friends."

There was a wistful longing in Susan's voice and Edna couldn't help but get an idea. While Susan was only in her midfifties, she *was* older in body and spirit than others her age. It seemed she had aged beyond her years when her husband passed away three years ago, a heart attack in the fields which unexpectedly took him home to God.

Perhaps, Edna thought, his death had taken its toll on Susan. Surely, she must be lonely and in need of companionship. But how to ask such a personal question without reminding her that she was aging, and not very well at that?

Her mind raced as she tried to figure out how to put her thought delicately. She didn't want to offend Susan, but if she didn't ask, how could she know how to help Susan? Quickly, she decided on the truth, for surely *that* was always the best policy. However, she found a roundabout way to get there. A way that wouldn't hurt Susan's feelings. "Speaking of my childhood friends, you remember Verna Bontrager?"

For a split second, Susan struggled to match the name to a face. Suddenly, she brightened. "From the Bontrager Hardware Store in town, *ja*?" When Edna nodded, Susan nodded, too. "She's a kindhearted woman. Her *sohn* Peter helped my husband rebuild our barn years back, and Simon donated quite a bit of the supplies. Lumber and nails. Remember that? When the barn burned down?" She shook her head and clucked her tongue. "My husband baled up and stored the hay too soon that year. The barn burned to the ground in a matter of minutes."

Edna *did* remember that. It had been the talk of all the local Amish communities, a harsh reminder to farmers about properly drying their hay before baling. There had also been whispers circulating along the Amish grapevine regarding Susan's now-deceased husband, a seasoned farmer who was blamed for allowing it to happen. Barn fires were a rare occurrence, but when they did happen, it was usually because the less experienced farmers baled too soon, anxious to get the crop inside. The older farmers knew better than to set damp hay inside before it had time to dry thoroughly in the sun. The moisture could cause a chemical reaction that would lead to spontaneous combustion.

"And her *dochder*, Myrna?"

Susan sobered and made an odd face. "*Ach*, *ja*, I remember her well. Found her in my pantry reorganizing the shelves. Funny one, that Myrna Bontrager."

"Verna's looking for some housework for the girl," Edna told her. "Mayhaps you know of someone who might need a helper? Or even a companion?"

This time, Susan took a deep breath and knit her brows together. Putting her hand up to her face, she repeated Edna's request. "A helper, eh? Companion . . ." She tapped her finger against her cheek and thought on it for a moment.

Watching her and feeling hopeful, Edna waited patiently. It was obvious to her, but apparently not so obvious to Susan.

Suddenly, the older woman's eyes widened, and a smile broke over her face. "Why, I know just the person!"

"You do?"

Satisfied with herself, Susan nodded. "*Ja*, I sure do."

Edna waited patiently for Susan to acknowledge that the person she knew was herself. But to her surprise, Susan didn't come to that same conclusion.

"Ezekiel Riehl!"

Taken aback, Edna took a minute to digest what she'd just heard. "Excuse me?"

Susan lit up. "Ezekiel Riehl. His wife, Katie Ruth, passed away last summer. I hear tell that Ezekiel isn't doing so well with those young ones."

Edna frowned. She knew a few Ezekiels, but the name Ezekiel Riehl didn't ring a bell. "Ezekiel?"

"Over in my *schwester*'s church district?" Susan gave the platter in her hand a final wipe with the now-damp dish towel. "Just south of Shipshe."

But that didn't help Edna. "I don't know him, I'm afraid. What happened with his wife?"

"Oh, terrible story, that. Katie Ruth passed away after refusing to get medical attention. Wouldn't let those doctors in the city operate on her." Susan shook her head. "So sad. She was just twenty-eight and had breast cancer." She whispered the words "breast cancer" as if just saying them might cause her to contract the disease.

"Oh help!"

Susan nodded. "*Ja.* Just up and refused treatment. Said God would heal her."

Edna caught her breath. While she didn't know Ezekiel Riehl and his family, she had heard about the young mother who passed from cancer. "Oh *ja*, I think I do remember that story," Edna said. "She was the bishop's *dochder*, *ja*?"

"Exactly. Some say it was her *daed*'s influence that made her refuse the treatment. Others said it was her husband's."

"So very sad," Edna whispered. She'd heard similar stories before, mostly about conservative Amish who shunned modern-day medicine and chose to rely on prayer instead. While she knew that prayer helped in all situations, she also knew that medicine had its place, too. *A little help never hurt anyone*, Edna always said.

"She left behind those little children," Susan continued, a sorrowful expression on her face. "Three boys and a little girl. A *boppli*, no less. Why, just for their sake alone, she should've gone to the doctor, regardless of what others advised."

Edna couldn't agree more, but she held her tongue.

"And Katie Ruth's youngest *schwester* was caring for the *kinner*, but I hear tell that she married last autumn and will be moving to her new *haus* in Middlebury soon. So that leaves Ezekiel without a helper."

"Surely his family will step in." Edna knew that was how it usually worked when a mother died, leaving behind young children.

"*Nee*, Ezekiel has no family in the area, I hear." Susan exhaled. "Not sure how he'll manage that farm with those little ones."

"He'll need to hire help, that's for certain." Edna wiped down the counter and carefully hung the towel over the edge of the sink. "Unless his *fraa*'s family will help. Don't you think they will?"

Susan took a second to respond, as if pondering the question. "I'm not sure he gets on so well with the bishop, and Katie Ruth only had the one *schwester*."

And that left the perfect opening for Myrna.

Edna caught her breath. *Could it really be so easy?* she

wondered. "If he's in need of someone to care for his *kinner* and *haus*," she said, "Myrna might be the person to help."

Susan gave her a broad smile. "You can stop by my *haus* and let me know after you speak to her *maem* on Wednesday." She paused. "It was Wednesday you said you'd be baking cookies again?"

Edna suppressed a smile. She suspected she knew what Susan was suggesting: stop by and bring cookies! "*Nee*, we'll be making baby blankets on Wednesday." When she noticed the disappointed look on Susan's face, Edna lowered her voice. "But I'd never stop by your *haus* to visit empty-handed."

Delighted, Susan clapped her hands as if she were a child. "Oh, *wunderbarr*! Mayhaps you might make your chocolate chip cookies this time? Or the oatmeal ones?"

Unable to hold back any longer, Edna grinned. "If Myrna gets this job, Susan, I can assure you weekly batches of both!"

On Wednesday, Edna could hardly wait to hitch the horse to the buggy and make the thirty-minute drive to the Bontragers' house. It had been quite some time since she'd visited Verna at her home. Life on the farm, especially during the tourist season when Edna served meals to the *Englische*, did not make visiting others easy. And, of course, during the winter months, Elmer often needed the buggy for running errands, and other times the weather didn't cooperate.

Edna was blessed that her friends were happy to travel to *her* farm. Perhaps they enjoyed escaping their own houses for their Friday afternoon gatherings as much as Edna enjoyed having them. The routine had been set long ago, and without anyone complaining, no one had felt the need to change it. Besides, Edna's large farmhouse kitchen accommodated them most comfortably, especially when it was cold outside and they could gather by the old stone fireplace in the kitchen.

However, when they had agreed to meet on Wednesday for an impromptu knitting circle—which hopefully no one would start calling a "knitting club," Edna thought wryly—they had agreed to do it at Verna's house. Edna had never been to Verna's before and found herself readily agreeing, curious to see where her friend lived.

When she pulled down the Bontragers' driveway, Edna found herself surprised by how small the property seemed. She paused the horse and buggy, staring at the small contemporary house on its small plot of land, and thought it couldn't be more than half an acre at best. There was a garden plot on the eastern side of the house, the earth recently tilled and ready for planting. And a clothesline hung from one corner of the breezeway to the back fence. Several bed linens hung there, the light April breeze causing them to flutter.

While everything was neat and tidy, it appeared far too modern for Edna's taste. She could never imagine living anywhere but on a farm.

She had forgotten what it was like for Amish families who lived near town. More and more of them were finding their livelihoods outside the family home. The ever-increasing cost of farm land and the decreasing price of milk made dairy farming a hard life, and it was harder and harder to support a family in the traditional way. Still, some Amish families chose to supplement their dairy by growing crops like hay, wheat, and corn. But, that, too, took land, which was hard to find. Many of the younger Amish were choosing to modify their lifestyles, adapting to the ever-changing ways of the world.

Even Edna had made concessions, like serving meals to the *Englische* during the tourist seasons—something she never would have imagined she'd do when she was a young bride. But, with farming becoming less and less lucrative, every gathering brought in much-needed income to help Elmer with the rising costs of running the dairy.

As for the Bontragers, they owned a local hardware store on the edge of Shipshewana. Most of their customers were Amish, but there were a few local *Englischers* who frequented the store as well. The Bontragers were one of the lucky families who didn't need to cater to tourists.

"Edna!" Verna opened the kitchen door, a broad smile lighting up her face. "You've arrived at last!"

As Edna walked into the room, she noticed that Wilma and Mary were already seated on the sunporch, busy working on their baby blankets for the MayFest sale.

"How is everyone today?" Edna asked as she set her knitting bag on the floor beside the sofa.

Settling in next to Mary, she leaned over and lifted the flap, withdrawing a skein of yarn and her crochet hook. Without skipping a beat, she began working on her blanket, a pale yellow and white design that reminded her of springtime. She had always preferred crocheting to knitting, just like Mary, and was glad they had that in common. But Wilma and Verna seemed to be partial to knitting, their long needles clacking loudly as they worked.

Before anyone could respond to Edna's question, a car horn blasted as it passed by the house. Wilma started, her large eyes practically bulging. "Oh help!"

Mary jumped at Wilma's unexpected shout. "My word, Wilma! It's just a car."

"I know that!" she snapped back. "I've no idea why they think they must do that! So noisy."

Edna glanced at Verna, who tipped her head, clearly fighting the urge to smile.

"Speaking of noise, those *dochders* of mine," Wilma started. She sat in the rocking chair, her feet planted firmly on the floor as she pumped back and forth, a fierce scowl on her face. "They're so competitive. Why, if I ask one to do laundry, the other one is practically running to do it faster and better! And bickering all the while."

Edna laughed. "Twins. I reckon that's something to be expected."

Wilma made a noise from deep in her throat. "I reckon they raced to see which one could be born first! Surprised they weren't pulling each other by the heel to try to squeeze past!"

At this comment, the other three ladies laughed, although Edna suspected Wilma spoke the truth.

"I just don't know where they get it from," Wilma continued. Suddenly, she stopped rocking and leaned closer to Verna. "How on earth did you get so far along? My word, Verna. You've just done twice as much as me in half the time!"

Verna responded with a soft smile.

Wilma began rocking again, fast and furious, as her needles continued clacking together. "I'll have to knit three times as fast to catch up."

Mary lowered her voice as she whispered to Edna, "And she wonders where her *dochders* get their competitive nature from?"

Wilma's needles stopped moving. "What's that?"

"Nothing, Wilma. Just admiring Edna's blanket is all."

"Hmph!" Wilma returned her attention to her knitting. "*Ja*, well, as I was saying about Rachel and Ella Mae"— she looked directly at Edna—"I was thinking—you know, about our discussion regarding our *dochders*?—with spring coming and all—"

Edna slowed her hands, feeling a pit form in her stomach.

"—tourists will soon flood the area, and I reckon you'll have an awful lot of customers wanting a home-cooked Amish meal."

Edna stiffened, knowing where Wilma was headed.

"Seeing that you don't have any *dochders* of your own—"

With three unmarried sons—all of them still living at home—Edna didn't need to be reminded of that painful fact.

"—mayhaps you'll need some spare hands setting out the meals?"

And there it was, in all its glory.

Edna didn't have to look up to know that both Verna and Mary were staring at her, quietly anticipating her response.

And how *could* she respond? The truth was that between readying the garden and tending to her chores, it *was* hard to find the time to do everything *and* prepare the nightly dinners for tourists. But how on earth would she get *anything* done if Rachel and Ella Mae were constantly bickering and battling each other?

"I . . . I suppose that's something to ponder a bit," Edna managed to say. It was her polite way of declining without upsetting her friend's feelings.

Wilma smiled to herself, clearly hearing what she wanted to hear. "You do that and let me know, *ja*?"

Edna nodded her head, then changed the subject, focusing her attention on Verna. "Speaking of working, how is Myrna doing?"

Verna frowned. "As well as can be expected. She's got an awful lot of ideas that Simon has no interest in hearing. Makes for some tense supper conversation."

Mary clicked her tongue and shook her head. "Oh help!"

"Exactly. That girl is just impossible, Edna. Sometimes I think her lack of tolerance for others' imperfections is most unchristian." She set down her needles, the beginning of the baby blanket resting on her lap. "I just don't know what to do anymore."

Edna gave her a knowing smile. "Well, funny you should mention that," she said in a deliberate manner. "After worship on Sunday, I may have heard about an opportunity. Thought of Myrna right away, seeing she needs a job, and it sounded as though it would be a right *gut* fit, too."

Mary caught her breath. "Already? My word, Edna! You work fast, don't you?"

"I didn't even have a chance to inquire after our worship service!" Wilma added, clearly feeling left out.

Verna, however, glowed. "Oh, Edna! I want to hear more details."

"It's caretaking for an Amish man with little ones. His *fraa* died last summer and he's got no one to mind them."

Edna didn't need to look at Verna to know that the color had drained from her face. "A widower?" She swallowed. "With *kinner*?"

It was a common story among the Amish when a young mother died: the husband would find a second wife before very long. Perhaps not because of love, but due to necessity. Edna wondered if Verna was concerned that he'd find someone to marry and replace Myrna. Verna, however, quickly explained her hesitation.

"Oh, Edna! I think you are *wunderbarr gut* to find something so soon," Verna said, her face still pale. "But can you see Myrna tending to *kinner* without the help of their *maem*? She knows next to nothing about childcare. It's one thing to be a mother's helper. It's quite another to be a stand-in mother. She simply has no experience, Edna, and that just worries me."

While there was some validity to what Verna had just said, Edna remained undeterred. "Verna, she has to learn sometime, and besides, sometimes learning on the job is the best way, *ja*? Besides, the opportunity presented itself, just when we needed it. Perhaps God placed it before us for a reason?"

"I don't know," Verna replied, her words slow and drawn out.

Wilma frowned. "What're you afraid of?" Her sardonic tone made Mary blanch. "They're just *kinner*, after all! And it's not as if she's likely to burn down the *haus*!"

Giving in to Wilma's argument, Verna sighed.

"So? What do you think?" Edna asked.

"Do you know the man, then?"

Edna shook her head. "*Nee*, I don't. Ezekiel Riehl's his name, I believe."

Verna seemed to think for a moment as if searching her memory. "Ezekiel Riehl? I'm not so certain I know of him."

Mary bent her head and focused on her crocheting, a tiny V-shaped wrinkle forming between her eyes. "Mayhaps Simon will know him, *ja*?"

"That's right!" Edna exclaimed. "Simon might know this Ezekiel! Everyone comes to his hardware store, ja?"

Even Verna appeared satisfied with that answer. "A *gut* idea, Mary. I'll ask him tonight."

"You do that and then you can let me know?"

Suddenly a dark cloud crossed Verna's face. "I wonder if Myrna might think we are trying to play matchmaker, if you know what I mean."

"Play matchmaker?" Edna hadn't considered that.

She knew nothing about this man, and given that he hadn't remarried yet—an unusual situation for a young widower—he was most likely still grieving and, as such, had no intentions of doing so anytime soon. "Oh, I should think she'd know well enough that's not our intention. But to expose her to some domestic training, why! She'd surely benefit from that. Besides, acting as the caretaker of the home, she could organize the *haus* and those *kinner* to her heart's content."

The darkness lifted from Verna's expression and she gave Edna a sideways glance. "Mayhaps you're right, Edna." A hint of a smile curved the corners of her lips. "Perhaps Myrna will be the right person for this Ezekiel Riehl after all."

Chapter Five

"Ezekiel Riehl?"

Wide-eyed, Verna sat in her rocking chair. In the dim light from the kerosene lantern, she stared at her husband as he leaned forward in his faded blue recliner.

Ever since she had spoken with Edna earlier that day, she'd wavered between excitement and worry. The idea of Myrna helping the Riehl family sat well with Verna. Not only would Myrna be doing something good for a grieving family, but the work would also help Myrna mature. The many responsibilities involved in tending children were much different from those of working in a store dealing with adults.

But Verna also worried, because she knew nothing about this Ezekiel Riehl. Some Amish men could be downright stern, and a widower who was overwhelmed might take advantage of someone as giving as her daughter. As much as Myrna could benefit from someone putting her in her place, Verna didn't want her subjected to an unfair man with unreasonable demands.

That was why she decided to ask her husband his thoughts on the matter.

She'd waited until long after supper to share the news

with him, not having wanted to say anything earlier when Myrna, Samuel, and Timothy were around. Now that the three of them had retired for the night, she only just found the perfect moment to discuss the matter with Simon and to see if he knew anything about this man.

From the way he'd repeated Ezekiel's name, Verna could tell he was fond of the man.

"You mean Zeke?" Simon grinned at her, which eased the concern she'd felt all afternoon. "Oh *ja*! He's a right *gut* fellow. Why! He was in the store just last Saturday." Simon paused and tugged thoughtfully on his beard. "I never once thought to ask him how he's faring since his *fraa* passed last summer. Been so long, it didn't cross my mind. Frankly, I forgot she'd been sick and all. And I haven't seen him since her passing."

Verna waited a moment out of respect for the young woman who'd passed. Then, when she felt it was appropriate, she asked, "Do you know how she died?"

"*Ja*, cancer." Simon frowned. "Breast cancer, if I recall."

Verna shook her head and clucked her tongue. "Shame they couldn't treat it."

Her husband paused and then held up his hand. "Now wait a minute. I seem to remember there was a bit of a hubbub about that." He tapped the side of his head as if trying to think back. "Something about the woman refusing treatment."

Verna gasped. "Oh my!"

"Not sure why," Simon continued, "but to refuse treatment when she had those little ones . . . such a shame."

It didn't happen very often, not in their area. But some Amish folks were naturalists and felt strongly that God would heal them. And if God didn't, then it was just their time to leave this world and enter God's kingdom.

Verna didn't subscribe to such thinking. "You don't think that Ezekiel is one of *those*, do you?"

Simon shrugged. "Doesn't appear to be so conservative, but I don't know him all that well. Not personally. However, what I do know about him is he's a kind man with a righteous reputation, more than giving to his neighbors, and hardworking, too."

Verna held her breath. "Do you think Myrna might do well with him?"

"Oh, *ja*! He's got a nice big farm and always pays his bills in cash. Never once uses one of those credit cards." Simon lowered his voice. "Not like some of the younger farmers."

Verna knew better than to inquire further. Like many middle-aged Amish men, Simon held to the principle that if there wasn't enough cash to buy something, it wasn't worth having. Once when the bishop and his family had come for supper, Simon had gone on a tirade about the younger men spending money they didn't have. The bishop had listened to Simon thoughtfully and, not even one week later he'd preached about that very subject at worship.

"But what about his personality?"

Slowly, Simon's smile dissipated. "Oh. I think I understand your question better now." He stood up and began to pace the kitchen floor. In the glow from the kerosene lantern, his shadow loomed large on the back wall of the gathering room. "I can't say I know much about him personally except that he's a bit reserved in nature. I haven't heard anything, either *gut* or otherwise." He paused and glanced over his shoulder at Verna. "But that's not unusual, considering he doesn't live in our district, or the neighboring one, either."

Patiently, Verna waited for her husband to sort out his thoughts as he began pacing again.

"She'll think we're trying to set her up, no doubt," he mused. "That's not it at all, of course. She'll just have to accept that."

"Of course," Verna repeated softly.

"I mean, Zeke's a right *gut* man from what I can tell, but that doesn't mean he'd be interested in a young feisty nineteen-year-old."

"She's twenty-one."

Simon grunted, and in the dim glow from the lantern, Verna thought she saw him flush, embarrassed about his error.

The floorboards creaked under his heavy shoes as he began walking back and forth again. "Still, no one will hire her in town, not the Amish-owned stores anyway. Why, just yesterday I ran into the *Englische* man who runs the Farver Bookstore, and even *he's* heard about Myrna's reputation." He gave a single laugh. "Not even the *Englische* will hire her now!"

"Oh help," Verna muttered under her breath.

Abruptly, Simon stopped and turned around, facing Verna with a resolved look in his eyes. "I think it's a *gut* idea, Verna. If Myrna tends to Riehl's *kinner*, she'll have a different type of responsibility than she's used to. She'll also learn the skills of working in the *haus*, which will be attractive to other young Amish men, especially if she keeps herself out of trouble. And she'll meet new people in the Riehls' church district, too."

"So she might do it then?"

Simon nodded his head. "*Ja*, I believe so. Edna Esh may have solved all our problems with this!" He moved back over to his recliner and sank into it. "Now, the big question is . . . who's going to tell her?"

* * *

"No!"

It was Thursday evening, and Myrna stood at the foot of the staircase, her hands crossed over her chest. She wore a dark expression, one that screamed defiance and anger. Verna knew that look far too well.

"Now, Myrna," Verna said calmly.

Only an hour earlier, she had hung up the phone with Edna. Oh, how delighted Verna had been to make that call! It had even been worth it to walk over to the *Englische* neighbors to ask about borrowing their phone, although she did have to sit afterward and hear about Joan's grandchildren for thirty minutes. She never could understand why the *Englische* insisted on talking about their grandchildren to people who'd never met them. Verna had smiled and nodded as Joan showed her photo after photo on her smartphone. So many pictures!

But Myrna knew nothing of the sacrifice Verna had made earlier. Instead, her daughter glared at her, a long, sour expression on her face.

"You should at least meet the man," Verna said in a pleading voice.

Myrna shook her head so hard that her prayer *kapp* came askew. "I will not care for someone's *kinner*. Even worse, you probably told him I'd clean for him as well. If I'm caring for anyone's *kinner* and cleaning *haus*, it's going to be my own, not some stranger's!"

Verna wanted to point out that there was no chance of Myrna ever *having* her own children or her own house if she continued criticizing everyone she met.

"Besides, you told me I'd be a companion or mother's helper!" Myrna's eyes flashed. "What you're describing is completely different. Why, I'd be in charge of everything.

I don't know anything about running someone else's *haus*! And a *boppli*?" She shuddered. "I've barely ever held a *boppli* for more than ten minutes, and that's only been at gatherings when someone needed a quick hand."

It was true—an unfortunate result of being born so close in age to her younger brothers. There were no lessons to be learned about tending to younger siblings. And the fact that they lived in a house on the outskirts of town— and near more *Englischers* than Amish—didn't help matters. Most of Myrna's exposure to children was brief, a few stolen moments at fellowship when a young mother needed an extra hand.

But that didn't mean Myrna *couldn't* do it. Verna had the feeling that her daughter could do anything once given the chance. *Well*, she corrected herself, *anything but working at a place where she has to deal with customers*.

Deciding to take a different approach, Verna attempted to appeal to Myrna's compassionate side. "The man's in a tough situation, Myrna," she said. "He has no one to care for his little ones."

"Surely he has family."

"His *fraa*'s *schwester* was tending to them, but she's recently married."

"So?"

"She's moving to another county next week."

"So?" Myrna repeated, clearly indifferent to Ezekiel's plight.

Verna tried to keep her impatience in check. "She'll live too far away to care for them." Taking a few steps toward her daughter, Verna held her hands out in a pleading gesture. "Have some compassion, Dochder. Think of the children missing their *maem*. How hard it must be on them. And the man. Why! He's a farmer, you know. And it's near impossible to run a farm or tend to chores with a *boppli* and small *kinner* underfoot."

Myrna rolled her eyes. "The community will help out. You know that."

"Myrna!" Verna couldn't believe how stubborn her daughter was behaving. "Do you truly think a rotating caregiver is appropriate?" She paused, trying to regroup her thoughts. Seeing Myrna's attitude, she realized that arguing with her wasn't going to get her anywhere. "It's not forever, Myrna. Mayhaps just until he finds someone else. He doesn't have time now to find anyone but you. Please."

Something shifted on Myrna's face. Her eyes narrowed, and she pressed her lips together in a fine, tight line. Verna held her breath, wondering what Myrna was thinking. From the looks of it, it was a deep thought indeed.

"You've already committed me to the job, haven't you?" Myrna said in a strangely calm voice.

"I—"

But Myrna interrupted her. "You committed me to working for this strange man."

"Well, not—"

"Oh, Maem!" Exasperated, Myrna threw her hands into the air and pushed past her mother. "How could you do that?"

"You need to work, Myrna. And it sounds like a fine opportunity. Even if it's only for a few weeks until he finds a permanent caregiver."

But Myrna wasn't so easily convinced.

"Look, Myrna, it's our duty to rally round our neighbors, and here is a man who could surely use your help." Verna glanced at the clock. How would Myrna react when she told her that they were scheduled to drive over and meet Ezekiel and his children on Monday?

There was a long moment's pause, and then, to Verna's surprise, Myrna's shoulders drooped, and she sighed. "Fine."

"Excuse me?" Stunned, Verna blinked rapidly. Had she misheard her daughter?

"I said fine!"

Verna couldn't help but feel a great wave of relief. She'd never expected Myrna to agree so easily. In fact, she had been prepared for a long, drawn-out battle. All day she had been practicing what she would say to her daughter and preparing herself for the backlash. But now, Verna heard herself laugh, relief washing over her like a wave of good tidings.

"Oh Myrna! That's wonderful!"

Myrna held up her hand as if to stop her mother. "But only until he finds someone else . . . until he finds someone more permanent. Surely this Riehl fellow can find a young woman who will be better suited for the job than I am." She lifted her chin in a subversive manner. "I can promise you I'm not about to be a mother to another woman's children for the rest of my life."

"They don't have a mother."

Myrna rolled her eyes. "You know what I mean. Besides, anything is better than being stuck in that storeroom at Daed's shop. I told you it's too cold, and he refuses to turn on the heat or provide better lighting. I've a headache from shivering and squinting all day. And my fingers are stiff from the chill!"

Verna waved her hand at Myrna in a dismissive way. She didn't understand why her daughter was always so melodramatic. "Oh, come now. I spoke to your *daed* about it and he told me that you're making a big fuss over nothing. He said it's not that bad!"

"It *is* that bad, I can assure you!" Myrna stretched out her fingers, then made a fist. "Why, if I was an *Englischer*, I'd complain to the authorities about those working conditions."

Verna rolled her eyes. "Then I reckon it's a right *gut* thing that you aren't *Englische*."

"Hmph." She started to walk up the staircase but paused in midflight. "I suppose I'm to meet this man before I start, *ja*?"

"Let's see if he can meet you Monday. We'll ride over together."

"And when would I start?"

"The following week. That's when the *aendi* is moving away, I'm told."

Myrna nodded. "So only one week left freezing to death at Daed's, then? Mayhaps you could see about trimming my hours back a bit." She glanced over her shoulder at her mother. "Since Daed insists on letting me freeze to death, I'd hate to catch pneumonia before I start working for Ezeriah."

"Ezekiel," Verna corrected.

"What. Ever." She tapped her fingers on the banister. "Can't be getting his *kinner* sick. I reckon *that* wouldn't win me any gold stars." She smirked. "Or any promotions. Oh, wait! Pretend mothers don't get promotions."

Verna pressed her lips together and gave Myrna a stern look. But Myrna merely continued making her way upstairs. When she heard the door to the bedroom shut, Verna exhaled and turned away from the staircase.

She was surprised that Myrna had so readily agreed to take the job. But she was also concerned that Myrna's flippant attitude might create problems for this Ezekiel Riehl. Surely, he didn't need a homemaker with such inappropriate behavior. She could only pray that Myrna would have enough respect for the man that she'd keep her opinions to herself and just do what was expected of her without trying to take undue control of his home and family.

"She said what?"

Sitting in her buggy, Verna laughed when she saw Edna's expression. "She said she'd do it!"

"Oh, glory day!" Edna clasped her hands together and lifted them toward the sky as if thanking God. "I just know this will be a *wunderbarr* learning experience for her."

It was Friday afternoon and, as soon as she'd finished her chores, Verna had hitched the horse to the buggy and driven over to the Esh farm, eager to share the news. "I thought we could ride over to your friend's *haus* and see if she might be able to get us in touch with this Riehl fellow to confirm."

Fifteen minutes later, they pulled into the driveway of the Schwartz household. Unlike the Eshes, the Schwartzes had a telephone on their property. Susan eagerly agreed to make the phone call and, while Edna and Verna sat outside on the porch, disappeared into the phone shanty to do just that.

"Monday still works fine for Ezekiel," Susan said as she rejoined them on the porch. "She should meet with him then."

It felt as if a weight had been lifted from Verna's shoulders. Perhaps Edna had been correct after all, she thought. Perhaps this was part of God's plan: a family in need of Myrna's help when she, too, needed theirs.

"I don't know how I'll get through the weekend," Verna said as she sipped at the glass of lemonade that Susan had served them. "This is all so exciting."

"So exciting, indeed!" Edna laughed. "Oh, Myrna will do just *wunderbarr*. I know it."

Chapter Six

Early on Monday morning, Myrna stood at the front door of the Riehls' house, her mother at her side. She felt like a child, having her mother accompany her, but Verna had insisted. Myrna couldn't help but wonder if her mother's presence was due to genuine concern for her daughter or to keep Myrna from saying something that would be deemed inappropriate.

Perhaps a mixture of both, she decided at last.

Verna knocked on the door and, after a brief wait, glanced in Myrna's direction. "I wonder if he remembered we were coming. Edna's friend Susan told us she'd arranged everything."

Myrna glanced around, taking in the muddy dirt road and the chipped paint on the porch railings. She wasn't impressed. Everywhere she looked she saw the lack of upkeep of the property. The cow paddocks were in desperate need of dragging—even *she* could see that!—and there was a pile of rubbish behind the chicken coop. To make matters worse, she noticed that the wheel for the clothesline was broken. How on earth had his sister been able to set the clothing to dry with a broken clothesline?

"Surely he remembered," her mother mumbled, a

panicked expression upon her face. "But no one seems to be home."

Myrna didn't wait for her mother to say anything else. "Oh, Maem! You just didn't knock loud enough!" Impatiently, Myrna stepped forward and pounded on the door with a closed fist.

Within seconds, it swung open, and Myrna heard the hinge squeak. She couldn't help but wonder what, exactly, this man did all day long. Rubbish in the yard. Manure piling up in the paddock. And a hinge that squeaked louder than any mouse *she'd* ever heard.

She was still contemplating this, her eyes staring at the rusty door hinge, when she heard the man speak.

"No need to knock so hard," he said, his voice quiet despite the reprimand. "Give a man a chance to answer the door," he added calmly.

Myrna was about to respond, irritated by his curt greeting, but as she raised her eyes to stare at his face, she caught her breath. This man was no stranger to her. "It's you!"

He narrowed his eyes and stared back at her. "Hm." That same noise, so guttural and noncommittal. She remembered it from their meeting at the store.

Myrna could sense her mother look first at Ezekiel and then at her, as if trying to make sense of the exchange between them. "You know each other?"

"We've met—"

"—We've never met."

His denial stopped Myrna midsentence. Had he forgotten? "*Ja*, we did," Myrna corrected. "At my *daed*'s store the Saturday before last. Don't you remember?"

He seemed to consider this. "Hm." That noise again.

"The *hardware* store?" she said, drawing out the word "hardware."

Something softened in his expression as he stared at her

with renewed interest, as if he'd found the memory tucked away in the recesses of his mind. "*Ja*, I reckon I do." He tilted his head and studied her, the intensity of his gaze catching Myrna off guard. "So, you're the *maedel* willing to help with my *kinner*—"

"Until you find someone more permanent," Myrna added quickly.

His eyes traveled up and down Myrna. "You look too young to tend to small *kinner*," he said, raising an eyebrow and meeting her gaze.

She bristled at his remark. "I can assure you that I'm not."

"Hm."

"Besides, as I said, I'm just helping out. Temporarily." She stressed the word. "It's my Christian duty." She stood her ground, her hands on her hips and a dark expression of determination on her face. She didn't want him to think she was one of those women who swooped in to rescue a recently widowed man, taking on the role of wife and mother, being pushed around and treated poorly like unpaid help.

Well, she corrected herself, at least she *was* getting paid.

Ezekiel's eyes shifted away from her. "Temporary or permanent makes no difference to me. A man's got to work to feed his family, and I can't do that with four little ones underfoot." He took a step backward and paused before he nodded, an indication that they should step inside.

Myrna entered first, walking past him as he moved to the side. Her shoulder brushed against his, and for a second, she caught his gaze, noticing a surprised look on his face. "Sorry," she mumbled, which only made her feel more uncomfortable. Her cheeks felt warm, and she bent her head, hurrying past him and into the kitchen.

Standing in the middle of the small space, Myrna waited for her eyes to adjust to the poor lighting. The kitchen was dark, with only one dirty kerosene lantern lit, which cast a soft glow on the kitchen table. She looked around, seeing pots and pans on the counter and dirty dishes piled in the sink and on the counters. There were two small boys sitting on a bench in the far corner, their faces pale and their eyes wide as they stared up at Myrna.

"This kitchen is a mess," she announced, turning around to face Ezekiel.

He leaned against the doorway, his arms crossed over his broad chest. But his expression remained relaxed. "Got too much to do outside to spend time washing dishes."

"I thought your *schwester* was helping you."

Something flashed in his eyes. Myrna couldn't quite place what she saw in his expression. Was it remorse? Mourning? Or, perhaps, simply unhappiness? "My *fraa*'s *schwester*, not my own," he corrected.

Myrna was about to speak, but her mother nudged her. Clearly, Verna or her mother was signaling her to say no more.

The man reached up and scratched at his chin. "She didn't come today. Too busy getting ready for the move to her new *haus*. Reckon she has a lot to do before she leaves."

Myrna chewed on her lower lip, her eyes scanning the room again. Nothing looked clean, that was for sure and certain. Clearly his sister-in-law was more focused on organizing her own life than *his*.

"But she's still helping you this week?"

He shook his head, a blank look in his eyes. "Reckon so." With that, he offered no more on the subject, and Myrna knew better than to inquire further. Asking additional questions would surely be prying into a private matter of which he clearly did not wish to speak. But Myrna couldn't help wondering why the women of the community hadn't stepped forward to assist him until he found another solution.

Something was definitely amiss.

Clearly Verna thought so, too, for she cleared her throat. "Reckon you wouldn't mind if I washed those dishes while we talk about how Myrna can help you?"

"Temporarily," Myrna was quick to add, not missing the opportunity to remind her mother that she had only agreed to work for him until he hired a permanent caregiver.

"Hm." There it was again, that short, throaty noise.

Myrna looked over at him and could see his eyes had narrowed. He stood in the doorway, watching them as they began to gather the dirty dishes.

Myrna helped her mother, all the while feeling his eyes flicker between the two women as they worked. She dried the dishes while her mother washed, the two boys quietly remaining on the bench. Myrna was relieved to see how well behaved they were but couldn't help feeling concerned for them. Shouldn't they be outside playing on this beautiful day instead of cooped up in the dark kitchen? She decided she would have to take charge of their activities, as it seemed their father was willing to let them remain idle indoors all day.

At least the sound of the running water made the house feel homier, and keeping her hands busy helped her relax so she could reflect on what needed to be done.

"Exactly what sort of help do you need?" Myrna asked, deciding that it was a good idea to see what Ezekiel's expectations were before she took control of the children and household.

He didn't answer right away, and Myrna glanced over her shoulder at him. When he caught her gaze, she felt a jolt run through her, noticing how his dark eyes had specks of gold in them which seemed to glow in the darkness. She quickly looked away.

"Well, caring for the *kinner*, to start. Hard to work the farm with little ones about, although David sometimes helps me." He paused to look over at the bench. "He's eight."

"And your *schwester*?"

"Katie Ruth's *schwester*," he corrected again, his tone flat. "She's moving to Middlebury."

Myrna already knew that from what her mother had told her.

"And housework, I suppose," he added.

"Well, that's to be expected."

"Hm." Once again, that short, guttural noise.

"What about gardening?" Verna asked. "Myrna's quite handy in the garden."

As Myrna listened, she noticed Ezekiel tugging at his beard. "Oh, that. *Ja*, if she'd like. We haven't had a garden for quite some time."

Myrna frowned. How could that be possible? From what she knew, his wife had been sick for only a short period of time. And she'd only passed the previous summer. Surely Katie Ruth had gardened before she fell ill. Providing fresh vegetables for the family was something that every Amish woman did. Well, most did, anyway. Had Katie Ruth been one of those rare Amish women who didn't tend to a garden?

It was a question Myrna didn't ask but wondered about nonetheless. Instead, she changed the subject and asked, "Where's the *boppli* now?"

"Napping. Just put her down so I could get the two older boys ready for *schule*," he offered while glancing at the bench again.

School. *Ah*, Myrna thought. That solved half of the

problem. Two in school meant she wouldn't have to worry about them during the day. That would be helpful, and since she didn't plan on staying through the summer, she wouldn't have to worry about keeping them entertained during the long summer months. Myrna's spirits lifted even further. So far, this job wasn't sounding like much work at all.

"And the fourth one?"

He motioned with his head toward the back of the gathering room. Myrna followed his gesture with her eyes and saw a door. Most likely the master bedroom, which, in the older farmhouses, was typically on the first floor. "Naps on a cot in the mornings along with his little sister."

"Two good sleepers?" Myrna asked hopefully.

"Sometimes they are."

There was something ominous about the way he said that, but there were more pressing things on her mind, and she didn't dwell on it further.

"So what, exactly will you need me to do in the house, Ezekiel?"

"Whatever women do in a home, I reckon." His eyes scanned the room. "Clean. Wash. Organize."

Organize? Myrna perked up. She liked organizing more than anything. There was no greater satisfaction than finding the proper place for all things. If a home wasn't organized, then it would never run efficiently, and from the looks of things, she knew the first week would be spent getting things in order.

"Like your *maem* said, gardening would be helpful," he added. "Canning." His eyes met hers once again. "Mayhaps helping with haying and baling."

"Well, I guess I can do all those things," Myrna said, feeling a bit overwhelmed. It would be difficult enough to mind the children and do the household chores as it was, but helping in the barn as well seemed a bit much for one person to handle. She wondered if her mother had known she would be expected to pitch in with the farm-work as well.

"Hm."

She frowned. What, exactly, did *that noise* mean?

Beside her at the sink, Verna looked over her shoulder. "Six days a week, then?"

Ezekiel shrugged noncommittally. "Would be *gut*, but I'll take what I can get."

Frowning, Myrna wondered at his statement. He had just rattled off a litany of chores, yet now he seemed unsure of her willingness to help him. With the lack of community support, she began to wonder if there was more to this man and his situation than met the eye. "How much is the pay?"

He blinked.

"You know, the wage for helping you?"

"Ah." A frown creased his forehead. "I hadn't thought that far," he admitted.

Before Myrna could speak up, Verna stepped forward. "Two hundred a week. Does that sound fair?"

Two hundred? Her mouth almost dropped open. Myrna knew better than to counter her mother in front of Ezekiel. To do so would risk him thinking she was difficult and, perhaps, she would lose the job. But two hundred dollars a week was far less than she'd have earned elsewhere. Why! She'd been earning almost ten dollars an hour at the grocery store!

But Ezekiel nodded a silent agreement to the suggested rate. There was nothing Myrna could say now. Inwardly, she sighed. Hopefully, at least, he would appreciate her efforts, unlike the others, who thought her too outspoken and opinionated!

"When should I start, then?"

He gave her a blank stare.

"All righty, then." She pursed her lips and exhaled through her nose. His communication skills surely needed improvement. "Monday it is."

Verna shut off the water and shook her hands dry. "You can bicycle over after breakfast and mayhaps Daed can fetch you when he leaves to come home around four thirty."

Her mother looked at Ezekiel and was about to say something else when they were interrupted by a wail from the room near the kitchen.

"Oh!" Verna tilted her head. "Is that the baby, then?"

He nodded. "Light sleeper," he said. "Always crying, that one. At least as of late."

"May I?" Verna didn't wait for a response before she headed toward the door at the back of the room, which led to the master bedroom.

Myrna frowned as her mother disappeared into the dark room. Left alone with Ezekiel, she felt uncomfortable. He watched her with a curious gaze. She couldn't help but wonder why he had said they hadn't met before. Well, she thought, in truth they hadn't really met. It wasn't as if her father had introduced her to Ezekiel that Saturday when he had stopped by the store.

A few seconds passed, and the baby stopped crying. Surely her mother was soothing the little one. Myrna took advantage of the newfound silence to scan the room once again, her eyes taking in the tattered sofa in the gathering room just off the kitchen and the dusty floorboards. The windows had fingerprints on them, and the calendar that hung on the wall was two months behind. What, exactly, had his sister-in-law done while helping the family?

Feeling his eyes on the back of her neck, she realized that Ezekiel was still watching her. The burning sensation caused her to turn and face him. It struck her that he hadn't moved from where he'd first stood; like a statue, he had remained rooted in place, offering little in the way of guidance.

For a moment she wondered if he didn't like her. Plain and simple. Perhaps he was aloof because he didn't care about her willingness to help. Just as he didn't seem to care about the state of his home or the care of his children. But then she remembered what her mother had said the other day. Something about having compassion for the man's loss.

That's when Myrna felt her heart swell, every vein in her body burning with sympathy. Surely, he was still mourning the loss of his wife. Why, from what she had heard, eight months had passed and he still hadn't stepped out to find a new wife. And from the looks of things, he was clearly not interested in doing so anytime soon.

Was it possible that he didn't plan on marrying again? Had he loved his wife so much that the thought of replacing her was too much to bear?

Oh, she had known many people who had mourned the unexpected passing of a spouse or child. But the Amish way was to focus on the living. After a funeral and burial, people moved on rather quickly. To openly grieve was, in a way, to question whether or not those who had passed were indeed in a better place. For the Amish, grief was locked away and life continued as usual.

Perhaps Ezekiel was one of those men who couldn't let go of the past.

Still, while she felt sorry for the Riehl family's loss, she knew that her sympathy was not what they needed. And she didn't give a hoot or holler if Ezekiel didn't care for her. All she needed was to bide her time until she could find a right proper job, and *this* time she'd learn to still her tongue and keep her opinions to herself.

"Best go see what Maem's doing," she muttered at last and hurried to the doorway where her mother had disappeared.

Inside the dark room, Myrna took a moment to let her eyes adjust to the darkness. There was a cot on the floor where a young boy slept. He was not more than two years old by her best guess, with a thin sheet carelessly draped over his tiny body. The crib sat against the wall near the doorway, and she easily saw the silhouette of her mother holding a baby in her arms.

"Oh, look at this sweet angel," Verna whispered so as not to wake the boy up. She leaned down and brushed her lips against the infant's forehead. "How long has it been since I've held such innocence?" Carefully, she resettled the baby against her shoulder and rubbed her back.

Myrna stepped forward and stared at the little face pressed against her mother. In the soft light, Myrna could see the cherubic cheeks and pursed lips as the baby's eyes fluttered shut. All it had wanted was to be held. Soft arms and a kind voice had lulled the baby back to sleep.

Suddenly, Myrna felt a wave of panic.

Who was she fooling? She knew nothing about caring for small children, and certainly not for a tiny baby. That child wasn't even one year old yet! And she was going to take on the responsibility—albeit temporarily—of running this household for a man whose heart was still filled with grief?

In that instant, Myrna knew she was not cut out for this responsibility.

"I . . . I can't do this, Maem!" Myrna insisted, her voice a hoarse whisper and filled with more than a hint of desperation.

Verna shifted the baby in her arms and turned to face Myrna. There was something in her mother's eyes that took her aback, a look of determination and purpose. "You can, Myrna, and you will. It's high time you gave of yourself a bit more," Verna whispered back. "This Riehl family needs someone." She tilted her head so that she was no longer looking at the baby but at her daughter. "And I have a suspicion that someone is you."

The adamant tone in her mother's voice told Myrna that now was not the time to argue. When her mother had that look in her eye and tone in her voice, there was simply no reasoning with her. Instead, Myrna knew she'd have to bite her tongue and help the Riehls for a week before broaching the subject again.

Maybe then she could convince her mother that this crazy plan had been a mistake.

For the rest of the week, Myrna worked at her father's hardware store in the late mornings and early afternoons when it was busiest. Her mother had managed to convince her father to cut back her hours. At least avoiding the early mornings and late afternoons meant that the storeroom wasn't as cold or dark.

And, despite still working in the back of the store, assigned to cleaning and organizing the shelves in the inventory room, Myrna didn't mind as much. Ever since leaving the Riehls' farm on Monday, she had been unusually quiet. She needed the isolation to think, and what better place to do that than the stockroom, where no one ever bothered her? Something about Ezekiel Riehl had stuck with her. Perhaps it was the intense way he had stared at her, as if studying her every move. It wasn't a look of interest, however. Instead, it was a look of apprehension, as if he didn't quite know what to make of her.

She wondered if he didn't trust her. But, after mulling it over, she knew that couldn't be true. Besides the fact that he didn't know her well enough to *not* trust her, he was hiring her to look after his four young children. Surely, he must think her responsible enough for the job if he was entrusting their care to her.

The children. A wave of panic flooded over her, and her heart began to race as one thought kept cycling through her mind: *how on earth was she going to take care of four children?*

She'd always been one of the youngest children, in both her immediate and extended family. While her older brothers were married, they didn't live nearby or have children of their own yet. She knew nothing about diapers or babies. Why had God thrown this challenge into her life? What was the unspoken plan that He had for her?

"Myrna!"

She looked up, wondering why her father was calling for her.

"*Ja*, Daed?"

He poked his head through the door. "I hate to ask you this, but . . ." Simon paused as if hesitant to continue. His eyes scanned the storeroom, and he took a deep breath, exhaling slowly. "Well, your *bruders* are not here, and I must run to the bank. I always make deposits on Thursdays, you know."

Wordlessly, she stared at him. Why was he telling her this?

Simon shuffled his feet and gave a nervous glance at the clock. "Well, I"—another pause—"need you to watch the front of the store."

Under normal circumstances, she would have been

ecstatic at the request. Today, however, she felt reluctant. For once, her mind was distracted, and the last thing she wanted was to interact with strangers who had silly questions or demands. Still, she knew better than to refuse her father, so she got to her feet, wiping her hands on her apron, and slowly plodded toward the doorway.

Watching her with a curious expression on his face, her father raised an eyebrow. "You feeling okay there, Myrna?"

"*Ja*, Daed." She didn't want to trouble him with her concerns. Even if she did, it wouldn't change the situation at all. She'd still be pedaling her bicycle to the Riehls' farm on Monday morning at six thirty.

For the next fifteen minutes, Myrna stood behind the counter, leaning against it with her back to the door. No one was in the store, and even though it was unlike her, she hoped that no one would come in. Her father wouldn't be long. He'd said he just needed to make a deposit, and how much time could *that* take?

When she heard the bell jingle over the door, she sighed. She craned her head but didn't see anyone. *A customer*, she thought, knowing her father would have called out upon entering.

"Good after—" she started to say as the sound of footsteps got closer and rounded the corner. And that's when she saw him. Ezekiel. "Oh!" It came out like a small gasp, a tiny puff of air. She felt her knees weaken as his dark eyes met hers. "It's you."

She thought she saw the corner of his mouth twitch, and, for the briefest of seconds, his eyes narrowed.

"*Ja*, it's me," he muttered in a low voice. As he stood on the other side of the counter, he placed his hands on the edge. "And I take it that's you."

Was he teasing her? Myrna blinked, trying to determine

whether he was being sarcastic or playful. Nothing about his expression indicated either. "May . . . may I help you with something, then?"

"Hm." That noise again, a noncommittal verbal cue that meant nothing and everything at the same time.

His eyes studied her, never leaving her face, and Myrna was glad that the counter stood between them. She needed it for support.

"I've come for some supplies, *ja*," he said at last, reaching into his pocket for a folded piece of paper. "But before you help me with those, I have something I need to say."

She swallowed.

He leveled his gaze at her. "It's kind of you to step in and help me with my *kinner*. It's an unfortunate situation for all of us."

Unfortunate situation. What a strange choice of words, she thought. She wondered what he meant by that. Was he referring to his sister-in-law leaving, she herself helping out, or the matter of his wife dying in the first place? Perhaps a bit of all three, she decided.

"The *kinner* have been through a lot," he continued, his voice softening. "Some of it preventable. But painful. Grief no parent wants their little ones to experience."

The torn expression on his face showed evidence of his enormous compassion toward others. Myrna felt her heart break for this man. Surely God had better plans for him, she thought, to bring joy back into his life.

He cleared his throat and leveled his gaze at her. "I'd only ask one thing of you."

While her curiosity had been piqued about his comment regarding the situation being preventable, she focused on the latter part of his little speech. "What is that, Ezekiel?"

"Two things, then. Call me Zeke, please." He frowned

and stared at the wall behind her. "Ezekiel sounds very old-fashioned. Reminds me of my *grossdawdi*."

She found herself smiling at his comment. "What's the second thing?"

His gaze shifted from the wall to meet Myrna's eyes. He wore a serious expression, one that spoke of sadness and fear. "I ask that you give me plenty of notice when you are ready to leave."

Now it was Myrna's turn to frown. What did he mean? "For the day?"

"*Nee*," he said, shaking his head. "For good."

"Oh." For a moment, she panicked. Had Ezekiel overheard her telling her mother that she couldn't work there? That she didn't know what she was doing with children? Or had her demeanor told him that she wasn't suited for this job?

Clearing his throat, he averted his eyes and she waited for him to explain further. There was something despondent about the expression on his face, and Myrna suddenly had the impression that it wasn't a hundred percent about his wife's death. "I don't mean to presume anything, Myrna," he continued in a soft tone, "but I'm not like other men in this situation."

He paused, and Myrna couldn't help but ask, "Oh? How's that?"

Slowly, he lifted his eyes and met her curious gaze. "I'm not looking to remarry."

Myrna caught her breath. Had he thought *that* was the reason she had taken the job?

Before she could say anything, he held up his hand. "I'm not saying that's your reason for agreeing to help," he said, as if reading her mind, "but I know how these older women work. A man becomes a widower and they all think he must remarry right away. I'm not like that."

She swallowed. "You must have loved your *fraa* very much."

He hesitated and glanced away. "We've all been through a lot," he said. "So, when the time comes to leave, I'll thank you to just let me know. A few weeks, mayhaps even a month or so."

"I . . . I can promise that."

He gave a single nod. "It'll help with the *kinner* if they have time to prepare for another change in their lives."

Myrna felt as if he had sucked out the air she breathed. How could she have been so selfish and self-centered? Her concerns had only been for herself, filled with worry and dread that Ezekiel would only want a replacement wife, to tend to his needs and look after the children.

What she hadn't considered was the children. First, they'd lost their mother, then their aunt had up and left. Now a stranger was coming to take care of them, but, she, too, would eventually leave.

Myrna shut her eyes for a long moment, trying to calm her erratic breathing. She had committed to taking this job. She couldn't back out now. But she also realized that she would be there longer than planned. Any sudden departure would hurt this man's children in a way that Myrna hadn't thought of before.

Surely Ezekiel was a good father, caring more for their needs than his own.

Swallowing, Myrna took a deep breath and exhaled slowly. "I'll stay, Eze . . . Zeke. As long as I can," she said.

"Hm."

Oh, how she wondered what *that* meant! Perhaps one day she'd learn more about this man and be in a better position to read his little nuances, especially that short, deep, guttural sound that he made so often.

"For the sake of the *kinner*," she added.

He dipped his head appreciatively. "*Danke.*"

"Now," she said, straightening her shoulders and smiling at him, "on to other business. What can I help you with today?"

Chapter Seven

On Friday afternoon, as the sugar cookies baked in the oven, the sweet scent wafted throughout the house. Outside the large picture window in the gathering room, the sky was gray and overcast. Early spring was often like that. Still too cold to want to work outside and too dark to want to be inside. But, with the light filtering in from the windows, it was just perfect for the women to spend time together, working on their blankets while the cookies finished baking.

Wilma's eyes widened. "So Myrna got the job?" She turned to look at Mary to see whether or not *she* had known this interesting tidbit of gossip before her. When Mary merely shrugged her shoulders, Wilma appeared satisfied that she was not the last to know. "When, exactly, were you going to tell us this, Verna? My word! We rode the whole way over here in your buggy and you said nothing about it! Was this a secret or something? Were we not supposed to know?"

"Oh, Wilma!" Edna gave her a stern look of reproach. "Simmer down a bit and give Verna a chance to tell you!"

"Hmph!"

Verna fidgeted a bit, taking her time to answer. "It's not

a secret. Frankly, I forgot to mention it because she hasn't
started yet."

"Not yet?"

"*Nee.* She starts this coming Monday."

"Heavens to Betsy, Verna!" Wilma exclaimed loudly.
"Seeing that Mary and I know nothing, why not start by
telling us how this came about so quickly? It was only
Wednesday last week when Edna told you about it!"

Verna paused for a moment as if thinking. "A week ago,
Thursday, I spoke with Myrna and she agreed to meet with
the widower."

"Hallelujah!"

Mary winced when Wilma shouted this.

Ignoring the ruckus, Verna continued. "I rode out to
Edna's on Friday to tell her, and together we went to see
Susan Schwartz—"

Wilma straightened. "Abram's Susan?"

"*Ja*, that's her."

"Hmph!"

Edna cast a curious glance in Wilma's direction. "What's
that about?"

"She took home my Tupperware from a gathering two
years ago and hasn't yet returned it."

Mary pressed her lips together. "Is that really important
right now, Wilma?"

"It is to me!" Wilma's eyes widened. "It was brand-new
and part of a set, given to me by one of my *kinner*!"

"Now, Wilma," Edna tried to soothe. "She's an older
woman, and that was most likely right after her husband
passed away. I'm sure she just forgot all about it!"

"I'll get you a new one," Mary sighed, "if you'll only let
Verna finish her story."

"That's not the point."

Edna counted to ten, then turned toward Verna. "Never you mind her," she said, encouraging Verna to continue. "Now, go on. I want to hear everything that happened after we left Susan's."

A look of relief washed over Verna. "Well, Myrna and I went to meet this Ezekiel Riehl on Monday."

"Ezekiel Riehl?" Wilma frowned. "I still can't say I'm familiar with him."

Mary shook her head. "Oh, I don't think I'd want my *dochder* working for a man I didn't know." A concerned look covered her face. "Aren't you afraid, Verna?"

Edna waved her hand dismissively at Mary. "Don't you be listening to her, Verna. Ezekiel's in-laws are very reputable."

"But is *he* reputable?" Mary asked. "Oh help. Just the thought. *Nee*, surely I would *never* send my Bethany to work for a stranger."

Wilma gave a little snort. "Of course not, Mary, because you'd never send your Bethany *anywhere* to work."

Edna shot her a dark look. While none of the women ever talked about it, they all believed that Bethany's shyness was due to her mother being so overprotective of her when she was a child. Even now, with Bethany nineteen years old, Mary still shielded her daughter from the rest of the world, refusing to let her work outside the home.

"Well, Simon knows this Ezekiel," Verna said directly to Wilma. "He says he's a fine man. Righteous and pays his bills in cash, which is more than he can say for a lot of other Amish men."

Edna coughed into her hand, trying to hide her smile at Verna's not-so-subtle comment. Everyone knew that Wilma's husband often ran up his bills and rarely, if ever, paid in cash.

Wilma scowled.

"What's he like, this Ezekiel fellow?" Mary asked.

"Seems nice enough. A bit overwhelmed since his *fraa* died last year." She lifted her needles again and began working on the blanket as she talked, the yarn moving slowly through her expert fingers. "The *boppli* is a sweet little thing, and all the *kinner* are clearly in need of a mother."

Both Mary and Edna clucked their tongues as they gave their heads a little shake.

"Poor little one, not even a year old," Verna said. "Just wants to be held."

That news worried Edna. When she'd told Verna about the opportunity, Edna had known that Myrna had very little experience with babies. Now, it dawned on her that she might have made a mistake. How on earth would Verna's daughter handle housework, three boys, *and* a baby? But she knew better than to voice her concerns at this late date. Like any new mother, Myrna would have to learn quickly, despite the fact that the children were not her own.

Clearing her throat, Wilma stopped sulking and leaned forward. "And is he handsome?"

"Wilma!"

She held her hands up as if fending off an attack. "I'm sure you want to know, Mary, just as much as I do!"

Pursing her lips, Mary's fingers flew even faster as she pulled another length of yarn from the skein. "And *I'm* sure that's not true!"

"Well then, *almost* as much."

"*Ach!*" Mary frowned and shook her head disapprovingly as she began unraveling the last row she'd crocheted. "Now look what you made me do!"

Edna took a deep breath. Clearly the afternoon was not going to be very productive for making baby blankets. However, now that Wilma had asked the question, she couldn't deny that she, too, was mildly curious. After all, it would be interesting to see how the relationship between Myrna and this Ezekiel progressed once she was working there every day.

Verna, however, didn't appear amused. "I can assure you that no sparks flew between Myrna and that man!"

"That doesn't answer the question," Wilma retorted smugly.

"What do his looks have to do with anything anyway?" From the way her shoulders had tensed, Verna clearly was not enjoying the direction the conversation was taking.

Wilma leaned back in her chair and began rocking again. "Well, if our plan was to help these *dochders* of ours develop skills and soften their rough edges with the hopes they would finally find a suitor," she said with false subtlety, "then it might expedite things if this Ezekiel *was* good-looking." She raised an eyebrow. "Especially since you said he seems—how did you put it?—'nice enough.'"

Picking up a skein of yarn, Verna tossed it at her. "Oh, Wilma! You're impossible!"

Edna couldn't help but laugh as Wilma caught the skein and promptly tucked it into her own knitting basket. "Now, now, Verna," she said, trying to soothe the woman's rattled nerves. "Stranger things have happened."

"Would be strange indeed if they *don't*, I'd say," Wilma added.

Verna narrowed her eyes and gave her a dark look.

"For now, however," Edna began, hoping to defuse a potentially prickly situation between the two women, "let's just rejoice that Myrna got the new job and pray that she does a right *gut* job at it."

"And likes it," Mary added.

"Amen."

After supper, Edna sat in her rocking chair, still crocheting her baby blanket. Too much talk had taken place during their visit that day, and she was anxious to finish at least one blanket. In the past, she'd always delivered five or six for the MayFest event. This year, she'd committed to delivering ten, and she was behind schedule for making them.

Elmer sat in his chair, his old leather-covered Bible on his lap. With the propane lantern hissing beside him, there was more than enough light to read the good book, but Elmer hadn't flipped a page in over half an hour.

Setting down her work, Edna peered over the rim of her glasses to watch him. "Something troubling you, Elmer?"

"Hmm?" He started at the sound of her voice. "Oh, *nee*," he mumbled. "*Ja*, mayhaps a little."

"Mayhaps you'd share your thoughts with me. Sometimes two heads are better than one when solving problems."

She watched as he put a sliver of paper in the Bible to mark his place. Then he laid his other hand on top of it. "It worries me, Edna, about our boys."

Nothing could have surprised her more. "The boys?" She almost laughed. Their three boys were men now, and each one was a blessing. There was no need to worry about any of them. Well, perhaps just the younger ones, Jonas and Jeremiah. Those two were rather rambunctious. But not one of them was ever in trouble, even though they were on their *rumschpringe*. "Whatever for?"

He shrugged. "Seems they should be courting already,

and from what I can tell, not one of them is even remotely interested in a girl."

"Oh help," she muttered. "And here I thought it was something truly important."

He gave her a weak smile.

"I suppose they'll settle down when they are ready," Edna said, returning her attention to her blanket. Another six rows and she'd be finished with it. "They're social enough, I imagine. Besides, both Jonas and Jeremiah are not even twenty-two yet. They've time."

"I reckon you're right," he said with a sigh. "But John?"

Edna hesitated before responding. Now that she thought about it, the oldest of her sons, John, was most definitely a concern. He worked at the auction house in Shipshewana, a job that kept him busy Thursday through Saturday, but his checks certainly helped with the bills at home. On the other days, he worked on the farm with his father and younger brothers. He was a hard worker and loved farming, apparently preferring that to courting young women. In fact, he rarely went out with friends. At twenty-five years of age, he should've already settled down.

But Edna didn't say that.

"He's a *gut* man, Elmer. I'm sure God has a plan for him. In His time, not ours."

"Quite true," Elmer said, his tone sober. "I know John wants to take over the farm one day, but how will he do that without a wife and sons of his own? It would be nice to start winding down a bit, don't you think?" He shut his eyes and rolled his head from one side to another. "A man's body grows weary after tending the land and dairy herd for so many years."

His words startled her. In all of their years of marriage, Edna had never once heard her husband complain. She studied him for a long few moments and realized with a start that he was no longer the young man she had married. His youthful face had been replaced with one that spoke of wisdom and weather. His hair had grayed out, with hardly any dark brown left at all on his crown.

When had he aged so much? Even more importantly, why hadn't she noticed?

Perhaps, she thought, *it's because I still see him as the Elmer Esh who came calling on me*. She smiled at the memory of Elmer in his Sunday best, nervously asking her to ride home from a singing in his buggy. She hadn't known it then, but Elmer had been nervous about asking her to step out with him. He had wanted to ask for several weeks, but he'd always been too shy to do so. It was only when he heard that Timothy Mast had interest that he finally mustered up enough courage to ask her.

They had married less than six weeks later.

Behind her, the clock on the wall chimed eight times. When it finished, a comfortable silence filled the room. She loved this time of the day. The house was quiet, John having already retired to his bedroom and the two younger boys out with friends. It was nice spending time alone with Elmer. It wasn't often that the boys weren't around.

"Did I tell you that Myrna will be working for Ezekiel Riehl?"

"Riehl, eh?"

She glanced up in time to see Elmer stroking his graying beard.

"Not familiar with an Ezekiel Riehl," he added.

Edna wasn't surprised. The Riehl farm was too far away for Elmer to know the young man. "He farms just south of Shipshe," she said. "Simon knows him, apparently. And Verna met him earlier this week. His wife died last summer."

"Oh *ja*?"

She nodded. "Cancer. Her father is a bishop, but I didn't think to ask his name." She made a mental note to inquire when she saw the women on Wednesday. Maybe their own bishop would be familiar with the Riehl family and know more about Katie Ruth's passing.

"But she had a baby before she passed?"

Edna knew exactly what her husband was thinking. She had thought the same thing. What a bittersweet moment for the young mother, giving birth to a child while knowing she'd never have the chance to see the baby grow. "Terrible tragedy," she added in a soft voice.

"As you said earlier, it's all about God's plan, not ours. Faith is more than just something we say; it's something we do."

She smiled. "Faith is a demonstration of complete trust in God."

He put the Bible on the end table, then stood up and reached for her hand. "And right now, I have faith that *you* are as sleepy as I am."

Setting aside the unfinished baby blanket, she laughed as she took his hand. "You know me so well, Elmer."

"Almost thirty years of marriage will do that to a man," he said and leaned over, planting a soft but chaste kiss upon her lips.

Chapter Eight

"Those *kinner* sure do like these sugar cookies," she heard someone say behind her.

Standing in the kitchen of the Hostetlers' house, where the table was laden with plates of cookies, pies, and cake, Verna turned around and smiled as Miriam Schrock approached her. "Mayhaps as much as I like making them."

It was Sunday and the Hostetlers' house bustled with people. The three-hour worship service had ended almost an hour ago and most of the congregation had already enjoyed their fellowship meal. Now the men stood outside, enjoying the early afternoon sun while clusters of women lingered around, some still seated at the long tables while others stood in groups near the open windows.

Verna had just put the last of the cookies on a tray to bring over to where Mary sat with some of the other women when Miriam had walked over to her.

Leaning against the counter, Miriam reached out to take not one but two of the cookies from a tray. She was an older woman, and a widow at that, who lived with her youngest son and his family just up the road. But, despite her advancing years, she was still as young and spry as they came.

"Now, Verna, you tell the truth, or I'll be reporting you to the bishop for fibbing!"

Verna's mouth opened. What had she said that would make Miriam say such a thing? The older woman was known to be a bit of a gossip, prone to sharing as much as (and sometimes more than!) she heard. The last thing Verna needed was to be the subject of Miriam's tall tales.

"Miriam Schrock! You know I'd no sooner lie than paint my face with makeup!"

"Mm-hmm." Miriam took a bite of a cookie and smacked her lips together. "Best sugar cookie I've ever tasted." She turned her steely gray eyes toward Verna. There was a mischievous glow on her face. "But I know that you enjoy the company you keep when making them more than just baking these cookies!"

It took Verna a few seconds, but when she realized that Miriam had been teasing her, she gave a relieved laugh. "Well, you do have a point there."

"Some of the other women are talking about making their own little clubs—"

"It's not a club," Verna interrupted. "I so dislike when people call it that." She couldn't remember when that had started. Calling their cookie-making visits a "club" made it sound as if they were excluding others or required a membership, and *that* was not true. They only wanted to enjoy each other's company—although Verna could've done without Wilma's taunting last Friday, that was for sure and certain.

Miriam laughed and patted her arm. "Now now, Verna. Don't you mind me. I'm just teasing you. And if other women want to start their own clubs, what harm would be in that? I, for one, would favor an Apple Pie or Peach Cobbler Club and my husband wouldn't mind an Apple Snitz Pie Club, either."

Sensing the lightness in Miriam's tone, Verna relaxed. "Well, I suppose there sure would be plenty of people who'd favor an Apple Snitz Pie Club."

"Exactly." Miriam finished one cookie and waved the other at her. "Me? I'd prefer to head up the Let Me Sample Your Sweets Club!"

Verna laughed. "That does sound like a fun club to belong to. Mayhaps we should start that one!"

"We'd have a waiting list, no doubt." Miriam chuckled. "So never you mind what people call your gatherings, Verna. There's nothing wrong with women getting together and sharing fellowship, especially given how long the four of you have known each other."

Since childhood, Verna wanted to add, but, once again, she didn't want to sound prideful. There weren't that many women in the community who had lifelong friends.

"Now, what's this I hear about your *dochder*?"

The sudden change of topic and the question itself made Verna's eyes widen. Oh, how she hoped Miriam hadn't heard about Myrna being fired from the grocery store! The last thing Verna wanted was more scrutiny concerning her daughter. Then again, *that* type of news always traveled swiftly. Leave it to the older woman to have nothing else to do but gossip about the unfortunate situations of others.

"Myrna?"

"Have you another *dochder* I don't know about?"

Verna felt heat rise to her cheeks. Her eyes scanned the room, and she saw Myrna standing beside Bethany. It warmed Verna's heart to see Myrna interacting with Mary's daughter. Bethany didn't have many friends. While Myrna had a few, she didn't socialize too often anymore— attending youth gatherings was her least favorite thing to do. She complained that most of her friends were married and she felt too old to hang around with younger women who had just started their *rumschpringe*.

Miriam leaned over and lowered her voice. "I hear tell that she'll be tending some *kinner* for a widower."

Verna gave an inward sigh of relief. "Oh, *ja*. She starts on Monday."

Nodding, Miriam appeared to approve. "Always makes sense to have young women care for those little ones, I say. How did that come about anyway?"

"Well, the other week, Edna heard about Ezekiel Riehl needing some help—"

Miriam's expression changed. "Ezekiel Riehl! A farmer from south of Shipshe?" When Edna nodded, Miriam clucked her tongue, an intense look about her eyes.

"You know Ezekiel, then?"

"*Ja*, I sure do. His *fraa* was the *dochder* of my second cousin, Daniel Gingerich, from this side of Nappanee."

Verna's eyes widened. She hadn't thought to inquire about Ezekiel Riehl among members of her own church district.

"A stern man, that one," Miriam continued.

Frowning, Verna tried to think back to when she met Ezekiel on the previous Monday. He hadn't seemed overly stern at the time. Sad, perhaps, and soft-spoken, but hardly stern. "You say that as if it's a bad thing."

Miriam shrugged. "Depends on how you look at it, I reckon. But I heard tell that my cousin didn't think too highly of him. Ezekiel's a farmer and all, but a poor one. Works hard, but didn't always take the greatest care of his family."

She took a quick breath and exhaled slowly. She didn't care for this type of talk. Gossip. That's all it was. Even if it were true, it meant nothing to Verna. "Have you met him?" Verna managed to ask.

"*Nee*—"

Verna interrupted her. "Then I reckon the rest is hearsay."

Miriam raised her eyebrows. "Reckon you're right." She reached out and took another cookie. "But my *gross-mammi* always said that where there's smoke, there usually is fire."

Verna pressed her lips together, unwilling to ask any further questions. She had the distinct feeling that Miriam wanted to tell her something, and Verna knew better than to egg her on.

"In fact," Miriam continued after taking a bite of her third cookie, "that Riehl fellow's not on speaking terms with my cousin—and Daniel's a bishop, mind you. I heard that he refused cancer treatment for his *fraa*." She made a noise of disapproval. "Can you imagine that? Refusing her treatment." She clucked her tongue and shook her head. "Such a shame. No wonder they aren't speaking with him."

At this, Verna caught her breath. Was it possible? Would a husband do such a thing? "Surely you're mistaken."

"*Nee*, I'm not." She took another generous bite, talking with her mouth full. "Wanted her to try natural remedies, which only made the cancer worse, I hear." She gave a little smirk as she leaned forward and added, "Or so they say—reckon that's why they call it 'hearsay.'"

After Sunday supper—a light meal, as Verna only re-heated leftovers on the Lord's day—she sat at the kitchen table, writing a letter to her cousin who lived in Sugar Creek, Ohio. She was happy to share the information about

Myrna starting a new job, but as she wrote the words, her mind wandered back to what Miriam Schrock had said.

"My word, Verna," Simon said as he set down his Bible. "That's the third time you've sighed in ten minutes. What's on your mind?"

Setting down the pen, she looked over to where he sat in his tattered recliner. The light from the large kerosene lantern washed him in brightness, a striking contrast to the little glow from her own tiny hurricane lamp.

"Do you really think Myrna will be okay with this Ezekiel fellow?"

Simon frowned. "Well, I'd no sooner send my child to a place that I felt wasn't safe than I'd take the Lord's name in vain."

Verna forced a quick, apologetic smile. "I don't mean it that way, Simon. I'm sure she'll be safe. It's just"—she bit her upper lip—"we don't know much about him, is all."

"Reckon if there was much to know, we'd have heard."

She fingered the pen on the table and spun it between her fingers. "I suppose."

"Verna?"

There was no fooling Simon. Verna sighed once again, and her shoulders slumped in defeat. She'd never been able to hide anything from her husband. "It's just that, well, Miriam Schrock made a comment about this Riehl fellow today. It just didn't sit well with me, Simon."

The corner of his mouth lifted as if he wanted to smile. "Miriam Schrock? You mean the largest root in the Amish grapevine?"

Verna cast a look of disapproval in his direction. "Seems to me that by saying such a thing, you're one of the roots, too."

He chuckled, but when Verna didn't join in, he sobered.

"All right, then." He adopted a serious expression. "What was it that she said?"

"Well, she said she'd heard about Ezekiel and his wife. That the wife died of cancer—"

"That's true," Simon interrupted. "Breast cancer, I believe."

"—but Ezekiel refused to let her seek treatment."

Simon froze. His eyes narrowed, and his brow wrinkled into deep-set lines. "Refused to let her get treatment? Why, I'd think her family would've had something to say about that."

Verna felt relieved at having set things straight. At least now Simon understood what was bothering her. While there were very conservative Amish families who preferred holistic medicine to hospitals or relied strictly on faith, such families weren't common in their area. After all, God made mankind intelligent enough to discover medicine—that *was* part of God's plan. To accept treatment wasn't a denial of faith, as some conservative Amish claimed. And if anyone thought such a thing, it surely spoke volumes about their true character.

"It just don't sit well," she repeated.

He tugged at his beard again as he mulled over what she had shared with him. "I suppose it wouldn't hurt for me to find out a bit more, but I do agree with you," Simon admitted slowly. "It does make me wonder, especially since this news doesn't seem to fit with the man I've come to know."

Chapter Nine

On Monday morning, Myrna lay in bed, staring at the ceiling while she waited to hear the familiar creaking of the stairs, a sign that her mother was up. Myrna always waited to rise until after her mother was already downstairs and setting the coffee to brew.

This morning, however, Myrna had been awake long before her mother. Her mind reeled. Why on earth had she agreed to help Ezekiel Riehl take care of his *kinner*? Four of them! What on earth did *she* know about children?

It wasn't as if her mother had given her much of a choice, though. The truth was that Myrna needed to work and no one else had offered to hire her. And Ezekiel Riehl was, indeed, in a bind.

True, at first, she'd been hesitant: Myrna knew how widowers behaved. A few months after losing their wives, they were on the prowl for a replacement. And Myrna was *not* looking for that job! Not with Ezekiel. Not with *any* man.

And yet, for some unknown reason, she'd still agreed to work for him.

She'd been a little relieved when Ezekiel had showed up at the store on Thursday, clearly intent on telling her that he had no interest in remarrying. While that gave her comfort, more than once, Myrna had found herself wondering if there was something wrong with her that he hadn't even *considered* her as a contender. Just as quick as that thought popped into her head, she dismissed it. Like Ezekiel, she, too, was not looking for marriage and, even if she were, definitely not to a widower with four small children, that was for sure and certain!

But then Ezekiel had made that strange request. Why would he be so concerned about her giving him proper notice? Did he really think that she'd leave him high and dry? Just not show up one day? Despite what everyone thought, Myrna loved to work. She just didn't like working in disorganized places or interacting with people who weren't the sharpest tools in the shed. Still, she had wondered about why he'd have asked that.

Her thoughts were interrupted when someone rapped at her door.

"Myrna?" her mother's voice murmured from the hallway. "You up yet?"

"*Ja*, Maem."

"Okay then."

Myrna waited until she heard her mother shuffle down the hallway before she willed herself to toss back the covers and swing her legs over the side of the bed. Despite not being thrilled at the prospect of tending to four small children, Myrna felt anything was better than working at her father's store. And she was never one to back down from a challenge.

God, please guide me today so that I say the right words and do the right deeds as I start this new job, she prayed as she sat on the edge of the bed.

In the darkness of the morning, she quickly dressed,

pausing for a brief moment in front of the small round mirror that hung over her dresser. She ran her brush through her hair with expert precision, then twisted and pinned it into a neat bun at the nape of her neck. Then she reached for her white prayer *kapp* and placed it on her head, securing it with one pin so it sat straight.

"There!" she said to her reflection. "Ready to face whatever the day brings!"

Despite her words, she felt apprehensive as she left the safety of her room and ventured downstairs to help her mother prepare breakfast before bicycling the four miles to the Riehls' farm on the other side of town.

When she arrived at the Riehls' farm, Myrna leaned her bicycle against the side of the porch before she made her way into the house. The quiet kitchen spoke of still-sleeping residents. Or, at least, children. Myrna suspected that Ezekiel was already in the barn, milking the cows and feeding the mules.

Better for her, she thought. She would clean up their supper dishes from the previous night and get started familiarizing herself with the house. Ezekiel's sister-in-law clearly hadn't kept things in order, and Myrna knew she had a full day of organizing before her.

It felt strange to be standing in someone else's kitchen. For a long moment, she stood in the center of the room and merely looked around. The calendar hung from the wall near the clock, the month still on November from the previous year. Had no one honestly thought to keep it current?

In the far-right corner of the kitchen was a large open doorway that led to a sunroom. A dark blue sofa rested against the wall underneath the windows. Next to it was a plant stand that held a giant fern, most of the stems devoid of greenery. Without doubt, it needed to be repotted and watered. On the end table next to the sofa was a pile of magazines. Even from the center of the room Myrna could tell that they were a mixture of *Family Life* and *Our Daily Bread* devotionals.

The windows were dirty, and there was a cobweb in the far corner of the kitchen over the cabinets. Myrna sighed. Definitely not the cleanest of homes, but certainly not the dirtiest, either.

She forced her feet to move, willing them to head to the mudroom in search of cleaning supplies. She needed to get started if she wanted to have the kitchen in shape by the end of the day. She'd worry about the other rooms tomorrow. One room at a time, she told herself, knowing that she didn't have much time before she should start breakfast for the family. She felt a bit overwhelmed and planned on asking Ezekiel what it was exactly that his sister-in-law had done. But then she remembered her promise to her parents about minding her opinions, keeping them to herself rather than risking offending Ezekiel—especially on the first day. There was no sense dwelling on others' poor housekeeping or complaining about the state of the house.

Finding a faded blue bucket, Myrna carried it to the kitchen sink. What she needed was hot water and a little Murphy's Oil to scrub the linoleum floor and invite the scent of cleanliness back into the house. When she was little, her mother had always claimed that a house wasn't clean unless it smelled of hard work and Murphy's Oil.

"You made it here okay, then."

Startled by the voice behind her, Myrna dropped the bucket of water. Fortunately, it landed upright, but enough water splashed out the side that she'd have to wipe it up. "Oh help!"

"Didn't mean to startle you none." He made a movement as if to help with cleaning up the spill.

"Well, you did." She waved off his help. "I got this. It's just water."

"Hm."

As she opened up drawers looking for a kitchen towel to wipe up the spill, she was too aware that he was watching her. She wondered whether he was thinking that he had made a mistake. After all, not even fifteen minutes in the house and she had already made a mess.

"Third drawer," he said quietly.

Sure enough, when she opened the third drawer, she saw a stack of poorly folded, mismatched dish towels. "Oh."

"Problem?"

Myrna glanced over her shoulder. "Well, to be honest, *ja*, there is."

His curiosity must have gotten the best of him, for he stepped forward and peered into the drawer. After a quick assessment, he stared at her with a bewildered expression. "What's wrong?"

"What's wrong?" she repeated. "Why! Just look." She wagged her finger at the contents of the drawer. "They aren't folded properly or even stacked in the right place. It just doesn't make sense! Who keeps their dish towels in the *third* drawer in the kitchen?" She pointed to the drawers to the right of the sink. "That's where they belong. And in the *top* drawer, so they are handy for drying."

Ezekiel raised an eyebrow. "Is that so?"

"Why, of course! Everyone knows that towels go to the right of the sink! Unless, of course, you're left-handed. But either way, they should *always* be in the top drawer. It's just easier access and plain old common sense."

"Hm."

"Organization," she said in a firm manner, "is the key to efficiency."

"I see." He stepped back and gave her a thoughtful look. "Well then, I reckon you'll want to move things around a bit."

Her eyes widened. Was he giving her permission to reorganize? "I'd like that very much," she stated. "Trust me when I tell you it will make life much easier."

She thought she saw a hint of a smile on his lips.

"Then, by all means," he said, gesturing to the drawer, "go right ahead and organize anything you want."

Good, Myrna thought. *That* was one thing she loved doing and knew how to do well. Perhaps working for Ezekiel wouldn't be so bad, especially if he kept out of her way while she did it.

He took a moment, standing in front of the sink and staring out the window. Myrna couldn't help but wonder what had caught his eye. Perhaps nothing, she thought, or perhaps it was the memory of his wife. Surely having a strange woman in the house must be as awkward for him as it was for her.

Sighing, Ezekiel leaned over and turned on the faucet. As he ran the water, Myrna couldn't help but notice how he methodically soaped up his hands, taking the time to scrub under his nails until they were free of dirt. Large hands. Hands that belonged to a farmer, that was for certain.

"The *kinner* will be awake soon," he said after turning off the tap. His back was still facing her, but she saw him reach for a towel to dry his hands. "After you feed them, David and Daniel will need to go to *schule*. It's down the lane and up the first dirt road. Henry and the *boppli* will stay home with you."

Myrna frowned. "I'm surprised Daniel's in *schule*. He's awfully young, ain't so?"

She saw his broad shoulders lift and fall, as if he had sighed. And then he turned around to face her.

For a long moment, he leaned against the counter, his hands still holding the towel. For the first time she noticed dark circles under his eyes that spoke of sleepless nights. Myrna wondered what kept him awake at night. The baby? Or memories of his deceased wife? Maybe a mixture of both.

"He started a few months early, *ja*. Under the circumstances, it was better for Daniel to be at *schule* than at home without his *maem*." His eyes narrowed at the mention of his late wife.

A moment of silence blanketed the room. Myrna looked everywhere but at Ezekiel. She felt uncomfortable, uncertain of how to continue with the conversation. Whatever she might say would most likely be wrong. Better to be safe than sorry and remain silent.

Finally, Ezekiel cleared his throat and glanced at the clock. "*Ja, vell*, best be getting back to my chores." He started to turn toward the door but paused. "Reckon you know what to do with the *kinner*. Breakfast, school, and then the house chores, *ja*?" His eyes met hers, and she had the awkward suspicion that he was studying her. Again. "David can help if you have trouble finding things."

Setting the towel back on the counter, he headed for the door. His heavy footsteps filled the emptiness of the room until he stopped. Myrna stared at his back, wondering why he had hesitated.

Without turning around, he mumbled, "Reckon I should thank you, Myrna."

For some reason, the sound of gratitude in his voice startled her. No employer had *ever* thanked her before, not even her father. She frowned. No, *especially* not her father. "For what?"

"For agreeing to help my broken family. Mayhaps you can help them heal. I know I sure can't."

And with that, he stepped outside and shut the door behind him, leaving Myrna in the solitude of the kitchen with her own thoughts. What on earth had he meant by *that*?

"Are you our new *maem*?"

Abruptly, Myrna stood up from peering into the oven and spun around. The sweet voice that had spoken startled her. Nearly forty minutes had passed since Ezekiel had left the kitchen, and during that time, she had been deep in thought as she worked.

Each cabinet had been opened and assessed, mental notes made as to what needed to be placed where. She couldn't believe that any Amish woman had lived in this house. It was far too disorganized and untidy, and, frankly, some parts were so dirty, she was sure they had never been cleaned. While she wouldn't fault Ezekiel's deceased wife, she certainly did fault his sister-in-law. What on earth had she been doing for the past few months besides tending the children?

The last thing on Myrna's mind, however, was the children themselves. So, when she heard those five words, she wasn't prepared.

Myrna stared at the small army of tiny faces that were watching her, and took a quick minute to digest the child's words. *New* maem?

"Heavens to Betsy!" she managed to say with a forced

laugh. They were, after all, just children. Three little boys, each one with a cherubic expression and wide eyes, stared back at her with more than just curiosity. There was hope in their eyes. Something about that irritated her. Was it possible that, despite his admission of having no interest in remarrying, Ezekiel had told the children otherwise?

"Are you, then?" the boy asked, an expectant expression on his face.

"*Nee*, I most certainly am not." Myrna put her hands on her hips and frowned at them. "Whatever gave you that idea?"

"Aendi said Daed was going to get us a new *maem*," the oldest boy said, his voice filled with disappointment. "We thought it might be you."

"She didn't seem happy about it," the other boy said. "But you seem nice enough!"

Surely, they meant Ezekiel's sister-in-law. Why on earth would their aunt say such a thing? And to children? If Myrna had been unimpressed before by the sister-in-law's lack of attention to the house, she was most certainly even less impressed by her poor judgment.

"Well, I hate to dash your hopes so early in the morning," Myrna replied, softening her tone. "But I'm only here to look after you for a spell. Until someone more permanent can be found."

The smallest boy's face began to scrunch up, and Myrna suspected that tears were imminent. Crying? She couldn't handle crying.

Quickly, she gestured toward the table, hoping that a distraction might make him feel better. "Perhaps some pancakes will change the direction of the day, *ja*?"

It worked. Immediately, the three boys rushed to the table, all of them climbing onto the long bench on the side farthest from the sink. Myrna watched them, amused at how the oldest child—David, she presumed—helped the smallest one. Things would go smoothly, she thought, if there was teamwork among the little ones.

She hurried back to the stove and began to lift the pancakes from the pan onto the waiting plate. A thin curl of steam rose from the short stack. Nice and hot, just the way breakfast should be served.

Placing the plate on the table next to the butter and syrup, Myrna stood back, giving the boys space to spear their pancakes and drop them on their plates. The smallest boy looked up at her, blinking his eyes as if waiting for something.

"Henry needs you to cut it," David whispered. "Aendi always cut his food."

"Oh. *Ja*, of course." She moved forward and grabbed his utensils, quickly cutting the pancake into ten bite-sized pieces. "How's that?"

Henry reached for the knife.

"He can't have a knife," David said, reaching out to push away his brother's hands. "He's only three and too little for knives."

Myrna frowned, reaching to snatch the knife from Henry's reach. She hadn't thought he was that old, but, either way, David was right. "I know that." She should've known better than to set it on the table in the first place. Her eyes scanned the kitchen, wondering just how many things that she took for granted represented danger for a three-year-old.

For a few long minutes, the boys quietly ate their food, their eyes wide and their mouths full. Myrna stood by the counter, chewing on the side of her thumbnail as she watched them. Silently she thanked God that two of them would be in school for most of the day. And the three-year old would most likely nap most of the afternoon and then play with his older brothers when they returned from the schoolhouse.

Then she remembered their sister.

"Oh help!"

Daniel giggled at her expression.

"What about your *schwester*?"

"You mean little Katie?" David asked.

"If that's her name, then that's who I mean," Myrna said sharply. "Is she still sleeping, then?"

David shrugged.

Myrna exhaled, wishing that David were a little more helpful. She hurried over to the bedroom door near the staircase and carefully opened it. Peeking inside, she let her eyes adjust to the dim light and looked in the direction of the crib.

Sure enough, two little eyes stared back at her.

"*Ach!*" Myrna hurried over to the crib and lifted the baby into her arms. "How long have you been awake, then?" She studied the baby, who smiled up at her. "Quiet one, aren't you? Not a peep from you for the past hour."

Carrying the baby over to the makeshift changing table on the low dresser, Myrna avoided looking at the unmade bed. Ezekiel had slept there and, for some reason, just being near it felt far too intimate for her. Perhaps she could convince Ezekiel that it was time for Katie to move to an upstairs bedroom. She was, after all, almost a year old.

Once the baby was clean and dressed for the day, she hurried back into the kitchen, with little Katie resting on her hip.

To her surprise, the kitchen was empty.

"Boys?" she called out.

But no one answered.

The plates were on the table and the chairs had been pushed back. Myrna took a deep breath and shut her eyes, counting to ten. This wouldn't do at all.

"Where did your *bruders* go, eh?" She looked at the cherubic face, which smiled back, and felt the baby's hand tug at her apron strings. "Now, now, let's find you something else to play with, shall we?"

Myrna looked around and realized there were no toys. No stuffed animals. No chunky books. No baby dolls. She shifted little Katie to her other hip, then wandered to the sitting area on the far side of the kitchen, her eyes scanning the nooks and crannies of the room.

"What on earth . . . ?"

She stared down at the baby and sighed. "Well, either I'm missing the toys, or you just don't have any. We'll remedy *that* soon enough, *ja*?"

The clock hanging over the sofa chimed eight times. Myrna took a deep breath. She needed to find those boys, get them off to school—they were late already!—and begin her day. Not even one hour into her new job and she already felt overwhelmed.

Grant me patience, Lord, she prayed once again, fully suspecting that it wouldn't be the last time this day that she asked Him for some extra help.

By the time the clock had struck five times, Myrna had already set the table for Ezekiel and the three boys. Little Katie had eaten earlier and was seated on a blanket, playing with some wooden spoons and a plastic container Myrna had found in the pantry. It wasn't much, but it was something.

The door to the kitchen opened, and Ezekiel entered. Quietly, Myrna watched him as he kicked off his boots and hung up his hat. His eyes never left the floor, not once taking in the room to see how neat and tidy everything was.

And clean.

"Daed!"

David was the first of the children to notice Ezekiel. The boy ran over to his father and then jumped up and down at his side. "Guess what Myrna made?"

At the mention of her name, Ezekiel looked up. He appeared almost surprised to see her standing there. When his eyes met hers, he paused, and for the briefest of moments, Myrna was sure she saw a hint of relief cross his face.

"I'm sure I couldn't guess, David," he responded in a quiet tone. "Why not tell me, then?"

"Sugar cookies!"

Clearly, he couldn't help it. His lips turned into a smile, even if his eyes still appeared tired and sorrowful. "Is that so?"

"I love sugar cookies!" Daniel wrapped his arms around his stomach as if hugging himself.

Henry imitated his older brother. "Me, too."

David gave him a stern look. "You don't even know what a sugar cookie is!"

"Do so!"

"Do not! Aendi never baked us anything!"

"Boys!" Myrna scowled and gestured toward the table. "It's supper time, and I'm fairly confident that your *daed* doesn't want to hear bickering at the table. So you best wash your hands and get seated for the prayer."

The comment about their aunt stuck with Myrna, but she knew better than to raise any questions now. Not in front of the children, and certainly not on her first day, especially since she wanted nothing more than to leave. However, Myrna knew that something wasn't right about an aunt who didn't make children cookies, especially given their situation. But instead of dwelling on it, Myrna made her way to the door, where she had her basket and shawl waiting.

"See you tomorrow, then," she said as she swung the shawl around her shoulders.

Ezekiel hesitated, seeming torn between sitting at the table with his children and walking her outside. The boys looked at him, pleading in their eyes. Obviously, they were hungry. But Ezekiel must have been raised in a very strict family, Myrna thought, where women were always seen to the door.

"Let me walk you out," he said at last. "You boys will have to wait."

Quietly, she followed Ezekiel through the door and out onto the porch. He stood against the railing, his hands on his hips as he leaned against the banister. Beyond him, the birds were settling down for evening, chirping and singing. She noticed that he watched them, his eyes following one particular bird, a bluebird.

"Pretty birds."

"What?" He glanced over his shoulder at her. When he saw her wiggle her finger at the bird who still sat atop a nearby branch, he nodded. "Oh, *ja*, definitely. My favorite bird, for sure and certain. God painted that creature with lovely colors, don't you think?"

She stared at him, startled by his words.

"Blue, so like the heavens, and touches of reddish gold like the sun. Whenever I see them, I think of God and how truly powerful He is." He turned his head to meet her eyes.

"And I realize how truly insignificant we all are. Humbles a man to think that way, to remember that we are here to serve others and not the other way around."

It took Myrna a minute to collect her thoughts. She tried to imagine one of her brothers speaking with such thoughtfulness and humility. No image formed at all. She gave her head a little shake as if to clear her mind. "I don't think I'll look at bluebirds in quite the same way ever again," she managed to say.

Suddenly he smiled, his face lighting up. "Is that so?"

She couldn't help but laugh at his eagerness. "That makes you happy, Ezekiel?"

"Hm. I asked that you call me Zeke. *That* would make me happy." Almost immediately after the gentle reprimand, the frown disappeared from his face, replaced by a more serene expression. "And I'm not used to people listening to my thoughts like that. Or caring, anyway. So, if my words touch you—perhaps even change you—then I am quite happy indeed."

Neither one spoke after that, choosing to stand in silence while watching the bird. Myrna glanced over at him, not once but twice, and found herself drawn to the man. There was something subdued about him that made her want to know more. It surprised her that he was such a reflective and thoughtful man, driven by inner thoughts that he obviously didn't share with many.

She wondered why.

Finally, he took a deep breath, inhaling the fresh evening air as his chest expanded. "Thank you for today," he finally said. "The house sure looks well-tended, and your meal smelled *wunderbarr*."

Appreciation? For what she'd done? Myrna almost

didn't know how to respond. For once in her life, she was speechless.

"Seems the little ones have grown fond of you, too," Ezekiel said in a low voice.

"I can't imagine why!" She gave a little laugh. "Had a hard time getting them ready for *schule*—seems they were more interested in sneaking outside to look for some new kittens."

He laughed. "Ja, they love those kittens. Never should've showed them to Daniel."

"And they put on quite a fuss when I made them help with the dishes and tidy their rooms. Seems they aren't very inclined to do 'women's work.'"

Ezekiel raised an eyebrow. "Is that what they call it?"

She nodded.

"Hm."

"Wonder where they learned that," she said so softly that she wasn't sure if he even heard her.

But he did.

"Not from me, I can assure you, Myrna." He pressed his hand against his chest defensively. "I was raised in a family where the men helped the women and the women helped the men. My *grossmammi* would have taken a strap to me if I had refused to work in the kitchen when help was needed." He chuckled to himself. "I've even been known to hang laundry on the clothesline." He glanced at Myrna and winked. "I like hanging it rainbow style."

"Rainbow style?"

"Why, sure thing! All the colors in order . . . black, brown, blue, green, yellow, peach, pink, and then red."

Myrna laughed at the image of Ezekiel standing on the porch sorting through the wet clothes in order to hang them on the line in a specific color order.

"You think that's funny?" But he was smiling, too.

"I do."

"Well, how do *you* hang your clothing?"

"Like with like, my *maem* always said."

He repeated what she had said and then nodded. "Well, Myrna, I can see the reason behind that. Easier to fold when you have all the pants, shirts, and dresses together. Mayhaps I'll try that sometime."

Myrna frowned. Wasn't *she* the one who would be doing their laundry? She had been planning on washing the children's clothes tomorrow. Was he already getting rid of her?

"I . . . I wonder about that," she managed to say. "If I'm working for you, isn't tending to the washing my job?"

"*Ach!*" Lightly, he smacked his forehead with his hand. "I reckon it is, Myrna. I just forgot, that's all. Been doing the wash for so long, it slipped my mind that I don't have to do it for the time being."

"Surely your *fraa*'s *schwester* did the laundry!" She hadn't meant to say it out loud, but Myrna's tongue had wagged before she could stop herself.

"Hm." He averted his eyes.

Myrna's mouth dropped open and she stared at him. "Are you saying that she didn't?"

"I don't recall saying anything about Linda." But the way he pressed his lips together so tightly told Myrna that the conversation was a sore one indeed.

"Well, I won't ask you any more questions," she said, choosing her words carefully. She could hardly imagine why Katie Ruth's sister wouldn't have done his laundry. Surely he was teasing for some odd reason. But then she realized that there couldn't possibly be *any* reason to make something up like that. "That's your story to tell, Ezekiel."

He looked at her in a reproachful manner.

"Zeke," she corrected. "Well, anyway, I . . . I best get going," she managed to mumble, slowly backing away from him as she headed toward the porch steps. "Have a good evening with the *kinner*."

She didn't wait for a response. Instead, she hurried to the place where she had propped her bicycle and began her journey home.

Chapter Ten

Even though Edna had just spent the previous Friday with Verna and would see her the following afternoon, she knew that she simply couldn't wait an entire second day to learn how Myrna had gotten on with Ezekiel and the Riehl children on Monday. Besides, Verna wouldn't share as much with both Mary and Wilma there, especially after Wilma had teased her so the previous week.

All throughout Monday afternoon and well into the evening, Edna had kept glancing at the clock, wondering if Myrna had returned home yet and shared the day's events with her mother. Now, on Tuesday morning, Edna found herself distracted beyond belief. She simply *had* to know what had happened yesterday or she'd get absolutely nothing finished for the rest of the day.

Tapping her fingers against the table, Edna tried to figure out if there was a way to get in contact with Verna. If she called the hardware store, Verna wouldn't receive the message until later that evening. Without a phone in the house, she'd most likely wait to speak to Edna when she arrived for their knitting circle anyway.

"What was that sigh for, Maem?"

Edna looked up and noticed her son John standing on

the bottom step, watching her with a concerned look on his face. "Did I sigh?"

"You sure did." He held an apple in his hand and bit into it. "*Ach!* Terrible."

"Me sighing?"

He held up the apple, his face twisted in exaggeration. "*Nee*, this apple. I sure can't wait until autumn when the apple trees are ready for picking. These store-bought apples aren't near as juicy or sweet as ours." Regardless of his complaint, he took another bite. "What's weighing so heavily on your mind?"

Edna couldn't help but smile. She'd always had a special relationship with her oldest son, John. Somehow, he had seemed to bypass his youth and gone right to being a man. A fine young man who cared more about others than himself. If there ever was a crisis, John was the first to step up and help. And he was handsome, too, with broad shoulders and a thick head of dark blond curls. The fact that, at twenty-five years of age, he was still single shocked Edna. Why! Any woman would be lucky to have him as her husband.

And yet, as far as she knew, he'd never courted anyone. At least not that she'd heard. He was old-fashioned like that, private and reserved—not like his younger brothers, who had driven many young girls home in their buggies.

"I'm just so curious to find out what happened with Myrna."

"Myrna?" he asked.

"*Ja*, Verna's *dochder*."

John held the half-eaten apple in his hand and stared at her. "Oh, you mean *that* Myrna."

She knew that John didn't care for Myrna. They'd met a few times over the years at summer picnics. Clearly, she had left an impression on him, and not a favorable one at that. Edna wasn't surprised. Myrna's outspoken personality would not be appealing to John. Or to many other Amish men, for that matter. Still, Edna didn't like the way he had emphasized the word "that."

"*Ja,*" Edna said sharply, "I mean *that* Myrna. She's started a new job taking care of Ezekiel Riehl's *kinner* and I've no way to reach her mother to find out how she fared yesterday."

John contemplated this for a moment before taking one last bite of the apple. For a few long seconds, he chewed in a thoughtful sort of way. "I know an Ezekiel Riehl."

Edna's eyes widened. "You do?"

"From the auction *haus, ja.*"

She wondered if it was the same man.

As if reading her mind, John added, "His farm's just south of Shipshe. Came to the auction a few times, most recently with two small boys in tow. Bought a new mule."

That must *be him*, she thought. "How well do you know him?"

John shrugged. "As well as anyone can know a client at an auction, I reckon. But he was soft-spoken and patient with those two boys. I remember that. It's not often young boys come to the auction without their *maem* along, too."

Eagerly, Edna pressed him for more. "What else do you know?"

"Not much. But when he bought that mule, I was there in the back. He spoke nice to the animal, unlike a lot of the other men, who act like an animal's no more than a box on a grocery store shelf." He grimaced, and Edna pressed no further. She knew how John felt about the animals being auctioned off. He was a bleeding heart when it came to farm animals and the way they were treated. Every evening, he spent well over an hour grooming his own horse, sometimes even walking it a spell to let it graze on the tender spring grass that was just now popping up.

"A man that treats his *kinner* well and speaks like that to a mule must be a right *gut* man," he said as he tossed the apple core into the small tin that Edna kept for compost. "Anyway, I'm headed into Shipshe right now. I could take you to visit with Verna. It wouldn't be a long visit, mind you. Daed needs me to fetch some oil for the buggy's axels. But it would be long enough, I suppose."

Oh! Such glorious news! Edna lit up and stared at her son. Leave it to John to make such an offer. Of her three sons, he had always been the most thoughtful. "Might you take me? Even if I could visit for just fifteen minutes—"

"—your curiosity would be quenched," he said, smiling.

Laughing, Edna tossed a hand towel at him, which he expertly ducked. "You're incorrigible."

John winked at her, his blue eyes twinkling. "I'll hitch up the buggy and be ready in ten minutes or so. Give you enough time?"

She gave him a sideways glance before nodding. "That should suit just fine, *danke*."

"What's this? A surprise visit?" Verna said, her face lighting up as she opened the front door. "Why, the other girls will get plain old jealous, Edna Esh, all this attention you're paying to me."

While Edna knew that Verna spoke in jest, she also knew there was some truth in her friend's words. At least as far as Wilma was concerned. "Mayhaps we can keep it our little secret, *ja*?"

The house was quiet, and the kitchen smelled like fresh baked bread. Edna took a deep breath, enjoying the warm, yeasty aroma.

"I've always loved that smell," Edna said, feeling a little nostalgic. No matter how many times she walked into a kitchen with the lingering scent of bread, she thought of her childhood. "Funny how it always makes me think of my own *maem*. She just loved to bake bread."

"Mayhaps that's where you developed your love of baking." Verna gestured to the table, indicating that Edna should sit.

"Oh, I can make cookies and pies just fine." Edna gave a little chuckle. "But the bread baking gene didn't get passed on to me."

Verna shooed away her words with a swat of her hand. "Oh, hush now, Edna. I've tasted your bread and it's just as delicious as anyone else's."

Pulling out the arm chair, Edna sat down. "Mayhaps, but it probably took me three tries to get it right."

Verna laughed.

"I've only a short time to visit," Edna said. "John's run to town and offered to drop me off. So don't be making a fuss over me."

Verna ignored her request as she carried a cutting board with a fresh loaf of bread to the table. "And I've some apple butter, too. Just opened it this morning."

Edna took the serrated knife and cut a large slab from the loaf. "I just couldn't wait until tomorrow to hear how Myrna's day went yesterday. Since John was driving this way, I took the opportunity to catch a ride."

Joining Edna at the table, Verna sat down on the chair opposite her friend. "She didn't say much when she returned last night, I'm afraid. But she went to bed without supper. Looked plain tuckered out."

"Oh?"

Verna gave a little laugh. "She's not used to tending *kinner*, I reckon. They must've run her ragged."

The image of Myrna chasing after four small children brought laughter to Edna's lips. "I can only imagine."

"But she was up bright and early this morning," Verna continued, "leaving just after six o'clock to cycle over there. I didn't even have to wake her."

Edna raised her eyebrows, impressed with this last bit of news. "Now that's something, wouldn't you say?"

Nodding, Verna agreed. "Not a complaint or comment was made. She just went about her business as natural as can be." Picking up a butter knife, Verna dipped it into the jar of apple butter and slathered it over her bread. "Mayhaps she's a good caretaker after all."

At this comment, Edna frowned and stared at her friend. "Why on earth would you think otherwise, Verna?"

"She's never shown any signs of wanting a family of her own," Verna said. "I don't even think she's ever courted anyone."

Edna wasn't surprised by that announcement, but she didn't say as much.

Verna sighed. "And I know that Myrna can be difficult. Opinionated and stuck in her ways. Some might call her a bit . . ." She paused before adding a quiet, ". . . spoiled."

"Oh, hogwash." Edna shook her head and clucked her tongue, disapproving of Verna's comment. "I'm not one to speak behind others' backs," she started slowly, "but don't you listen to Wilma and her talk of your *dochder* being spoiled."

"You heard that, then, the other week?"

Edna rolled her eyes and nodded. "Heard it and let it roll right off my shoulders. Just like you should've, too. Myrna's a hard worker, never one to lounge around when there's something that needs to be done. A bit opinionated, as you say, but her intentions are always good, ain't so? I've no doubt that she'll be a *wunderbarr gut* caretaker to this Riehl fellow's *kinner*." She leaned forward and covered Verna's hand with her own. "Otherwise I wouldn't have recommended her for the job and soiled my own good name. Did you think about that?"

A grateful smile crossed Verna's face. "*Danke*, Edna."

"Don't you think twice about it. Why, Myrna's a compassionate young woman. Anyone can see that. And, mayhaps, this Riehl fellow will see it, too."

"Edna!"

The surprised expression on Verna's face made Edna's eyes widen, just a bit. She hoped that she hadn't trodden on forbidden territory with her friend. But, to be truthful, Edna had hoped that Myrna might find herself in a courting situation with the widower. It wasn't uncommon. Why, in the neighboring church district, Bishop Brenneman had helped match Nathanial Miller and Katie Mae Kauffman together, and those two were as unlikely a love connection as any she'd ever seen.

Surely Verna had secretly hoped the same for her own daughter! It wasn't as if suitors were clamoring to take Myrna home from youth gatherings in their buggies. Sure, she was one of the prettiest girls in the church district, but she was also one of the most outspoken.

"Now, Verna, I can't say that I haven't thought a little about it. Haven't you considered such a thing?"

Verna pursed her lips. "I'm not so certain we should worry about such things. God seems to be the best matchmaker. Best to let Him handle all of that." She forced a small smile. "Besides, you have your own three boys to worry about."

Edna laughed, sensing that Verna was on edge about any suggested romance between Myrna and this Ezekiel Riehl. "Oh help! I sure do, don't I?"

But Verna wasn't finished. She raised an eyebrow and, with a mischievous smile on her lips, said, "I know!

Mayhaps you could marry them to Wilma and Mary's girls."

Immediately, Edna stopped laughing. The last thing in the world she would want was to have her sons involved with Wilma's twin daughters. Their competitive nature—so like their mother's—would drive her crazy during family gatherings. And she couldn't imagine any of her boys being remotely interested in them anyway.

"Well, now, I reckon it is time for them to settle down," she said politely. "But you're right—mayhaps it's best to let God help them find their own matches."

Chapter Eleven

On Tuesday evening, Verna sat on the front porch and enjoyed watching the setting sun. She'd already had supper with Simon and the boys, who were now busy tending to the evening chores.

Verna had decided to wait outside for Myrna to return home, and since the light was still good enough for her to catch up on her knitting, she worked on a blanket for the charity.

It was close to six thirty by the time she heard the sound of the bicycle approaching the end of their driveway. Verna set down her knitting needles and peered toward the mailbox, knowing it had to be her daughter.

When she saw the familiar pale blue bicycle turn and approach the house, she smiled.

"You must be starved, Myrna!" Verna called out as soon as her daughter was within earshot. "I've kept a plate warm for you."

She watched as Myrna set the bicycle against the edge of the porch, then slowly trudged up the walkway toward the house. "*Danke*, Maem," she mumbled as she climbed the three steps to the house. "I'm exhausted, but

I wouldn't say no to some warm supper, that's for sure and certain."

Verna stood up, then held open the door. "Go sit down and I'll fetch it for you."

Inside, while Myrna collapsed into one of the ladder-back chairs at the table, Verna hurried over to the oven. She had made fried chicken, mashed potatoes, and green beans for supper with a side of chow chow and applesauce. The plate had been kept warm while the two bowls of cold food sat wrapped in the refrigerator.

"Now, you be careful with this plate, Myrna, you hear? It's going to be hot to the touch." She set the plate down in front of her daughter.

Myrna rested her head against one hand and poked at the food with her fork. "I'm so hungry, but I'm so tired," she complained. "I don't even know if I can stay awake long enough to eat this."

"My word!" Verna slid into the chair next to her. "Mayhaps this job is just too much for you."

"*Nee!*" The firmness of Myrna's voice and her quick response surprised Verna. "That's not it at all, Maem."

"Oh?" Now Verna's curiosity was piqued. She thought back to Wilma's words the previous week and wondered if her friend's comments, so irritating to Verna then, might have a ring of truth to them after all. "Then what is it?"

"It's . . . it's just an adjustment, that's all." She dug into the mashed potatoes and lifted the fork to her lips, and her face lit up as she savored the taste. Closing her eyes for a moment, she groaned. "Your potatoes are always so light and fluffy, Maem. Mayhaps you would show me how you make them so. The boys sure would enjoy them," she said.

"Sounds like you're developing a soft spot for them, then," Verna said, feeling hopeful.

"*Ja*, I guess they're right *gut* boys," she answered while cutting into a piece of chicken. "But it sure is nice to be waited on," she said before she took a bite.

Verna patted her daughter's arm. "Seems to me that you're just bone weary. I can assure you that those potatoes are no better or worse than any others I've made in the past."

"I *am* bone weary," Myrna admitted. She stared at her mother, a look of wonder on her face. "It's hard work tending to *kinner* and a *haus*. I don't know how you get everything done!"

Verna couldn't help but laugh. "Well, I couldn't argue with you there. But women have done it for thousands of years."

"But how do you do it all?"

Taking a deep breath, Verna exhaled slowly. "You *do* get into a routine after a while, Myrna."

"Well, I would hope so!" Myrna speared some green beans with her fork. "But I can't see how, not with that baby always wanting to be held and the boys underfoot. I was sure glad when they went to *schule* this morning, but the time flew by! They were home before I knew it."

"If anyone can do it, I know it's you. But it will take time, Myrna, to get into a routine. This *is* only your second day, after all. And you're in someone else's *haus*. It's bound to be different and takes some getting used to. Plus, they probably have their own way of doing things." She paused, watching as her daughter devoured more mashed potatoes. "How is Ezekiel, anyway?"

Immediately, Myrna perked up. "Zeke?"

Something about the way Myrna shortened his name made Verna catch her breath.

"Why, he seems kind enough. He's even fine with me reorganizing everything—"

"Oh help!" Verna tossed her hands in the air. "What can of worms has he opened there!"

Myrna ignored her mother's playful comment. "—and seems appreciative of what I'm doing. Why, he even thanked me—twice!—for cooking his supper!" This time, it was Myrna who laughed. "It's as if no one's cooked for the man since his *fraa* died."

Verna frowned. Surely the members of the community had brought over food for the family. The women of the church always stepped up to help when someone passed away, especially when those left behind were a man and his young children. "Well, I'm sure that's not true."

Myrna shrugged. "Just telling you how it seems."

"And the *kinner*?" Verna prodded. "How are they taking to you?"

"Fine, I suppose, especially now that they understand my rules." Her eyes flickered toward her mother's. "God gave them two hands, I told them. They can carry over their plates after eating and tidy their rooms, even if they *are* boys." She took another bite of the chicken. "They called it women's work." She gave a single laugh. "Can you imagine such impudence?"

No, Verna thought, she couldn't imagine. Nor could she imagine the firestorm *that* comment had evoked in Myrna. Surely her daughter had given the boys an earful after hearing them speak those two words. It was a wonder that Myrna was still employed. "Seems to me that you're doing just fine with the little ones," Verna said carefully, not wanting Myrna to be put off.

But, to her mother's surprise, Myrna didn't react defensively. Instead, she agreed with her mother. "You know, Maem, I am. It's hard work, but I like it. I mean, as you said, it's only been two days, but Zeke doesn't bother me or tell me what to do. He approved my reorganizing the kitchen—land's sake, it was a mess!—and he seemed pleased that I made little Katie some toys to play with."

"Well, those are all good things, don't you think?"

"Exactly. They *are* good things. I'd sure not like it if he made me follow a bunch of silly rules that make no sense like at the tea store or grocery market. Instead, he seems right thankful." She glanced up at her mother, a thoughtful expression on her face. "No one's ever made me feel appreciated before."

Verna didn't doubt her daughter's words.

Suddenly, Myrna sobered, the glow fading from her eyes. "But something does bother me, Maem."

"Oh?" Verna tilted her head. "What's that?"

"If he's so happy with the changes I've made, why didn't he make them before?" Myrna made a face. "I mean, he's not a lazy man. He's hardworking. And he seems to care a lot for his *kinner*. But I've never heard of a family not having toys for their *boppli*!"

That *was* strange indeed. Verna thought back to what she'd heard about Ezekiel Riehl and his sick wife. She didn't want to spread more gossip, so she hadn't shared it with Myrna. But she did wonder if there was any truth to the tale. Perhaps Ezekiel was from one of those ultra-conservative Old Order Amish families who followed Scripture in the strictest form.

"Well, you're just getting to know him, Myrna. Mayhaps you'll understand more as time goes on. Until then, it's not up to us to judge him or even question him." She placed her hand over her daughter's. "We can't even imagine what he's been through, losing his *fraa* with those young ones. It's a terrible thing."

Myrna seemed to mull over her mother's words before

she sighed. "I reckon you're right. He's been through an awful lot. No sense in questioning things that can't be answered just yet."

In the morning, Verna shuffled out of her bedroom door and into the kitchen, surprised to smell coffee already brewing. The sun hadn't risen yet and a kerosene lantern glowed from the kitchen sideboard. Normally she was the only person awake at this hour.

"What on earth?"

The answer came in the form of Myrna walking out of the downstairs bathroom, her red hair neatly combed back and her prayer *kapp* already placed firmly on her head. "I didn't wake you, did I, Maem?"

Startled, Verna tried to appear nonchalant, but she couldn't remember the last time her daughter had risen this early, and without a reminder! "*Nee*, not at all. But I'm surprised to see you up so early."

Myrna shrugged. "Couldn't sleep, I suppose."

Curious, Verna watched as Myrna peeked at her reflection in the small oval mirror that hung on the wall by the bathroom door. Her fingers reached up and straightened the long white strings of her prayer *kapp*.

"And you made coffee?"

Myrna nodded. "*Ja*, I did."

"Shall I fetch you a cup, then?"

Without waiting for an answer, Verna moved over to the coffeepot and started pouring two mugs of coffee. The sound of the liquid hitting the bottom of the mug and the steam that rose, brushing against her cheeks, warmed her.

When the mugs were full, she carried one over to her daughter. "So, you couldn't sleep?"

With a gentle lift of her shoulders, Myrna shrugged as she took the mug. "My mind was racing, that's all."

"Oh?"

She nodded. "*Ja*, I was thinking of all the things I need to do today. There's an awful lot of dirty laundry piled up. I think I'll follow your schedule, Maem. Clothing on Mondays and Fridays. Linens on Wednesdays. Works well enough for you." She sipped at her coffee. "As Mammi Bess always said, don't fix it if it ain't broke."

Verna couldn't keep herself from beaming at the compliment.

"And I think I'll inventory the pantry and see what canned goods are left. Mayhaps I'll even see if I can borrow the buggy and go to the grocery store."

"Don't you think it's a bit soon, Myrna?" She kept her tone soft and uncritical. "You don't know the man so well to borrow his horse yet. Besides, do you think it'd be wise taking two young *kinner* to town? They'd be quite a handful."

Myrna froze. "*Ach!* I didn't think of that." The excitement faded from her face. "Well, at least I could make a list for Zeke, I reckon."

Sipping at her coffee, Verna couldn't help but notice again the way her daughter called him Zeke and not by his formal name. She also contemplated her daughter's reaction, knowing her only too well. She was all about approaching a project head-on. This time, however, Verna suspected that Myrna needed to take a slower approach. Even God took six days to create the world and all its creatures.

"Might I make a suggestion, Myrna?"

A single nod was her response.

"Mayhaps you might take a more . . ." She paused, searching for the right words so as not to offend her daughter. ". . . practical strategy."

Myrna sat silent, an expression of curiosity on her face as she waited for her mother to continue.

"Focus on one thing a day. Just one. If you can do that—and do it well—you've done a lot. You'll be working there for some time." *We hope*, she thought to herself. "You're not on any deadline for organizing that *haus*. In fact, that's not even your primary job. It's to care for the *kinner*, first and foremost. So, remember this: Small steps will contribute to the larger picture and be less wearisome in the long run."

Myrna groaned, leaning her head against her hand. "Small steps? Oh, Maem! You know that's hard for me, especially when there is so much to contend with."

"You'll have to try," Verna said encouragingly.

"But there's just so many things that need to be addressed." She sighed. "How on earth do you decide what to do now and what to leave for later?"

"One thing," Verna repeated, holding up her finger. "With small children, sometimes you can't even do that."

At this suggestion, Myrna snorted. "We'll see about *that*!"

Verna lifted the coffee mug to her lips and suppressed a chuckle. "We'll see about that, indeed," she said, her eyes staring over the rim of the mug to peer at her daughter.

Chapter Twelve

After sending the two boys off to school the following Monday morning, Myrna could barely wait to start with the wash. She needed little Katie to take a nap so she could gather all the clothes and begin sorting. Henry might be too young for school, but Myrna had every intention of showing him how to help her with the chores.

The previous evening, she'd lain awake and stared at the ceiling in her bedroom. She'd replayed the last few days in her head, trying to think of ways she could be more efficient in managing the Riehls' household.

And then it struck her.

Just as she had mentioned to her mother the other morning, Myrna knew exactly what she had to do—she just didn't know *how* to do it. She needed to create a schedule and stick to it. No matter what happened. If she stuck to a routine, she'd stay ahead of the chores and, hopefully, wouldn't be so exhausted at the end of the day.

The idea excited her—organization was definitely her thing!—and she began mentally mapping out how each week would go. Wash clothing on Mondays and Fridays, clean the kitchen and bedrooms on Tuesdays and Fridays, wash linens and towels on Wednesday, and focus on special projects each Thursday. On Saturdays, she'd tidy up and prepare a meal for Sunday, her only day off.

She'd awoken in the morning feeling renewed and refreshed, eager to get started with her plan.

But as soon as she and the two younger children returned to the farm after dropping David and Daniel at school, Henry sat on the floor, tugging at his ear and crying.

"What's this?" She stood before him, her hands on her hips. She glanced at the clock on the wall. Eight thirty. She needed to get the clothing washed and on the line before ten o'clock, otherwise it wouldn't dry before the rain rolled in later that afternoon.

"My ear."

She knelt and gently pushed his hands away from the side of his head. "Let me have a peek, Henry." Despite not really knowing what she was looking for, Myrna peered into his ear. It was a little red, but she figured it was probably from him rubbing at it.

"Oh, I'm sure you're just fine."

"It hurts."

"Now, now." She took him into her arms and held him for a few minutes, rocking him back and forth, her eyes flickering to the clock nervously. As the long hand moved, she felt a tightening in her chest. Finally, she leaned back and pushed his hair away from his forehead. "Listen, Henry. We've a lot of work to do today. If you help me a spell, then we can make sugar cookies again. Won't your *bruders* be excited if they come home from *schule* to find sugar cookies again?"

He sniffled and nodded.

"That's a right *gut buwe!*"

She stood him up before she got to her feet and brushed off the front of her black apron.

"Let's start upstairs, *ja*? While your *schwester* sleeps, I'll gather your *bruders*' clothing, and you can gather the hand towels in the bathroom for me." *That's simple enough for him*, she thought. "You can do that?"

He sniffled again, his chest catching twice. But he nodded and then reached his hand up to take hers.

The gesture startled Myrna. Feeling his small, warm palm in hers, she felt a moment of tenderness for the small boy.

"Come along, then," she said in a soft voice. "The sooner we finish this, the sooner we can bake those cookies!"

Upstairs, Myrna hurried into the bedroom that the three boys shared. One double bed and one twin bed were pushed against the walls. The plastic hamper in the corner was empty, for their dirty clothing was scattered on the floor. It took her a few minutes to gather everything, since several pairs of socks had been kicked under the bed.

Plopping everything into the hamper, she carried it to the hallway, but, before she went downstairs, she paused.

The previous week, she'd spent most of her time on the first floor. When Henry was busy and little Katie napping, Myrna had focused on cleaning and organizing the kitchen until the floors practically shone and everything found its proper place. She hadn't really explored the second floor.

Now, however, the two other doors in the hallway beckoned to her.

Setting down the hamper, Myrna let her curiosity get the best of her. She walked to the first door and opened it. The room was empty, but the perfect size for a large bed or two smaller ones. A green shade, half-drawn, filtered the light. She shut the door and turned to the other door across the hallway.

To her surprise, this room was not empty.

Two boxes sat against the wall and four dresses hung

from a peg. And there was a large wooden chest, beautifully carved on the top. Myrna swallowed, realizing that it was probably Katie Ruth's hope chest.

Quietly, Myrna backed out of the room.

Two unused rooms that Ezekiel and Katie Ruth had probably thought would be filled with children one day. Dreams that had been lost when Katie Ruth passed not even a year ago. The thought troubled Myrna.

But she didn't have time to wallow in sadness for what the Riehl family had lost, because she was interrupted by the sound of a loud crash.

"Oh help!"

She grabbed the hamper before hurrying down the narrow staircase to see what had happened.

"Henry!"

He sat on the floor near the counter, a toppled chair by his side. The cabinet above was open and a broken bag of flour lay on its side. And everything was covered in white.

"My word, child!" She dropped the dirty clothes and hurried over to him. "Are you okay?"

Tears began to slide down his cheeks.

"Are you hurt?" She checked his arms and legs for any sign of injury and then touched his head. He didn't seem to be in pain, but his tears kept flowing. "What on earth were you doing?"

"Making c-c-cookies," he sobbed.

Myrna frowned. "But you were supposed to collect the towels from the bathroom, Henry."

"C-c-cookies."

Inhaling, Myrna shut her eyes and counted to ten. "That wasn't the agreement. It's work before play, Henry." Unfortunately, cleaning the kitchen *hadn't* been on her list today, and now all her plans were upended. "Now I have to sweep up this mess, and not only won't we have time for making cookies, we certainly don't have enough flour."

When Henry heard this, his upper lip started to quiver, and his crying grew even louder.

"You should've done what I asked and not something else," she scolded.

For a few minutes, she ignored his cries while she worked to clean the floor. But the more she tried to sweep it up, the worse it seemed to get. The task overwhelmed her and, with Henry's caterwauling, she couldn't focus.

"Oh help," she muttered and leaned the broom against the counter. She went over to Henry and opened her arms. The sobbing child dove into them. The way he hugged her, his little arms tightly clasped around her neck, warmed her heart. "There, there," she murmured. "It'll be okay." She rubbed his back and rocked him, just a little. "It's nothing that can't be fixed. And mayhaps we can send your *daed* to town for some more flour, so we can make those cookies after all."

Upon hearing this, Henry shuddered and his cries began to subside until she felt his soft breath against her neck. For a few minutes, she held him like that, gently rocking him back and forth.

"I think he's sleeping," a whispered voice said from the doorway.

Slowly, Myrna turned around, surprised to find Ezekiel standing in the doorway. How long, she wondered, had he been watching?

Quietly, he crossed the room and took the small boy from her arms. As he held his son, his eyes scanned the mess in the kitchen. Inwardly, Myrna cringed. She didn't even want to think about how the place must look to him. Surely he would think she was incompetent.

"What happened here?"

There was no accusation in his voice, for which Myrna was thankful. Had he appeared angry or spoken sharply to her, she might have broken down and cried just like Henry.

"He wanted to help make cookies," she whispered.

"Hm."

Myrna glanced down and realized that, just like the counters and floor, she, too, was covered in flour. Her cheeks grew hot, her embarrassment clearly evident. "He . . . he fell down."

Ezekiel ran his hand up the boy's back and gently placed it behind Henry's neck. He waited a few seconds before he shook his head. "*Nee*, he's fine. No injuries, anyway." His dark eyes met hers. "Probably just a wounded ego from being scolded."

Without another word, Ezekiel crossed the kitchen and disappeared into his bedroom. She stood there, alone in the kitchen, and felt terrible. How could she have scolded a three-year-old child? Perhaps she wasn't cut out for this, she thought. Surely Ezekiel would not want her returning to care for his children. Only a week into the job and already everything seemed a disaster.

Seconds later, Ezekiel emerged and quietly shut the door behind him. He took a deep breath and ran his hands through his hair. His dark curls stood up, making him look as if he'd just awoken.

"I'm sorry that I yelled at him," she said at last.

He nodded.

"I . . . I just didn't think, I suppose."

"Hm." That grunt again! "Reckon he owes you an apology, too."

His words surprised her. An apology? From the child? Myrna had expected that Ezekiel would be upset with her. She certainly hadn't expected that he'd be *understanding*!

"Reckon there's been a lot of change for him." He rubbed

at the back of his neck and glanced toward his bedroom door. "Too much excitement for a little one like that. He'll sleep now, for a while, anyway. Seems he naps better on the cot in my room." He exhaled. "I could hardly get him to go to bed last night. David and Daniel, too."

"Oh?"

He gave a small smile. "All they wanted to do was talk about you. *Myrna* this and *Myrna* that."

She flushed and averted her eyes. "A few sugar cookies and their hearts are all mine, it seems."

When he laughed, she realized that she hadn't heard him laugh before. He was always so serious and somber. But the sound of his laughter filled her with a type of joy that was completely new to her. It was as if she had given him the gift of laughter, and just knowing that, Myrna felt blessed. She had brought a brief moment of joy to his day. She had a terrible suspicion that his laughter had remained hidden for far too long.

"Well now," he said, returning his attention to the white-coated kitchen. "Why don't we tackle this mess, *ja*?"

Surprised, Myrna didn't know how to respond. Why would Ezekiel offer to help her? After all, she was paid to tend to the children, and it was her fault that Henry had spilled the flour. She hadn't been watching him properly. Under her care, he had gotten into the cabinet, and it was her mess to clean up. Besides, surely Ezekiel had chores to do in the barn or pastures. And yet he had volunteered without any hesitation. She knew that she couldn't allow him to help.

"*Nee*, Ezekiel—" she started, but he interrupted her with a raised eyebrow. "Zeke," she corrected. "I don't mind cleaning it—"

"Neither do I."

And with that, the matter was put to rest. She knew better than to argue. Not over something like this.

He walked to the pantry and pulled out a dustpan. In silence, they swept up the flour, mopped, and wiped down the counters. With Ezekiel's help, it only took about twenty minutes before everything was put back in order.

"There now." He rinsed the cloth and wrung it out, hanging it from the side of the sink.

She leaned against the mop handle and watched as he reached into the top drawer to the right of the sink and pulled out a dish towel to dry his hands. It made her smile that he remembered she had put them there. "*Danke*, Zeke."

He gave a single nod, then he gestured toward the door to his bedroom, where he had laid Henry to nap. "Well, enjoy the quiet before they both awaken," he said, giving another smile before he left to work in the fields.

Myrna stared after him, wondering at the moment they had just shared before realizing that she didn't know why he had come into the house in the first place.

"No cookies?"

As they walked down the driveway, Myrna fought the urge to roll her eyes as David gave her a despondent look. Ever since they had left the schoolhouse, Myrna pulling the wagon with Henry and little Katie inside while the two older boys trotted alongside, the entire conversation had been about cookies. Clearly she had indeed won their hearts one cookie crumb at a time.

"*Nee*, David," she said, hoping that she sounded just as sorry as they felt. "We had a mishap with the flour this morning and there's not enough left to make cookies today." She knew better than to admit what had happened. Brothers could be hard on one another, and Henry was too little to be subjected to any teasing from his older brothers.

"Tomorrow?"

She gave a shrug. "It depends whether your *daed* can get to the store before then. But he's busy with farmwork, so it might not be until next week."

He scowled and kicked at the dirt.

Myrna laughed at the disappointed expression on his face. "My word, David!" She remembered what she'd been told on her first day and, still not believing it, probed a little. "Surely your *aendi* must've made you cookies every day."

To her surprise, he shook his head. "*Nee*, she did not. We told you that already."

Daniel pouted. "And we like *your* cookies, Myrna!"

She glanced over her shoulder to make certain little Katie was okay. "That's nice to hear," she said. "I learned from my *maem*. She makes cookies with her friends on Fridays for Sunday worship. All the little children love to eat her cookies."

Daniel's mouth opened.

"Best be careful or you'll catch flies," Myrna teased. Then she tentatively asked, "Mayhaps your *maem* made you cookies, then?"

He squinted and gazed upward into the sky as if looking for her. Myrna took advantage of the moment to study the young boy. He didn't look much like his father, so she could only imagine he resembled Katie Ruth. If so, his mother must have been very pretty.

"Maem was sick a lot," David said as if merely stating a fact. There was no emotion in his voice. "She didn't cook."

"Someone must've cooked for you!"

"Daed."

Myrna stopped walking. "Your *daed* cooked for you? While your *maem* was sick?" When he nodded, Myrna tried to wrap her head around this information. With three small children and a sick, pregnant wife, Ezekiel cooked for the family? She couldn't imagine that was possible, given the amount of work there was on the farm. "I wonder that the community didn't help out," she said slowly. "Surely they did, and you just didn't know it, David."

"*Nee*, they didn't, Myrna!" David shot back, his eyes narrowing. "Daed did it," he insisted.

"And Daed can't cook so good," Daniel whispered. "We like your cooking better." He peered up at her and gave her a grin. "Just like we like your cookies! Mayhaps we can go to *your* church service sometime."

Despite the disbelief she felt at David's confession, Myrna couldn't help but laugh at Daniel's eagerness. "Well, if it means that much to you, we can surely make cookies for *you* to bring to *your* worship next time. I'm sure your friends will appreciate it."

As they approached the farm buildings, Myrna caught sight of Ezekiel. For a split second, as she saw him dumping a barrel of manure into the sludge pit, she felt a wave of compassion for the man. If what David had told her was true—and she wasn't certain she believed him—no one had stepped up to help Ezekiel care for his three small children and sick wife. But surely, after she passed and there was a newborn baby, someone must have offered to help besides his sister-in-law?

Her compassion for him grew twofold. Raising four young ones—and tending a farm as well!—would be a difficult task for anyone. She could hardly imagine how hard the past few months had been on him. Suddenly, she felt a desire to make him a special meal, one that would show him that *someone* cared, even if it was only her.

"Let's go inside," she coaxed the children, hoping to distract them. "We can see about making something extra special for your *daed* tonight. And we can see if there's enough flour left over to make a pie, *ja*?"

Daniel, however, noticed his father as he returned to mucking the dairy barn. "Daed!" He ran away from Myrna and headed toward his father. David quickly followed.

Myrna kept the same pace, pulling the wagon with Henry and Katie. She hoped that David and Daniel weren't bothering their father about flour. If so, she'd have to sit them down and remind them not to interrupt Ezekiel with things as unimportant as cookies.

Earlier that day, after the flour incident, she had managed to wash the family's clothing. As she walked down the driveway toward the house, she could still see the items flapping on the clothesline. Fortunately, it hadn't rained. She'd have to settle down the boys so she could fetch them, or there would be nothing for them to wear tomorrow. Hopefully David would mind Henry for a while so she could finish her chores before starting on supper.

As she approached the dairy barn, she saw Ezekiel pull a handkerchief from his back pocket and wipe his forehead. Even though the weather wasn't too warm, it was hard work shoveling manure.

"What's this I hear?" he said as she neared. "The shortage of flour seems to be of concern to young David and Daniel here."

Myrna caught her breath and pressed her lips together tightly. "So it seems."

"We want cookies!" Daniel jumped up and down.

"Myrna makes the best cookies!"

Ezekiel gave a soft chuckle. "Well, I wouldn't know," he

said, "seeing that there were none left when I came inside last week."

This news caught her off guard. Putting her hands on her hips, she stared at the two young boys standing beside their father. "What is this? You ate *all* of those cookies?" She had specifically told the boys to save some for dessert after their supper. "It's a wonder you didn't get sick! Mayhaps I won't make any more cookies if you can't control yourselves."

At once, she saw the crestfallen looks upon their faces. Daniel's eyes began to fill with tears, and from the wagon, Henry began to cry again.

Why was nothing going right today? she wondered.

Ezekiel frowned, his gaze shifting from his boys to Myrna. But he said nothing.

David stomped his foot. "But you said we'd make some for worship Sunday! You promised."

Before Myrna could say anything, Ezekiel rested his hand on his son's shoulder. "Now, David," he said in a soft but firm voice, "you best listen to Myrna now. If she told you to save some cookies and you didn't, well, she has the right to be upset. Gluttony is a sin, you know. Mayhaps if you do your chores and behave properly, she'll change her mind. But in the meantime, there's nothing to be done about it today." He gave David's shoulder a gentle squeeze. "Now, go on inside and do your chores. No back talk, or we'll have our own little private discussion later," he warned sternly.

Without arguing, both David and Daniel scampered toward the house. Myrna watched them disappear inside before she turned her attention to Ezekiel. To her surprise, he had been studying her, and once caught, he averted his gaze.

She felt her cheeks grow warm, but she realized that

she didn't mind that he had been looking at her. In fact, she found his attention suddenly agreeable. There was something about this man that intrigued her, and *that* awareness made her cheeks flush even redder.

"If you make a list," he said quietly, "I'll take you to the grocery store in the morning." He looked up. "If you'd like, that is."

When she met his gaze, Myrna felt as if her throat closed up. Her breath felt short and her chest tightened. She knew that she could go food shopping by herself, even with both Henry and little Katie in tow. But at that moment, his dark eyes staring into hers, Myrna realized that she wanted nothing more than to spend more time with Ezekiel, to get to know him better, and to make up for the uncharitable people in his church district.

"I'd like that very much," she heard herself say.

His mouth twitched as if he wanted to smile, but he caught himself. "Best be getting back to my work," he mumbled and hurried off to the dairy barn.

Myrna forced herself to walk toward the house and not look back. Was she holding hope that Ezekiel might be interested in her? And, if so, why did she care? She tried to convince herself that she *didn't* care, but deep down, if she was honest with herself, she knew she did.

He was, after all, a wounded bird, and she was always the first one to help those injured birds heal.

Chapter Thirteen

Edna wasn't the biggest fan of grocery shopping, especially when she needed to shop in Shipshewana. She always made certain to avoid going there on the weekends. It was always so busy then, mostly with local people—*Englischers*, of course—who clogged the aisles with their carts and children.

On Tuesday morning, she decided it would be a good day to tackle the chore. She needed to replenish her supplies for the cookie group. She scolded herself for not having gone before or after she visited with her friends at Verna's.

"Oh help," she muttered. She'd just washed the last of the breakfast dishes but hadn't finished before her oldest son, John, had left for his job. She'd meant to ask him to hitch the horse to the buggy for her. Now he was gone, and Elmer was already in the back pasture mending a fence.

Sighing, she leaned against the counter and noticed that Jeremiah and Jonas still sat there, Jeremiah scanning the newspaper as they both lingered over a final cup of coffee.

"What's wrong, Maem?" Jeremiah asked.

"Oh, I just forgot to ask John to hitch up the horse."

"Where y'going?" Jonas asked, a mischievous gleam in

his dark chocolate eyes. "Anywhere good? Mayhaps I'll ride along and keep y'company."

"*Nee*, you will not," Edna scolded. The youngest of her sons, Jonas was always the first one to try to sneak out before doing his chores. "You've got to help your *daed* with the fencing in that paddock. Can't have those cows wandering into the hayfield." Her eyes stole a glance at the clock. "*Ach!* It's almost seven thirty! I'm surprised you're not out there already."

Both young men groaned, but knew better than to linger further. They got up, carrying their coffee mugs to the sink.

"I'll hitch up the horse," Jeremiah offered as he reached for his straw hat, which hung from a wooden peg on the wall. "Jonas can get started helping Daed." Plopping the hat onto his thick, dark blond curls, he made his way to the door, gesturing for his younger brother to follow.

Jonas, however, made a face and dragged his feet, half in jest.

It always made her wonder at the little jokes God played on people. Her three sons were as different as could be and yet they seemed to blend together along the edges. In some ways, her middle son, Jeremiah, resembled John in the way he looked out for her. The only difference was that John thought of things to demonstrate his attentiveness without reminders, while Jeremiah needed that gentle nudge. And yet, he also resembled Jonas, who was carefree and tried to get out of doing his chores at the first opportunity.

Thankfully, the store was not crowded. There was nothing worse than a crowded grocery store with gawking *Englischers*. With tourist season starting again, it was that time of year. But tourists helped all of the Amish businesses stay profitable, so Edna knew better than to wish things were different. In fact, with her own little business serving the noon meal to tourists on Thursday, Friday, and Saturday, she tried to be forgiving of their awkward stares and silly questions.

"Edna Esh!"

She squinted, trying to make out the figure of the woman approaching her. Her farsightedness was getting so bad that she couldn't tell who it was until the person grew near. "Miriam Schrock?" Edna smiled, even though, if truth be told, it was a little forced. The older woman was known as a gossip, and from what Verna had told her, Miriam hadn't wasted any time after worship to speak poorly of Ezekiel Riehl. "Why, I haven't seen you in ages!"

"Land's sake! You must be keeping yourself busy," Miriam exclaimed. "The only time I ever get to see you is at weddings and funerals."

Edna wagged a finger at the woman. "And MayFest."

"Ah, *ja*! That's right." She snapped her fingers as if she had completely forgotten. "MayFest. Why, that's just in another week, ain't so?"

A wave of panic washed over Edna. Was that all it was? Just a week? She'd have to get busy to finish the last two baby blankets. "I believe it is, Miriam." *And* danke *for the reminder*, she wanted to add.

Just then, a child bumped into Edna's legs. Thankfully, she was leaning against the cart as she talked to Miriam, so she didn't stumble forward.

Reaching out her hand, Edna steadied the young boy. "Careful there, now."

"Henry?"

Both Miriam and Edna looked up as a young woman in a dark purple dress hurried around the corner of the aisle, a deep frown on her face as she scanned the area for the missing child.

"There you are!"

Her hand still resting on Henry's shoulder, Edna greeted Myrna with a smile. *How fortunate*, she thought. Now she could inquire directly about how Myrna was enjoying her new job. "Myrna! What a surprise!" She glanced at Miriam. "You remember Miriam Schrock, *ja*?"

"Oh, *ja*, I do." She gave the other woman a quick smile before responding to Edna. "She's in our *g'may*, you know."

Of course! Edna should've remembered that Myrna and Miriam were in the same church district.

Myrna knelt before Henry. "You shouldn't run off like that," she scolded before she held his hand and, with an exasperated sigh, turned toward the two women. "I just don't know how anyone keeps track of their little ones! Balls of energy and always on the run!"

Miriam raised an eyebrow. "I heard you were watching the Riehl *kinner*," she said, an odd tone in her voice.

"*Ja*, I am."

With a curious look on her face, Miriam glanced around as if seeking someone. "And the other *kinner*?"

"*Schule.*" The single word was Myrna's only reply as Henry began to flop onto the floor, tugging at his ear. "Henry! Please."

"And how're you getting on with Ezekiel?"

Myrna lifted Henry into her arms and held him, his head pressed against her shoulder. "I . . . I don't see much of Zeke. I mean"—she gave a small laugh—"he works outside, and I work inside."

Edna pursed her lips, considering Myrna's response. There was something in the way Myrna spoke, a bit of nervousness, when she responded about Ezekiel. And she had called him by a very familiar nickname. But before she could inquire further, Miriam leaned over and placed her hands upon Henry's cheeks, twisting his head around so she could get a better look at him.

"He's got an ear infection," she announced after a quick ten-second inspection.

Edna couldn't resist looking into Henry's ears. "Oh help! He sure does." She looked at Myrna. "Best tell Ezekiel to take him to the doctor."

At this, Miriam bristled. "Won't do you any good, you know. Best to treat it on your own."

Myrna's eyes widened. "What do you mean?"

Miriam puffed out her chest a bit, and Edna rolled her eyes. She knew exactly what was coming: a long stream of busybody gossip. "Why, Ezekiel's the one who wouldn't let Katie Ruth get the care she needed when she had the cancer. I wouldn't think he'd take his son to a doctor for a simple ear infection, then."

Edna frowned and gave a short *tsk, tsk* while glancing at Henry. But he was already asleep, his hand on his ear as he snuggled against Myrna's shoulder.

Lowering her voice, Miriam continued. "Katie Ruth's *maem* is my cousin, you know." She paused. "Was, anyway."

"I'm sorry."

Miriam bristled. "Not your fault. However, I have this on good authority. He all but . . ." She scanned the aisle before she mouthed the words, ". . . killed her."

"That's hogwash!" Edna exclaimed.

But Miriam remained adamant. "And *you're* familiar with the family?"

While she had a point, Edna didn't like such ugliness spoken about anyone.

"Anyway, you'd best be buying some wax burning

candles for his ear," Miriam suggested. "Won't do you any good to think Ezekiel will take him anywhere. He's one of those who believes God heals everything without the help of doctors, who we all know only learned medicine by God's grace." She made a scoffing noise. "Why, my cousin said that he had quite a temper about the whole thing. Frightened Katie Ruth terribly."

The conversation ended abruptly when a man walked around the corner, pushing the shopping cart with a baby seated in the front section. "Myrna?"

Edna noticed that Miriam blanched, the color immediately draining from her face. *Serves you right*, Edna thought. *Gossiping like that!* From Miriam's reactions, Edna didn't need an introduction. She knew right away that the man who approached them, his eyes lighting up when he saw Myrna, was none other than Ezekiel Riehl.

He looked at Edna and smiled. When his eyes fell upon Miriam, something about his countenance changed. His jaw tensed, and he visibly stiffened. He barely nodded his head at her. Instead, he focused on his son.

"You found him, I see." Ezekiel leaned over and brushed his hand across the back of Henry's neck as if straightening the collar of the child's shirt. "Let me hold him, *ja*? Boy's heavy for you, don't you think? Then you can finish gathering the items on your list."

Curiously, Edna watched as Myrna handed over the boy and started to say something, as if about to mention Henry's ear. But, for some reason, she clearly thought better of the idea. Instead, she clamped her mouth shut and let Ezekiel cradle the now-silent child.

Well, Edna thought, if *that* didn't come as a shocker. For once, Myrna didn't open her mouth to speak out? Had Miriam's warning kept her silent?

Myrna waved goodbye and followed Ezekiel down the aisle, pushing the cart behind him. With great curiosity, Edna watched as Myrna stopped and leaned over, whispering something to the baby, who grabbed Myrna's *kapp* string, which hung over her shoulder.

Edna smiled. She remembered the days when her children used to do that. Now, as she saw Myrna gently withdrawing the string from the baby's hand, it dawned on her that something had changed in the young woman. In the few days that Myrna had been working for Ezekiel, she had grown up.

Oh, she thought, as she watched Myrna trailing behind Ezekiel, hurrying to catch up, she could hardly wait to speak to Verna. Stranger things had happened than a young woman falling for a widower or a widower falling for his children's caregiver. From the looks of it, the wheels were in motion already, and Edna suspected that it was taking root on both sides.

Perhaps the cookie club's idea to help tame the boldness in Myrna was already working!

Chapter Fourteen

Nothing could have surprised Verna more than opening her door Tuesday afternoon to find Miriam Schrock standing there. Or so she thought. When Miriam shared her news, Verna thought she'd just about faint on the spot. Surely Miriam was not standing before her to discuss Myrna being at the store. Something must have happened there. But her brain couldn't wrap itself around the shock of seeing Miriam and her surprise at hearing that Myrna had gone to Shipshewana.

"Who's watching the *kinner*?" she asked, her heart racing. "Has something happened?"

The older woman pushed her way into the house, making her way to the kitchen table. "Heat me up some coffee and I'll tell you all about it!" she ordered as she plopped into a chair and slipped off her shoes.

"I went to the food store earlier," Miriam explained. "You can imagine our surprise when Myrna walked around the corner and Ezekiel followed!"

Verna frowned. "What do you mean by 'our' surprise?"

"Edna and I."

A chill went through Verna. For some reason, she had a feeling that this story wasn't going to end well.

"I ran into Edna and we were talking a spell, you see, and then Myrna came around the corner all flustered and chasing after Ezekiel's boy." She sipped at her coffee. "We were talking a bit and then Ezekiel showed up." Her expression changed, clearly showing her displeasure with him. "Why, he had no manners whatsoever, scooped up that little one, and practically marched away with nary a word!"

Ezekiel was rude? She could scarce believe it, but why would Miriam tell a lie? No, Verna didn't like the sound of that one bit. "What did Myrna do?"

Miriam set down the coffee cup. "That's the strangest thing about it, you see. She trailed after him, her head hanging down, a good two steps behind that man as if scared of him!"

Verna gasped. "Oh help!"

Miriam nodded. "Exactly. That sure ain't like your Myrna. And I'm just wondering what's going on at that *haus*." She ran her finger over the top of the coffee mug. "How long's she been working there?"

"Why, just a week or so."

"Stranger things have happened," Miriam mumbled. "And the boy has an ear infection, you see, but Ezekiel's against *Englische* medicine . . . or, rather, any medicine at all!" She clucked her tongue. "Well, I picked up some ear candles and a small bottle of apple cider vinegar to swab the ear afterward." She reached out and pushed the bag across the table toward Verna. "Mayhaps you could give them to Myrna when she gets home. He shouldn't suffer like that."

Verna reached out for the bag and slowly opened it. The paper crinkled in the quiet of the kitchen. She peered inside, and sure enough, there were ear candles and a bottle of apple cider vinegar. "That was awful kind of you, Miriam," Verna said. "Let me pay you for that."

Dismissively, Miriam waved her hand. "*Nee*, not necessary. It's for the boy. He was such a sweet little thing and giving Myrna such a start when he ran off. But when I saw that red ear, well, I just wanted to do something." She reached again for her coffee and lifted it to her lips, peering at Verna over the rim. "But you might be wanting to chat a spell with your *dochder*. I know that Ezekiel, and he'll be looking for Katie Ruth's replacement. You sure don't want Myrna to end up the same way Katie Ruth did!"

Verna's mind wandered while Miriam quickly changed subjects, the energy of the coffee having kicked in. She began talking about Jenny Hostetler and a fight she'd had with her sister over the best way to clean the house for the upcoming worship service. Verna barely listened to one word that Miriam said—she already had heard about the disagreement and thought Miriam to be exaggerating, anyway—as she mulled over about this new information she'd learned.

Was it possible that Ezekiel was trying to woo Myrna? While he'd seemed like a nice enough man, she also knew that dark secrets were often hidden by the most surprising people. And what about Myrna? She was someone who was always trying to help others, mending the wing of every broken bird—even when the wing was only sprained. It would make sense that she'd fall for Ezekiel, especially since he had given her permission to reorganize everything in his house. Had that one sanction won her heart so easily?

Verna knew she needed to talk with Simon the moment he returned home from work. Only he would understand her concern and help her sort out the matter.

* * *

At six o'clock on the button, Verna stood on the porch, waiting for Simon to arrive home.

Inside the house, a plain white linen cloth covered the table, which was already set for dinner. A plate of freshly baked bread—sliced in thin pieces—along with a bowl of homemade jam looked lonely without any other platters of food. But the table wouldn't be so empty for long. Dinner was cooking in the oven, and the entire house smelled of maple ham and sweet potato casserole.

But Verna wasn't going to let one person eat a morsel of food until she'd had a moment of private time with her husband.

After Miriam's visit, she wanted to get to the bottom of this situation with Ezekiel. Frankly, she had forgotten to ask Simon if he'd learned of any other news about the man. Shame on her, she thought wryly. But she'd noticed that Myrna seemed happy with her new job—though tired—and that made her want to push aside this negative scuttle-butt about Ezekiel. She'd never subscribed to Miriam Schrock's "where there's smoke, there's fire" philosophy.

All of that had changed after today, however. She could no longer ignore the stories floating around about Ezekiel Riehl. She needed to get to the bottom of the rumors. A man who refused his wife treatment for cancer and didn't want his child's ear infection addressed was not a man Verna wanted her daughter working for. Especially if she was forced to follow him around a grocery store while pushing a shopping cart!

"What ho! What's this?" Simon asked as he emerged from the horse and buggy. "A welcoming committee today?" The bright smile on his face gave no indication that he suspected his wife had something important on her mind. But that changed when she hurried down the porch steps and across the yard to speak to him before he had a chance to unhitch the horse.

"Simon! Have you managed to ask anyone about this Ezekiel fellow?"

His hands stopped as he unbuckled the traces. "Back to that again, eh?"

"Indeed!" Verna put her hands on her hips and lowered her voice. "Miriam Schrock stopped by today and—"

Simon's eyebrows knit together, and he gave her a sharp look. "Miriam Schrock has an awful lot of time on her hands, Verna, and we both know what God says about idle hands."

She clucked her tongue. "She ran into Myrna *and* Ezekiel at the grocery store today."

Simon raised an eyebrow. Clearly, this news appeared to intrigue him. "Oh *ja*? Interesting . . ." His voice trailed off as he focused on unhitching the horse.

"And Myrna was pushing the cart behind him like a . . ." She paused, trying to think of the correct word. When none came, she pressed her lips together and said, "Well, like an obedient wife, I suppose! He was telling her what to buy, Miriam said, and she was just trailing along, with that *boppli* hanging on to her *kapp* strings, according to Miriam."

"She *is* working for him," Simon reminded her. "But it's interesting that a farmer would take time from his day to go grocery shopping."

For all her fluster, Verna froze upon hearing his words. "What's that supposed to mean?"

Simon tried to hide his smile. "Mayhaps he's a bit *ferhoodled* with our *dochder* after all."

"*Ach!*" Verna flung her hands into the air. "Don't say such things, Simon Bontrager! The last thing we need is our twenty-one-year-old *dochder* suddenly married to a man with four young *kinner*—"

"And what's wrong with that?" he asked, interrupting her. Resting his arm across the horse's back, Simon stared at her. "Many a good marriage came from a man and a second wife."

Verna flushed. She had forgotten that Simon's mother was a second wife and had borne his father six children to complement the two that he'd had with his first wife. "If you had let me finish," she snapped, "you'd have heard me say a man with four small *kinner* who doesn't believe in modern medicine!"

"Back to that silly story, huh?" he mumbled. "Ironically, the source, once again, is Miriam Schrock!"

Verna stepped closer to her husband. "Simon, I don't want my *dochder* working for one of *those* types of Amish." She met his gaze head-on. "They're too strict, and I want better for her. I'm sure Katie Ruth's family wishes they'd learned more about him before they gave their blessings on the union. Maybe she'd still be alive." She paused before adding, "Lord knows I never want to be in that same position in two or three years, would you?"

Chapter Fifteen

On Wednesday morning, Myrna peered into the brown paper bag, trying to make sense of its contents. She pulled out a long, thin, cream-colored candle, wrapped in waxy paper, and examined it carefully.

Incredulous, she looked at her mother. "I haven't seen one of these in years! I think since Mammi Bess was alive. Where did you get this ear candle?"

Her mother fussed with the ties on her apron. "Miriam."

At the risk of sounding insolent, Myrna groaned. Leave it to Miriam Schrock to take it upon herself to butt in when no one asked for her advice.

Upon hearing this, her mother said, "Now Myrna, she's just trying to help."

"Really?" The sarcasm dripped from Myrna's voice. "I seriously doubt that."

"Myrna!"

Spreading her hands out before her, the candle still between her thumb and finger, Myrna couldn't help but say what she felt. "Maem, she saw me at the store and came all the way over here to give you this? An ear candle?" She reached into the bag and withdrew the bottle of apple cider vinegar. "And this?" She read the label. "What's this for, anyway?"

"Ear infections."

Irritated, Myrna dropped it back into the bag. "I've never heard of such a thing."

Her mother, however, remained adamant. "First of all, if you rub a little in the boy's ear with a cotton swab, it will help heal the infection. Secondly, I think it's nice that she stopped by. It's not every day that someone is so concerned about another person's child."

Then where was Miriam after Katie Ruth died? Myrna wanted to snap back. But she held that truth close to her heart, not wanting to circulate stories that weren't her business to spread. Besides, she hadn't asked Ezekiel whether they were true or not. Even more importantly, she felt protective of him and didn't want her mother to know *his* business.

She tossed the ear candle into the bag with the bottle of vinegar. "I'll be certain to try it," she forced herself to say. In her mind, she simply could not see herself swabbing little Henry's ear with apple cider vinegar. After having almost two weeks under her apron, the children certainly liked her well enough. She didn't want to ruin it by burning a candle or dousing his ear with smelly vinegar!

"And you'll thank Miriam when you see her at worship this weekend?"

She pressed her lips together, trying to keep her tongue from lashing out. "Maem, Miriam Schrock is a nosy gossip. I'll not be thanking her for anything."

"Myrna!"

"I'm not using this . . . this"—she gestured at the bag— "this silly old wives' tale on a child!"

Verna gave her a stern look of disapproval. "These old wives' tales, as you call them, have survived all these years because they work! And if this Ezekiel fellow doesn't believe in modern medicine, he certainly can't argue with traditional medicine, can he now?"

Myrna rolled her eyes.

But her mother wasn't about to give up. "There's no sense in having a little one in pain, Myrna. Little Henry needs something to help him get better. Why, I remember how your *bruder* Samuel always had earaches."

"*Ja*, and I remember how Mammi Bess used one of those ear candles and fell asleep, almost setting his hair on fire!"

Verna made a face. "Well, there was that. But it *did* work."

Taking a deep breath, Myrna knew she couldn't argue with her mother. There was no getting through to her. Besides, she didn't have time, not if she wanted to get to the Riehls' to make breakfast before she took the children to school. "Fine, Maem."

"You'll try it, then?"

Myrna sighed. "*Ja*, I'll try it."

She grabbed the paper bag and started toward the door.

"Oh, and Myrna?"

Pausing, she turned toward her mother. "*Ja*?"

Verna smiled at her. "Don't fall asleep."

"Come, Henry," she coaxed. "I've brought something that mayhaps will help your ear."

He watched her with great suspicion.

"It's nothing that will hurt," she said, a smile on her face. "But you're going to have to lie still. Can you do that for me?"

Henry swallowed and watched as Myrna pulled out the ear candle. She showed it to him. "See? It's just a candle."

His older brothers stared at it, wide-eyed. "Not medicine?"

She shook her head. "*Nee*, Daniel, it's not medicine."

"He's not allowed medicine," David replied. "None of us are," he added before losing interest and wandering off.

Myrna took a deep breath, watching David sulk away while wishing she could find out more about the young boy's comment. But she felt it wasn't her place to question him on the subject. Myrna knew there was nothing wrong with *Englische* medicine. And from the way David had left, she could tell that he'd been privy to discussions between his mother and father. Knowing that his father had refused his mother treatment must have hurt David, Myrna thought. For that reason, she forced herself to keep silent, not wanting to speak ill of Ezekiel to his children, and not wanting to raise painful memories for his young son. What she wished she could do, however, was speak to Ezekiel.

None of it made sense. He seemed so caring and loving toward his children. Even though she'd only worked for him just a short time, Myrna held Ezekiel in high regard as a parent. He'd been very kind and appeared grateful for all that she did, too. It just didn't make sense that such a warm, tenderhearted, and thoughtful man would be so opposed to seeking help from *Englische* doctors.

An ear candle, however, was *not Englische* medicine. In fact, it had been used by many Amish for generations, probably even dating back to when the communities lived in Palatine. Surely Ezekiel wouldn't complain about that, would he? To be on the safe side, however, she'd decided not to tell him about it. She just hoped that it would work so Henry would feel better.

An hour later, just as she was about to remove the candle and blow it out, she noticed Henry staring over her shoulder, focusing on something behind her. For a moment, she started to turn, wondering what he was looking at. But even as she glanced over her shoulder, she already knew.

Ezekiel stood in the doorway.

"Zeke!"

Quickly, she grabbed the candle and, moving it away from Henry, extinguished the flame.

A dark cloud blanketed his face. "What's going on here?"

Holding the candle in one hand, Myrna knew that she couldn't deny what she had been doing. Something about Zeke's expression frightened her, and she knew she had to be truthful. She wished she hadn't listened to her mother's advice. "I . . . I thought I'd try this to help soothe Henry's earache."

"You thought you'd try to help soothe his earache," he repeated in an incredulous tone. "But you clearly did *not* think to mention it to me, his father."

Slowly, Myrna moved her hand so that the candle was hidden from view.

"I control the care my *kinner* receive," he said, raising his voice. "Not you or anyone else, Myrna. I do."

She felt the color drain from her cheeks. It was true that she'd intentionally not consulted him. Her fear of his refusal to help Henry had stemmed from what she'd heard about his refusal to permit his wife to treat her cancer. But Ezekiel was right, of course. This child was not her son, and she had no right to treat him without permission, despite her desire to make him feel better. If Ezekiel didn't care for medicine, that wasn't something she could change. Simply put, it was not a decision she could make on the child's behalf. How could she have been so foolish?

"I'm terribly sorry, Ezekiel," she whispered.

"You should be!" he snapped and, without another word, stormed out of the house.

For a long moment, Myrna stood there, the candle still

in her hand. Somehow, Henry had not cried when his father had scolded her. For that, Myrna was grateful.

And yet, she wondered at Ezekiel's anger. It seemed disproportionate and so out of character for the man she had grown to know.

She'd heard the stories about Katie Ruth's passing and how it was Ezekiel who refused to let her try conventional medicine. Now she understood why Katie Ruth would have succumbed to his demands. If the normally subdued and kindhearted Ezekiel could turn so quickly and with such vengeance, it was no wonder his wife hadn't fought back.

Going against Ezekiel's wishes was a mistake Myrna would not make again.

By the time she'd finished her afternoon chores, Myrna was more than ready to leave the Riehl farm. She wanted nothing more than to put distance—and a lot of it!—between herself and Ezekiel Riehl.

For the rest of the day, Ezekiel hadn't come into the house. In fact, she thought she heard the horse and buggy leave the property when she was fixing the children a snack. Knowing that he was gone gave her a little bit of breathing room. She needed that break after what had happened earlier.

Still, she knew that she'd have to face him. After all, she couldn't leave the house until he came in at the end of his afternoon chores. For the past two weeks, she'd *always* waited until he came into the house before she bade him and the children goodbye. It was the unspoken passing of the children's care from one person to the other.

Now, as Myrna stood at the kitchen window, chewing on a fingernail, she waited for any sign that Ezekiel was finished working for the day. But she saw nothing, not even a hint of where he might be at that moment.

"Myrna, can you color a picture with me?"

She took a deep breath and forced herself to leave her station at the window. "*Ja*, Daniel, I'd love to."

Walking over to the table, she saw that he'd spread out his box of half-broken crayons on the table, a pile of the prettiest colors neatly set aside for her. His thoughtfulness warmed her heart.

Once she sat down, Daniel pushed a piece of paper toward her. On it was the outline of a horse standing behind a chunky wood fence.

"Is that my picture, then?"

He nodded. "You can color it any color you want."

Myrna poked at the crayons he had assigned to her pile. "Hmm, I don't see any brown here."

Daniel gave her an odd look and then burst out laughing. "Girls like pink, not brown."

"But you can't color a horse pink," she teased.

He giggled as he picked up the brown crayon from his pile. "Here, use that one."

She smiled and then took the crayon and set about filling in the outline of the horse.

Just as she was about finished coloring the horse, she heard the sound of the buggy wheels on the gravel driveway. She looked toward the window. Had Ezekiel truly been gone that long? She had thought he had returned a long time ago. Clearly not. *Where could he have gone?* she wondered.

A few minutes later, the kitchen door opened. Silently, Ezekiel entered, pausing to shut the door behind him.

"Daed!"

Ezekiel held his finger to his lips, indicating that Daniel should lower his voice. "Where's your *bruder*?"

"David? He's outside."

But Ezekiel shook his head. "*Nee*, Daniel. I meant Henry."

Myrna finished coloring and put down her crayon. "He's sleeping. Been napping on and off all day." Pushing her chair back from the table, she stood up. "I believe he's feeling better."

Ezekiel's eyes followed her as she went to fetch her things.

"Daniel, I'll see you tomorrow."

"Aw. You gotta go?"

She nodded. "*Ja*, I do. I have my own family to sup with tonight."

He grumbled under his breath but quickly returned his attention to his coloring book.

"Myrna."

Though she wanted nothing more than to flee from Ezekiel's steady gaze, Myrna did the opposite. She planted her feet firmly on the floor and faced him, making certain to hold her chin high.

"I'm sorry about earlier," he said when she finally made eye contact with him. "I didn't mean to raise my voice."

She nodded, grateful he had apologized but still ready to hold her ground if need be.

"It's just that . . ." He appeared nervous, shuffling his feet and clearing his throat. "Well, I reckon after everything that happened with Katie Ruth, it just caught me off guard when I saw you using that . . . that thing on Henry."

"I'm sorry, too." She forced a small smile. "I should've discussed it with you. I suppose I just didn't want to bother you." As soon as she spoke, she knew it wasn't true. But she didn't want to tell him the truth. It would do no one any good to remind Ezekiel that he, and he alone, had stood in the way of his wife getting treatment.

A look of relief washed over him, and she thought she saw him sigh. "So, we'll see you tomorrow, then?"

Myrna frowned at him, an incredulous expression on her face. Had he truly thought that she'd neglect her responsibilities and commitment to the children? "Unless you tell me otherwise," she said tersely.

"*Nee*, I'm not saying that." He gave her a small smile. "The *kinner* sure do care for you."

As she rode her bicycle home, Myrna found herself replaying the events of the day in her head. How could a man be such a mixture of conflicting personalities? Until that morning when he'd walked in on her candling Henry's ear, Ezekiel had impressed her with his care of the children and his kindness toward her. In fact, she had almost forgotten about the rumors regarding his hand in his wife's death. Now, however, she'd seen a whole other side to him, a side that left her wondering whether he was a true chameleon or not. Could someone really hide their true personality behind feigned virtues?

Chapter Sixteen

"I understand you ran into Myrna in town earlier this week," Verna said. "She's supposed to be at the Riehls' tending the *kinner*, not shopping."

Edna laughed in a light, good-natured way. "Oh, relax, Verna. She had the *kinner* with her. I take it she told you that she saw me, then?"

"*Nee*, Miriam stopped by and told me." Verna exhaled. "Myrna didn't tell me because she knows I thought it was too soon. Taking a *boppli* and a three-year-old shopping?"

"Oh now, Verna, there's no need to fret so much. After all, Ezekiel was with her."

Wilma wore a smug look. "No wonder Myrna didn't mention seeing Edna."

While Verna had no idea what *that* meant, she wasn't about to poke the bear and take Wilma's bait by asking.

Mary, however, set down her crocheting. "You saw him? What's he like, Edna?"

"Tall, dark, and handsome?" Wilma quipped.

"Oh hush!" Mary scolded.

Edna laughed again. "Well, Wilma, I must confess that

he *is* a rather nice-looking man, and he seems quite humble. In fact, he was pushing the shopping cart instead of Myrna."

Mary gasped and clasped her hands before her. "Like a courting couple!"

At this comment, Wilma tossed a ball of yarn at her. "Now *you* hush! What courting couple goes grocery shopping, anyway? Sounds more like a *married* couple to me."

Abruptly, Verna stood up. "Excuse me," she said and hurried into the kitchen.

She needed a moment to think. Alone.

Was it possible that Myrna was developing feelings for this man? She pretended to check on the cookies baking in the kitchen, but her mind was reeling. It might have only been two weeks, but stranger things happened all the time. Why, she had known she wanted to marry Simon after only two buggy rides!

She stood at the kitchen sink and stared out the window. In the distance, just beyond the edge of the backyard, she could see a neighbor plowing his field, a team of four Belgian mules pulling the harrower.

"Verna?"

She didn't turn to face Edna. Instead, she continued watching the farmer drive the team along the long, straight rows of dirt. "Not one of my *kinner* was raised to farm," she whispered. The warmth of Edna's hand on her arm startled her, and Verna turned to face her friend. "It's a hard life, Edna."

"I know," Edna replied. "I live it every day." Her lips turned up at the corners. "But if anyone could do it and do it well, it's Myrna."

Verna sighed. "I reckon she could."

"But let's not put the buggy before the horse, eh? One shopping trip in town does not mean you should start planning a wedding."

"Oh *ja*, there's truth to that," Verna said. "But I have a feeling, Edna. You just get those sometimes with daughters."

This time, Edna's smile was small and poorly hid her own pain at never having enjoyed the pleasure of raising a daughter. Verna watched as Edna rejoined the other two women, but there was a noticeable silence about her as she picked up her knitting needles and continued working on the baby blanket for MayFest.

On Sunday, Edna sat on the hard wooden bench, half listening to the bishop preaching in his singsong way about how Jesus tended to his followers as a shepherd tends his flock.

"And we as a community must take care of one another and tend to those in need . . ." the bishop was saying as Edna's attention began to drift.

With so little time left until MayFest, she had enough on her plate with finishing the promised baby blankets and organizing a baking bee so that they'd have enough cookies to sell at the event. *If the bishop wants to preach to the congregation about taking care of others, he needn't preach in my direction*, she thought.

There was so much to do and so little time to do it. With the days growing longer, Elmer and the boys were busy prepping the fields, spreading manure and raking the soil. In just another week, they'd seed the fields for corn and, shortly after, tend to their first cutting of the alfalfa in the back fields. It was a busy time of year, that was for sure and certain.

And, on top of all that, MayFest was the unofficial kick-off to the tourist season and the end to Edna's quiet season. Soon she'd begin hosting midday meals for the

Englische tourists again. While she only cooked for them on Thursdays, Fridays, and Saturdays, it took a lot of planning, organizing, and time.

Frankly, Edna dreaded it, but the family needed the extra income.

First, however, Edna knew she had to survive her commitment to helping with MayFest.

An hour later, the three-hour worship service ended with the final prayer and genuflection at the wall. Edna could hardly get to the kitchen fast enough. Her mind had been reeling throughout the service, and her backside ached from having sat for so many hours.

"That was a long one today, eh?" someone mumbled into her ear.

Edna stifled a laugh when she recognized the voice as belonging to Susan Schwartz. "*Ja*, a bit long. I much prefer Preacher Mast's sermons, to be honest," she admitted in a low voice.

Behind them, the room was being transformed from a place for prayer to a fellowship hall. The younger men brought in large wooden trestles while the older men lifted the bench legs to slide into them. The smaller boys scampered around the room, collecting the chunky black hymnals and placing them in two wooden crates. Those would be loaded into the bench wagon that waited outside the kitchen doors.

Suddenly, the room no longer had forty benches, but two long tables, ready for the congregation to enjoy a fellowship hour.

Once the men finished, the younger women began setting the tables with plates and cups while the older women worked in the kitchen.

"Preaching about serving others," Susan scoffed as she

placed sliced bread onto serving plates. "I feel like that's all I do anymore."

Edna knew the feeling.

"Speaking of serving others, how's that Myrna Bontrager making out with Ezekiel Riehl's *kinner*?"

"Land's sake!" Edna had forgotten that Susan was the catalyst for Myrna's new job. "I'm getting addle-brained, Susan. I clear forgot to update you!"

Susan gave a tired laugh. "Happens to the best of us, I'm afraid."

"Seems like Myrna's making out right *gut*," she said to Susan. "In fact, I saw them in town the other week." Edna paused before she added, "They were grocery shopping."

Immediately, Susan stopped working and gasped. "Grocery shopping? Together? In town?" Her eyes widened. Edna didn't need to be a mind reader to know what Susan was thinking. The older woman clucked her tongue and pressed her lips together in a mischievous way. "Well, wouldn't that be something?"

Susan wasn't one to gossip to others, so Edna didn't mind sharing her thoughts with her. After all, Edna had thought the very same thing.

"Well, they *did* look rather comfortable together, I suppose," she admitted. Was it too much to hope that Myrna might have found more than a job at the Riehls' farm? Of course, knowing how fastidious Myrna was, Edna had her doubts. "But he's a bit older than her, and she might feel she's far too young to start off with four young *kinner*."

"Oh now, Edna! Stranger things have happened," Susan replied, a knowing gleam in her aging eyes. "Why, my own *schwester* married an older farmer with five *kinner* and went on to have six of her own!"

This time, it was Edna who gasped. Having only three sons, Edna couldn't imagine raising such a large brood of children. Times were tough enough with the decreasing price of milk. How on earth did a farmer feed so many mouths?

"Eleven *kinner*? Oh help!"

"And my eldest *bruder* took on a second wife who was about Myrna's age, and they were happily married until he passed away four years ago." Teasingly, she wagged a finger at Edna. "So don't 'Oh help!' me." She picked up the platter and began carrying it to the table. "God works in mysterious ways, don't you agree?"

Indeed she did.

By Wednesday, Edna could hardly wait to visit with Verna. She'd thought quite a bit about Susan Schwartz's comments after worship the previous Sunday.

Now that Myrna was in the middle of her third week, Edna was curious if there were any signs of a serious attraction between the two young people. After all, Myrna *had* seemed unusually amenable and dutiful when Edna had seen her with Ezekiel at the grocery store. Surely Verna would recognize such a change in her daughter, too!

But, to Edna's surprise, when she sat with her friends at the Bontragers' house, working on the baby blankets for MayFest, Verna merely shook her head at the suggestion.

"I don't know, Edna," Verna said. "I get the feeling that she just doesn't like it!"

"Like it? You mean the job?"

Verna nodded. "*Ja*, that's what I mean. The first two weeks, she seemed so eager to leave for the Riehls' in the morning. Why, I only had to check on her that first day to make certain she was up!"

"And now?"

Verna shrugged. "She's been awfully quiet this week and doesn't talk about the *kinner* anymore."

None of this made sense to Edna. How could that be possible? "I don't understand," she mumbled. "She was so . . . so different the other week."

"*Ach!*" Wilma cried out as she unwound a row of yarn from the blanket she was knitting. "Remind me next year that I don't want to donate so many baby blankets!"

"I wonder what's happened since last week," Mary said, ignoring Wilma's outburst. "You said she seemed so content working for Ezekiel."

The room fell silent and Edna realized that Verna was visibly focused on her knitting. Suspecting that her friend hadn't shared something, Edna probed further. "Verna, do *you* know what might have happened?"

"Well—" Verna practically squirmed under Edna's intense scrutiny. "There was the ear candle situation . . ."

Both Edna and Wilma made faces as they simultaneously cried out, "What?"

Mary clucked her tongue. "I don't even want to know."

Wilma, however, did not share that opinion. "This ought to be good."

Edna scowled at her. "Wilma!" she exclaimed. "This is serious." She turned her attention back to Verna. "What on earth are you talking about? Ear candles?"

"It was Miriam Schrock," Verna said point-blank.

At the mention of Miriam Schrock, Edna groaned.

Verna sighed and set down her knitting. "On Thursday, Miriam stopped by my *haus*. She'd brought an ear candle for the little boy. Said she noticed the little one tugging at his ear and crying. Thought he had an ear infection and the candle might help some."

If Verna had said she'd seen Martians falling from the sky, Edna couldn't have been more surprised. Leaning forward in the chair, Edna rested her elbows on her knees and stared directly at Verna. "Excuse me? Did you just say what I thought you said?"

Next to her, Wilma chuckled. "I knew this would be good."

"Well—"

Edna held up her hand. "Verna. Please do not tell me that you actually bought into Miriam's suggestion and told Myrna to use the ear candle on Ezekiel's son!"

"I—"

Mary shook her head. "I'd *never* do that to Bethany."

Wilma snorted.

"But it works!" Verna insisted.

"What. Ever!" Edna lifted her hand and waved it at Verna. "Let me guess. Myrna tried it and Ezekiel found out." She shook her head. "You know how he feels about medicine, Verna. Why would you even suggest such a thing?"

"Modern medicine," Verna was quick to correct. "An ear candle isn't modern medicine. Nor is apple cider vinegar."

Edna's eyes widened. "Apple cider vinegar?"

"*Ja*, you swab the ear to kill infection."

Wilma burst out laughing and slapped her knee. "I've just about heard it all today."

Edna shot a stern look of reproach toward Wilma.

"I'm not so certain how I'd feel if someone did that to my *dochder*," Mary said softly. "And I'm all for medicine."

A defensive expression covered Verna's face. "She only meant to help."

Leaning back in her chair, Edna remained silent as she continued crocheting. No wonder Myrna was so subdued. Helping others was one thing, but treating someone else's child without discussing it with the parents was quite another.

Edna suspected that any hope of a love match between Ezekiel and Myrna was just a pipe dream now. She made a silent vow that if Myrna lost this job, she'd not put herself out to recommend the young woman for another. If word got out about what Myrna had done, surely Edna's own judgment would be questioned, if not by everyone, then at least by Susan.

She made a mental note to apologize to Susan Schwartz the next time she saw her at worship in two weeks.

Chapter Seventeen

By Friday, Verna felt ten times worse about having listened to Miriam. Why had she allowed herself to be influenced in such a way? She knew better than to butt in to other people's business, especially when it came to children. And she certainly knew better than to listen to Miriam Schrock, of all people!

In hindsight, Verna knew that Mary had been correct: Verna never should have suggested that Myrna treat the child. And Edna's silence spoke of her own disappointment in Verna's interference.

But the worst was Myrna.

Every evening that week, Myrna had returned from the Riehls' farm barely talking at all and only responding to questions with monosyllabic answers. Even her two brothers had commented in private to Verna that something was wrong with their sister.

"Is everything all right?" Verna had asked Myrna on more than one occasion, only to have her daughter respond with a simple "*Ja.*"

But Verna suspected that things were *not* all right. From the way her daughter withdrew and looked so forlorn, Verna began to suspect that there was truth behind her intuition that Myrna had developed feelings for this Ezekiel.

And *that* made Verna feel even more terrible.

Myrna wasn't the type of young woman who spent a lot of time socializing. She certainly didn't ride home with young men from singings, mostly because she tended to avoid going to singings altogether. So how, exactly, was Myrna supposed to meet a young man? Now, if she had actually started to take a shine to Ezekiel, had the ear candling episode ruined her chances?

Verna couldn't stop beating herself up about it. She had to find out what, exactly, was going on at the Riehl house to make her daughter so downhearted.

So, after she had finished hanging out her laundry on Friday morning, she decided to hitch up the horse to the buggy and ride over to the Riehls' farm. *Perhaps*, she thought, *I can correct this wrong*.

The drive to Ezekiel's felt painfully long. She tried to imagine her daughter bicycling all that way, pedaling through back roads and then Shipshewana to get to the southern side of town where the Riehls lived. Despite passing all the pretty farms, she found little to improve her mood.

Upon arriving, Edna tied the horse to the side of the barn and stood there, just for a minute, looking around. Everything appeared neater than she remembered from her first visit. The piles of wood had been removed from the side of the barn and the fence line had been trimmed of weeds. She wondered at this improvement to the property.

"May I help you?"

She turned around, surprised to see Ezekiel emerge from the dairy barn.

When he saw her, he abruptly stopped. "*Ach*, it's you." He greeted her with a broad smile and reached out his hand to shake hers. "I didn't recognize you there," he said apologetically. And then a concerned look crossed his face. "I hope nothing is wrong."

Verna forced a nervous smile. "*Nee, nee*, everything's fine. I . . ." She paused. She hadn't thought she'd run into Ezekiel at this hour. Shouldn't he have been working in the fields? Preparing them for planting? Quickly, she tried to come up with an excuse for having intruded unannounced. "I . . . I was nearby and thought I'd stop in. See how Myrna's faring."

"Hm." He walked up to the horse and ran his hand along its neck. "She's in the *haus*."

"Everything is well?"

"Oh *ja*, I reckon so." He patted the horse's shoulder, avoiding Verna's eyes.

She glanced around the barnyard. "You've tidied up a bit, I see."

He nodded. "With Myrna helping out, I've more time to work outside."

His comment startled her, and Verna's eyes narrowed, just briefly, as she wondered if she'd misheard him. Surely he'd had enough help before Myrna started working there. After all, hadn't Katie Ruth's sister watched the children? "So, things are working out, then?" she prodded.

"For sure and certain. The *kinner* love her." And then he smiled again, his eyes lighting up. "Especially her cookies."

When she saw the glow on his face, Verna managed a small laugh.

"You're practically a celebrity with the boys," Ezekiel continued.

"Me?"

He nodded. "*Ja*, for having taught Myrna how to bake so many different types. They'll be rather put out that they missed meeting you." He dropped his hand from the horse. "Perhaps another time, *ja*?"

That sounded promising. If Ezekiel intended to terminate Myrna, he wouldn't have asked for his children to meet her, Myrna's *maem*. "I'd like that for sure." She began feeling at ease in his presence. "Although I expect their *aendis* and *grossmammi* make them cookies that are just as tasty as mine, if not better."

Suddenly, the expression on his face changed, as if a dark cloud had passed over him. "Hm." His eyes flickered toward the house. "I best get back to work. Myrna's inside if you wish to visit with her." Without another word, he turned and headed back into the dairy barn.

Inside the house, Verna noticed that everything looked cleaner and brighter. The cabinets practically shone from having been freshly oiled, and the room smelled fresh from Murphy's Oil. There was nothing on the countertops, and everything looked orderly. Even the table was already set for the noon meal.

Myrna's doing.

Standing in the middle of the kitchen, Verna couldn't help but feel a touch of pride. Her daughter's tendency to overorganize had finally found a place where her efforts could be appreciated.

"Maem?"

Verna turned around in time to see her daughter emerge from the downstairs bedroom, little Katie attached to her hip.

"What're you doing here?"

Verna smiled at the sight of her daughter holding the baby. There was something natural about the way Myrna's arm wrapped around Katie, her hand cupping the child's bottom in a protective way. "I just thought I'd see how things are going," she admitted. "You've been so quiet at home as of late."

Myrna pursed her lips.

"I . . . I wanted to make certain you're truly all right."

"I'm fine, Maem." Myrna gave Katie a little jiggle, and the baby laughed. "Getting the hang of taking care of the *kinner* and the *haus*. It's starting to run like clockwork. And the boys . . ." She smiled. "They're such a handful, but so entertaining. Henry's napping, or I'm sure he'd be here, climbing onto your lap. Why! You'd think these little ones never had any attention before!"

Verna frowned.

Immediately, Myrna added, "Not Ezekiel!" She sounded defensive about her employer. "He's very attentive and kind to the *kinner*. But no one from Katie Ruth's family has stopped by. Not once since I've been here. You'd think *someone* would want to check in on them."

"That is rather strange," she admitted.

"I thought so, too. But I like working here very much. Truly I do. It's so"—she paused—"rewarding."

Verna studied the way her daughter stared into the baby's face as she said those words. "That's *gut*. A job should be rewarding."

"*Ja*, I reckon."

Verna couldn't help but notice the lackluster look in her daughter's eyes. "But something *is* wrong, isn't it?"

Myrna took a deep breath and exhaled slowly.

"Myrna, whatever it is, please tell me."

As she did, her shoulders drooped just a little bit. "I'm afraid I've upset Ezekiel, Maem."

Just as Verna had expected. "Let me guess." A fresh wave of guilt washed over her. "The ear candle?"

Myrna nodded. "*Ja*, the ear candle."

"Oh, Myrna." Verna stood up and walked over to her. She placed her hand on Myrna's shoulder as she apologized. "I'm so sorry. It's all my fault."

At this comment, Myrna shook her head. "*Nee*, Maem. I'm an adult. I should've known better. I should've trusted my own judgment." She stepped away from her mother and moved toward the rocking chair near the far window. Verna followed and sat in the chair next to Myrna.

"I never should've pressed you to do that," Verna admitted. "I never should've listened to Miriam."

At the mention of the woman's name, Myrna frowned. "I'm just as guilty."

"I spoke to Ezekiel just now." She glanced toward the door. "Outside. He seemed pleasant enough."

Myrna stiffened.

"Things are sour between the two of you, then?" Verna asked in a gentle tone, and then, withdrawing her hand, she retreated back to the chair. "It's what I feared."

"*Nee*, that's not it," she replied. "But something's changed. He's more silent than usual. Doesn't come into the house as much as before. I'd like to think he's just busy and working, but I'm afraid that's not it at all." She hung her head. "I can't understand why I am so affected by what happened. *Ja*, that's it. Affected. Why, in the past, I've always stood by my decisions, right or wrong in the eyes of others."

Verna gave a small smile. There was something sweet in her daughter being so unaware of her own feelings. What was so obvious to her mother was obscure to Myrna. Verna, however, wasn't about to avoid the reality of the situation.

"Mayhaps you're affected, as you say, because you're a little *ferhoodled*, Dochder."

Myrna snapped her head upward and stared fiercely at her mother. "*Ferhoodled!*"

"*Ja*, that's what happens, Myrna, when you start falling in love."

Myrna shifted the baby in her arms. "I'm *not* in love with anyone!"

"I didn't say anyone, Myrna," Verna countered softly. "But mayhaps you are with Ezekiel."

She watched as Myrna's mouth opened, her eyes widening as she stared at her mother. After too long a pause, she finally shut her mouth and shook her head. "*Nee*, Maem. I'm not."

Verna didn't believe that for a heartbeat. "Mayhaps not yet, and certainly not ever, if you don't apologize to him, Myrna." Verna gave her daughter an encouraging smile. "I think this is one of those times where least said is *not* soonest mended."

Chapter Eighteen

When she arrived at the Riehls' farm on Saturday morning, Myrna set about her chores right away.

She hadn't slept at all the previous night, tossing and turning in her bed as she mulled over her mother's words. She was most certainly *not* in love with Ezekiel Riehl. Why! She wasn't even certain if she liked him, not after he grew so angry about Henry and the ear candle. Thankfully, the boy's earache had gone away, whether on its own or from her treatment. Regardless, Myrna's relief that Henry was no longer in pain was countered by her irritation over Ezekiel and their confrontation.

What sort of man would shun medical treatment in such a way? She knew that she couldn't answer that question, not only because she just didn't know, but because Ezekiel did not seem to be anything other than an extraordinary father to his children. It created a strange puzzle indeed.

Throughout the night, she'd told herself over and over again that she shouldn't care. People raised their children based upon their own values and beliefs. Even among the Amish, some lived very conservative lives, while others were more lenient and worldly.

During her bicycle ride to the Riehls' farm, Myrna

convinced herself that she had to honor Ezekiel's strange belief system about medicine. He wasn't the only Amish person to feel that way. Why, last spring, Susie Hostetler refused to get surgery for her foot after it was crushed by a Belgian mule! Now she walked with a limp and most likely would for the rest of her life.

Despite not agreeing with him, Myrna knew that she needed to respect Ezekiel's ideology that everything happened according to God's plan, including illness.

It was almost seven thirty when she went outside to sweep the walkway. She knew that the children would be up soon, and then her day would be busy, indeed. On Saturdays, she kept her chores to a minimum in order to focus on the children.

"There you are."

Startled, she spun around, surprised by the sudden appearance of Ezekiel behind her.

Her hand rose to her throat and she clutched it. "You frightened me!"

"I'm sorry, Myrna. Didn't mean to."

She managed to smile. "I know that. You just caught me off guard."

He reached out to her shoulder and plucked something from her dress. He held it up, and she saw it was a small green inchworm. "A new friend?"

"I suppose so."

He took it over to a bush and put it on a branch. Slowly, it inched away.

When Ezekiel turned back to face her, he hooked his thumbs behind his suspenders. "Wanted to ask you something."

She blinked.

"It's been—what?—three weeks now." He rocked back

and forth on his heels as if nervous and unsure of himself. "How do you like being here?"

His choice of words gave her a moment's pause. She would have expected him to ask how she liked *working* there. But he had specifically said *being* there. And then she wondered if he was going to let her go. Despite his apology the previous week, perhaps the incident had festered and now he was going to terminate her employment.

It struck her that she didn't like that idea at all.

"I rather like it," she confessed, opting to be truthful. "It's much nicer than working in one of those stores in town, following all of their silly rules or selling bad products to the clients." She scowled.

He chuckled, which surprised her.

Looking up, she noticed an amused expression on his face. Quickly, she tried to regain her professionalism. "I'm terribly sorry about the incident with Henry and the ear candling. I feel that it's come between us."

His eyes narrowed for just a split second.

"But I've tried to focus on my work. Now that the kitchen and pantry are organized, not to mention my weekly cleaning routine, everything runs much more smoothly."

He glanced toward the barn as he nodded. "I noticed that."

"Are you pleased with my work?" she asked point-blank, figuring that there was no sense beating around the bush. "Or are there things you'd like me to do that I'm not currently doing?"

Ezekiel coughed into his hand, his eyes wide with wonder. "*Ach*, Myrna! *Nee*, you're doing everything perfect."

She caught her breath. Perfect? No one had ever said such a thing to her.

"Why, it's such a pleasure to know that the house and

kinner are being cared for." He exhaled and let his shoulders droop. "It's a relief, actually. Having you here."

"A relief?" She could hardly believe that he hadn't even one complaint or suggestion.

"*Ja*, that's right. A relief." He swallowed, and his eyes avoided meeting hers. "I cannot thank you enough for your hard work, Myrna. Having you here has made a positive change in all of our lives."

She blinked. Another compliment? She wasn't used to such flattery.

For a few seconds, they stood there in silence, Ezekiel unable to look at her and Myrna unable to look anywhere else but at him. She wanted to ask questions, to learn more about Katie Ruth's sister, Linda. All Myrna knew was that Linda didn't bake for the children, definitely didn't do laundry, and now, apparently, didn't do much of anything at all.

But Myrna had told him that she would not pry.

Clearing his throat, Ezekiel pointed to a small fenced-in area of the yard. "I was wondering," he said, "if you might walk out with me."

She looked at him, her eyes widening.

"I mean, to see the plot of land for the garden."

When she thought she heard him chuckle, she knew that color had flooded to her cheeks.

"*Kum*," he said in a gentle tone. "This way."

Myrna followed him as he led her to the white picket fence, which was in sore need of a fresh coat of paint. Side by side, they walked around the fencing until they came to the gate.

Ezekiel opened it and then stood aside for Myrna to pass through. Then, he followed her.

"It's big enough," she said as she paced off the width. "At least twenty-five feet, *ja*?"

He nodded. "About that."

"And what about length? Fifty feet?"

He held up his hand, pinching his thumb and forefinger together but not touching. "Little more, I think."

She began walking across the garden. It was weedy, having been overgrown the previous year. But one day of everyone helping out, she told herself, would solve that problem. And she'd have to teach the boys how to hoe the weeds on a regular basis. But with daily attention, it would bring forth a bountiful harvest.

"It's not part of your job," he said, leaning against the fence as he watched her bend down to touch the soil. "But I thought it might be something the boys could help with. They're old enough for some responsibilities like this."

Myrna couldn't agree more. "I don't mind, Eze—" She stopped herself. "Zeke. I like working outside."

He looked relieved. "*Wunderbarr.*"

"I think I can get Daniel and David started on weeding today. Henry can collect any stones in the soil." She stood up and let the soil fall from her fingers. "It's probably going to need a good amount of manure worked into it."

She turned to face him and saw him studying her. Feeling conspicuous, she reached up and touched the side of her prayer *kapp*.

"Your *daed*'s not a farmer."

She shook her head. "*Nee*, he owns the hardware store."

"Hm." He gave a single nod. "That's right. We talked there twice." His lips twisted into a half smile. "How could I forget?"

"Why did you ask about Daed?"

He pointed toward the soil. "You know a lot about prepping the garden. I'm surprised."

She laughed. "Just because we don't live on a farm doesn't mean we don't have gardens."

But he was insistent. "*Nee*, it's more than that. I can see it in how you examined everything."

"Well, if people are going to garden, they should do it properly, don't you think? Why waste your time and energy if you don't set it up for success? Dry soil won't have the nutrients. Old weeds will overgrow the plants. And if you pull them out now, before spreading fertilizer, it's much easier to maintain on a daily basis." She pointed to the side of her head. "Common sense."

She wiped her hands on her black apron and crossed the garden toward the gate.

"If you point me in the direction of your tools, I'll have the little ones out here right after breakfast."

"Can't we stop?" Daniel whined. "I'm tired."

But Myrna was on a mission. Ezekiel had given her more responsibility, and she didn't take that lightly. And, from the looks of it, the family hadn't benefited from a home garden in at least a year, perhaps longer.

"No rest for the weary," Myrna sang out cheerfully. "This garden will feed you all next year!" She smacked the hoe into the ground, chopping up the soil. "Ooh! Henry, look here! More rocks!"

To his credit, Henry ran over and knelt down, quickly sifting through the dirt for the rocks.

Myrna leaned over to look at them. "Those are good ones. Nice and round. Go put them in your bucket for later."

David threw the trowel he'd been using on the ground and stood up. "I have to go to the bathroom."

But Myrna wasn't about to fall for that. "You've gone three times already," she said. "And we haven't even been out here an hour. Back to work."

Both Daniel and David groaned, but that only made Myrna laugh.

"This is God's work," she said to them. Leaning against the hoe, she rested her chin on the back of her hand. "Don't you see that? We're taking care of God's earth, and in turn, it will help take care of us. Even better, we're taking care of one another."

"But I don't understand why we have to do it all today?"

Of course not, she thought. "I suppose you'd prefer to drag it out a few days, maybe even a few weeks, *ja*?"

Both boys nodded.

"That's a terrible idea," she said, frowning. "And I'll tell you why. It's called 'procrastinating,' which means putting things off. It's akin to being lazy, and you know that laziness is a sin." She swept her arm around, gesturing toward the plot of land. "Besides, it's almost the end of April. We're late to plant some of the crops that like colder weather. You like broccoli, David, right? And Daniel likes radishes. Well we're going to plant some of those seeds. But we can't plant them if the ground isn't prepared."

Henry dropped a rock into the bucket. It clanged against the other rocks. "What're you planting for me?"

Myrna tapped her chin with her finger. "Good question. Let's see." She pretended to think. "Hmm, how about cabbage?"

"Ew!"

"Cauliflower?"

"Double ew!"

She laughed. "Then how about strawberry plants? We can plant those in May."

The three boys cheered at that news.

"What's all this about?"

Myrna turned around and saw Ezekiel standing by the corner of the fence. He wore a smile, one that she hadn't seen on his face before. It lit up his eyes and plumped his cheeks.

"I thought you were supposed to be working," he said in a teasing voice. "But here you are laughing and having fun."

"Aw, Daed," Daniel said, kicking at the dirt. It scattered before him. "Don't you know that you can work and laugh and have fun at the same time?"

Ezekiel tugged at his beard, his dark eyes sparkling. "Is that so? Mayhaps you might have to show me how." He tipped his head in Myrna's direction. "That is, if you don't think she'll mind?"

The boys cheered again, racing toward their father while Myrna tried to hide her smile. Ezekiel entered the garden and walked over to her. He reached out to take the hoe and, when he did, his hand brushed against her fingers. For the briefest of moments, Myrna met his gaze, and it felt as if the rest of the world evaporated. No one else was nearby, not the baby who was napping under the shade of a tree or the three boys clamoring around Ezekiel. At that particular moment, it was just her and Ezekiel.

Finally, he took the hoe and backed away, his eyes still set upon hers.

No, she thought as she stood back and watched the four of them digging up weeds and collecting rocks. *Myrna would not mind at all.*

Because it was Saturday, Myrna didn't have to work all afternoon. But by the time two o'clock rolled around, she didn't really want to leave. Most of the area was weed-free, and Ezekiel promised that he'd spread some manure for the boys to rake into the dirt later that afternoon. By Monday, Myrna would be able to start planting seeds.

She could hardly wait.

"Why do you have to go?" Henry cried, clinging to her legs.

Myrna laughed as she tried to disentangle herself from him. "Because this isn't my home, Henry. I have my own home with my own family." She knelt down before him. "Remember? You met my *maem* yesterday when you woke up from your nap."

He sniffled and wiped his nose with the back of his hand.

"And now, young man, you will go wash your hands." She stood up, turned him around, and marched him toward the sink.

She gathered her things and started out the door, Henry quietly crying as he followed her.

Outside, a playpen had been set up under the shade of a tree, and little Katie sat there, playing with the yarn doll that Myrna had made for her. Daniel and David were following their father, who was already spreading the manure. The two boys raked it into the soil, each one racing the other to keep up with their father.

She took Henry's hand and guided him back to the garden. While she'd been inside cleaning up the dinner dishes, Ezekiel had hitched the mules to a large wagon that was filled with manure. Now it sat in the middle of the garden, the back gate of the wagon hanging down so that he could shovel the contents on the soil, scattering the manure so that it wasn't too thick, but there was instead just enough to add nutrients into the soil.

Lifting her hand to shield her eyes, she squinted as she watched him work. "I'm leaving now," she called out. "So, I believe I must turn this one over to you." She scooted Henry into the garden.

Ezekiel set down his shovel, leaning it against the side of the wagon and walked over to where she stood. He glanced over his shoulder to make certain the boys were still working, Henry having now joined them.

"I can't thank you enough," he said in a low voice. "I meant what I said earlier."

She lowered her lids, her eyes downcast. "*Danke*, Ezekiel."

"And I hope you realize that nothing has come between us," he said softly. "I understand why you did what you did for Henry. Your intentions were honorable, Myrna." He waited until she looked up, and then he reached out, pressing his hand on her arm. "And I respect that."

His touch sent a wave of electricity throughout her, and she jumped, just a little. Quickly, he dropped his hand and took a step backward.

"You have a right *gut* rest of the weekend, Myrna."

For a few seconds, she stood there, staring after him as he returned to the boys. She watched as he picked up his shovel and began tossing out manure from the large wagon. The muscles in his shoulders rippled underneath his dirty white work shirt.

Had his touch actually sent an electrical charge through her body? Was such a thing possible?

Slowly, she backed away from the gate, her eyes still upon the Riehl men. She'd have to give more thought to what her mother had said, because, as much as Myrna wanted to deny it, she knew that she'd never been around a man who made her feel the way Ezekiel Riehl did.

Chapter Nineteen

"*Ach*!" Edna felt as if she might jump out of her skin when Wilma dropped a metal bowl onto the floor, the loud, clanging noise piercing her ears. "Careful, Wilma! You near about gave me a heart attack!"

"Why on earth did we agree to make cookies for this MayFest after we made all those baby blankets?" Wilma grumbled as she tried to bend over for the bowl. "I can't get that! My back'll give out, and then what good will I be?"

Mary hurried over and knelt down to fetch it. "And this weekend is a worship Sunday," she said remorsefully. "We have to make twice as many cookies this week!"

"And at least we get to see each other again!" Edna tried to sound cheerful. With MayFest just a few days away, they'd agreed to meet up again on Wednesday to bake cookies for people who visited their display.

Peering over the ingredients that Edna had set upon the table, Wilma asked, "What kind are we making today?"

"Oatmeal cookies and chocolate chip." She'd decided on those because they hadn't made oatmeal cookies in a while and the chocolate chip cookies were always a favorite with the children.

"Hmph. I should've known." Wilma reached down and picked up the yellow bag of chocolate chips. "First clue."

"Aren't you afraid that chocolate chips will melt?" Mary asked.

"*Nee*, only if it's hot, and it's not likely to be."

For sure, Edna had been checking the weather every day, monitoring the newspaper to see what the forecast was. Rain would ruin the event, and then they'd be stuck with forty baby blankets!

Everything was ready, so the women set to baking, Edna and Mary working at the table while Verna and Wilma stationed themselves at the counter. To Edna, there was something special about working alongside her friends, the quiet noises of wooden spoons hitting the sides of bowls the only thing breaking the silence.

Perhaps because she didn't have any daughters to cook with, Edna especially appreciated the time she shared with her friends.

"I can't believe that MayFest is finally here," Verna said. "Time sure does fly, doesn't it, now?"

"Speaking of time, it's almost been a month that Myrna's worked for Ezekiel." Edna plopped a spoonful of cookie dough onto a baking sheet.

"Three weeks," Verna replied. "More or less."

"When's the wedding?"

"Oh, Wilma!"

Mary and Edna stole a secret glance and smiled at each other.

"Have things settled back down after the ear candling incident?" Edna asked.

Verna nodded. "*Ja*, I believe so. It's just a strange situation. Why, he must be very conservative in his beliefs, but when I went there last week, he was pleasant as could be."

"Just because someone is conservative doesn't mean they can't be pleasant, too," Edna pointed out.

"Oh, I know that. But you hear about those conservative Amish." She lowered her voice. "The Swartzentrubers."

Edna made a face, and Wilma groaned.

Edna remained silent, despite having a lot to say. She'd never been a big fan of Swartzentruber Amish. Their ultra-conservative lifestyle gave the Amish in general a bad name.

"Well, he's not Swartzentruber, I can assure you," Edna said at last.

"Oh, I know that. After all, he uses a mechanical milker for his cows and has running water in the *haus*."

Wilma clucked her tongue. "Can you imagine? How can they live with no running water? Or a toilet?" She shook her head, a look of disdain on her face. "I'm surprised they permit motorized washing machines!"

Edna sighed. "To each his own, I reckon."

"Which leads me back to Ezekiel and this medicine situation." Verna finished dropping oatmeal cookie dough on her two baking sheets and turned around, the spoon still in her hand. "It just doesn't make sense."

"Well, Verna," Edna began, "you know that some Amish just don't like *Englische* medicine. That's not so unusual."

"Oh, I know that. But an ear candle? That's more traditional medicine."

Edna gave her a stern look. "You know that he was probably more upset that she didn't speak to him first."

Verna hung her head, hiding her eyes from Edna's.

"But you said that everything was fine now, so I wouldn't fret about it anymore."

"It's not that I'm fretting," Verna said. "It's just that his behavior in that instance doesn't seem to match his character."

"What you *know* of his character," Wilma added.

"That's true, I suppose." Verna paused thoughtfully. "But Myrna surely knows his character."

"And she's not concerned," Edna interrupted, pointing her spoon at Verna. "Nor should you be. No more interfering. Let them figure it out if it's meant to be."

Wilma leaned over, pressing her cheek against Verna's shoulder. "Once again, wise words spoken by our fearless cookie leader!"

Verna pressed her lips together. "I reckon people ought to call our meetings cookie therapy rather than a cookie club."

Edna laughed at her friend. "Not a bad idea at all."

That evening at supper, Edna retold the stories from that day, mentioning again about the mysterious Ezekiel Riehl.

"I just can't believe no one knows anything about this man," she said, staring first at Elmer and then at her son John.

Elmer kept his head bent over his plate. "Seems everyone knows more than enough by now."

John bit into a roll. "How's Myrna making out there, Maem? She doing okay with this fellow's *kinner*?"

It was always John who took interest in the details. She smiled at him. "*Ja*, she's doing right *gut*. Has taken well to tending the *kinner*. And seems to get along well with Ezekiel, which is why I'm curious about his true nature. I'd hate to see Myrna involved with a less than righteous man."

Jonas scoffed. "Myrna."

Edna jerked her gaze to stare at her younger son.

"She's a handful, that one." He shoved a mouthful of mashed potatoes into his mouth.

"Besides being unkind, that's also untrue," Edna reprimanded sternly. "She's changed quite a bit since she started working for this Ezekiel."

He laughed as if he didn't believe her.

"And she's not a handful. She's just overly . . ."

"Opinionated?"

Edna narrowed her eyes at Jonas. "Organized. She likes things done in a particular way, that's all."

He rolled his eyes. "What. Ever."

Elmer glanced up. "You can 'whatever' your *maem* all you want, Jonas. But one day someone will come along and clip your wings, mark my words."

"Ha!"

Edna shook her head at him.

"When I find someone, she's going to be quiet and docile, like a little mouse in a barn."

Jeremiah elbowed him. "More like a big rat, I think."

Jonas returned the push.

"Boys!"

They both straightened up and stared into their plates at the sound of their father's booming voice.

"None of that at the supper table," he snapped before he leveled his gaze at his wife. "And as for this Myrna and Ezekiel, best to let God handle that situation. If something happens there, we'll all know soon enough about the true nature of this man." He reached out for a roll and began slathering apple butter on it. "Besides, I'd think you had enough going on with your MayFest this weekend and then the tourist season starting up."

With that, the conversation about Myrna and Ezekiel was finished.

Edna sighed, picking up her fork and pushing her food around her plate. Elmer's reminder about the tourist season made her heart palpitate. She'd need to start planning for her first customers the week after MayFest. And the week after that and the one after that. Elmer was right; she had much more important things to do than to worry about Myrna, at least for the moment.

Chapter Twenty

"Are you *still* making those baby blankets?"

Verna looked up as Simon walked into the room. Her eyes followed him as he crossed the kitchen floor to join her in the sitting area. "*Ja*, I am. And I'm just about sick of it, let me tell you." She held up her knitting needles to show the pretty yellow blanket that was half-finished. "My last one, thankfully! Remind me not to do this next year."

Simon laughed at her. "Your charitable heart is showing," he teased.

"Oh hush!" But she couldn't help smiling.

Outside, footsteps approached the porch and, after a brief hesitation, the sound of someone walking toward the door interrupted their conversation.

"Myrna? Is that you?"

She appeared in the doorway, setting her handbag on the counter. "*Ja*, just me."

She sounded tired. Sitting up, Verna leaned forward and glanced at the clock. "You're home awful late."

Myrna followed her gaze. "*Ach!* It's almost seven! I hadn't realized." She gave her mother an apologetic smile. "Sorry."

"Seems he's working you rather hard over there," Simon

said. Verna heard the inquisitive tone to her husband's voice. He wasn't accusing but fishing for information; only Verna wasn't certain what information he sought.

Myrna quickly jumped to Ezekiel's defense. "*Nee*, it's not Ezekiel. It's the little ones. Henry fusses something terrible when I leave. Cries and carries on."

Simon chuckled. "Attached to you, eh?"

She nodded. "Very." She walked over and sank into the sofa next to her mother. Peering over Verna's shoulder, Myrna made a soft noise. "That's pretty."

"*Danke.*"

"The color is different. Pale." She reached out to touch the blanket. "I like it."

Verna smiled at her. She hated to admit it, but she missed Myrna. Now that she worked every day for Ezekiel, she was rarely around, and when she was, she often slept as only young adults are prone to do. But it wasn't just that she missed having Myrna at home. It was that she missed having *this* Myrna at home. Ever since she'd started working at the Riehls', Myrna seemed much more pleasant to be around. Her temperament had evened out, and she wasn't as prone to disrupt things by trying to reorganize or improve them.

"We each made ten blankets to donate to the Amish Aid table at MayFest," Verna said. "This fine blanket"—she held it up—"is my last one."

"By 'we' I trust you mean the Cookie Club?"

"*Ach!*" Verna dropped her knitting onto her lap. She gave Myrna a look of exasperation. "Will you people ever stop calling it that?"

Simon laughed. "Just get used to it, Verna. You'll never get everyone to stop."

Myrna stood up and stretched. "Well, considering it's

Thursday night and the fair starts tomorrow, it's a *gut* thing that it's your last blanket."

"We'll work the vendor table on Saturday for a spell, so I still have time to finish this one." She picked up her knitting needles and began to continue with her work. "Will you be attending MayFest?" Verna asked.

"*Nee*, Maem. You know I've got to work." She walked back to the kitchen and took a piece of bread. "And speaking of work, I'm exhausted. Going to bed."

Verna watched as her daughter climbed the stairs and disappeared into the darkness of the second-floor hallway.

"Hmph. She comes right home and goes to bed only to get up and leave again. It's a wonder she doesn't just move there," Verna mumbled.

Simon winked at her. "Mayhaps you'll get your wish sooner than you think."

Everyone gathered at Mary's house on Friday to prepare the blankets and more cookies for the weekend. The Amish Aid table would be manned by different groups of ladies during the two-day MayFest event. Set up near the food section at the corner of Main and Morton Streets, it was destined to be busy, and the blankets would sell quickly.

"At least we don't have to be there for the parade at nine o'clock," Wilma said. "I just can't stand parades."

Edna laughed. "How is that possible? Everyone loves a parade."

Thrusting both her thumbs at her chest, Wilma wrinkled her nose. "Not this gal. I can't stand them."

"That's so funny. I never knew that about you, Wilma."

Mary set her pile of blankets on the kitchen table. "I reckon it's the noise. The fire trucks and all."

Wilma gave a noncommittal nod. "And last year we

were near that main tent." She shuddered. "Remember that loud music? I hated it."

Mary sighed. "I'm not partial to the crowds. But it's only one day of the year, and I do like seeing all those families out and about together." She glanced over to the side room, where her daughter, Bethany, sat in a rocking chair, reading a devotional. "I don't know when the last time was that I went anywhere with my *dochder*."

Verna followed her gaze. It had always surprised her that Bethany was so painfully shy. She was a pretty girl with dark hair and big brown eyes, an interesting contrast to her own daughter's fiery red hair and green eyes. Plus, she was petite, a small wisp of a girl. But she hated going out to town and had yet to work outside of the house. How she'd ever get married was beyond Verna's comprehension.

"So, we're to arrive there by ten o'clock," Edna said, interrupting Verna's thoughts. "We'll relieve the women who are working the table in the morning, and we're to stay until three o'clock. Five hours. It shouldn't be too bad."

"And we should sell a lot of these blankets." Verna ran her hand along the edge of the box. "Forty blankets for forty babies."

"Don't forget the cookies!" Wilma added as she set three plastic containers beside the box of blankets.

Verna laughed. "How could I forget the cookies? I bet half the people come to our table for those rather than the blankets."

"Undoubtedly," Edna said. And then, popping off the lid of the container, she grabbed a chocolate chip cookie and took a bite. "Mmm. I don't blame them. These *are* good cookies!"

"Of course they are," Verna said, feigning an angry expression. "Why else would they call us the Amish Cookie Club?"

Chapter Twenty-One

When she entered the Riehls' kitchen on Saturday morning, Myrna noticed that there was coffee brewing already. The dishes had been washed and were neatly stacked on the side of the sink. Clearly Ezekiel had been busy that morning. Despite her apprehensions, she caught herself smiling.

"Morning, Myrna."

She started at the sound of his voice coming from the doorway of the master bedroom.

"Zeke!" She pressed her hand to her chest as she turned around to face him. "You frightened me."

He stood there, his big frame filling the open space, and stared at her. "Didn't mean to."

When he made no move to enter the room, Myrna gestured toward the coffee. "You've been up early, I see. Care for me to pour you a cup?"

He nodded.

"Have a seat, then." She felt strange telling him what to do. He was her boss, after all, and this was his house. Busying herself with pouring the coffee, Myrna couldn't help but wonder what was on his mind. Clearly, he had something he wanted to discuss with her. Myrna just couldn't imagine what it might be.

"I . . . I wanted to ask a favor of you," he said, the coffee mug cupped between his hands and his eyes focused on the liquid inside of it.

From the somber expression on his face, Ezekiel looked as if the matter were truly serious. For a moment, Myrna panicked. Had something happened? Was one of the children sick? "Of course, Zeke. What is it?"

He ran his thumb along the side of the mug as he collected his thoughts. Whatever this favor was, he was clearly troubled by having to ask it.

"I . . . I was wondering if you might forgo working today."

Startled, Myrna caught her breath. She'd thought they'd gotten over the whole ear candling episode. Had she done something wrong? "Well, I suppose if you don't need me—"

"Oh, it's not that," he interrupted her. "It's just that, well . . ." He fiddled with his coffee mug. "It's been a hard year, you know. And, well, I haven't done much with the *kinner* in a while." He paused and frowned. "Long while. Anyway, today's the last day of MayFest, and I wanted to take them." He lifted his eyes and met hers. "All of them, including little Katie. Make it a fun family day and all. But I can't handle the boys and the *boppli* by myself." He paused. "Truth is, I don't even know if I'd want to."

She bit her lower lip.

"They always have so much fun when you're around," he said. "And you're so good with them. I guess what I'm trying to say is that I'm hoping you might join us."

She blinked. "Oh, to help with the children."

"*Nee!*" He held up his hand and then immediately went back to toying with his coffee mug. "I mean, *ja*."

"I see."

He shook his head. "*Nee*, Myrna. I don't know what I'm saying. My tongue's all twisted and words aren't coming out right. I guess what I meant to say is that I'd like you to come, too."

As soon as he said it, Myrna felt her heart beat faster. She'd never been invited anywhere like that by a man. Of course, she reminded herself, despite his invitation, she was going as part of her job, not as part of a courtship. Still, the idea of actually going somewhere and having fun in the company of a man did not displease her. Even if it was Ezekiel.

She bit her lower lip and corrected herself. *Especially* because it was Ezekiel. It might have only been four weeks that she had been working for him, but Myrna knew there was something truly special about the man. And she also knew that she was beginning to regret the fact that he wasn't looking for a wife.

Still, even if they could only be friends, Myrna thought that an outing with the children and Ezekiel was not an unpleasant way to spend the day.

"That sounds right nice, Ezekiel," she heard herself say. "I think the boys will surely love such an outing."

Ezekiel gave a half smile and averted his eyes. "Me, too."

As she sat next to Ezekiel in the buggy, little Katie upon her lap, Myrna felt a renewed sense of excitement. Her arms wrapped around the child and she hugged Katie to her chest, loving the sweet lavender scent that wafted from her little pink dress.

Out of the corner of her eye, she thought she saw Ezekiel glance at her. He made that all-too-familiar noise, the guttural sound that she had come to translate as one of satisfaction, and Myrna tried to continue staring ahead.

He had startled her by asking that she accompany the family to MayFest. She was even more surprised that Ezekiel even wanted to go at all. It had been a long week for him, cutting, drying, raking, and baling the hay. David and Daniel had tried to help after school, but Myrna suspected their contribution was in effort only.

David poked his head between Ezekiel and Myrna's shoulders. "I hope they have cotton candy!"

"Me, too! Me, too!" Henry jumped up and down in his seat.

"Aw, you don't even know what it is!"

Ezekiel chuckled. It was a sound that Myrna wished she heard more often. "I'm sure they'll have it, David, and Henry will soon learn that cotton candy is like eating a sweet, sugary cloud."

"Yummy!"

Myrna laughed and, without thinking, bent down to place a soft kiss on Katie's head. "Mayhaps you'll get a taste, too," she whispered into the baby's ear.

When she straightened, she noticed that Ezekiel had been watching her. There was an intensity to his gaze as his eyes studied her, even after she caught him looking at her. He didn't seem to care. Instead, he squinted his eyes and tilted his head just a little.

"What?" she asked, her voice low. "What is it?"

For a moment, she thought he was going to respond. His mouth opened and then shut again.

"Ezekiel?"

"I . . . I just realized that . . ." He paused and shook his head.

Reaching out, Myrna placed her hand on his arm. "Tell me."

He looked down at her hand for a second and she started to pull it away, afraid that she had invaded his private space. But immediately, he covered her hand with his as if asking her to keep it there.

"I realized I'd never seen anyone else kiss Katie."

She withdrew her hand. "Did I?"

"Just now." He pointed to the baby. "You kissed her head."

"I did?" She would have laughed but for fear that she'd offend him. It wasn't common for the Amish to show affection like that. Perhaps a husband and wife might kiss each other in private, but certainly not when other people were around. And children might be hugged and kissed by their mother or grandmother, but it wasn't something that was done all the time, and certainly not by other people.

"It caught me off guard," he admitted.

"I'm sorry. I don't even remember having done it."

"*Nee*, don't be sorry." He gave her a small smile. "Everyone needs a little love and affection from time to time."

She couldn't help but wonder if he truly meant everyone or if he might have been referring to himself.

Chapter Twenty-Two

Edna sat at the table, the baby blankets laid out on display for the people passing by to examine. Wilma was arguing with Barbara Brenneman about the best way to set up the display, which made Edna smile as she bent her head over her crocheting. Leave it to Wilma to argue with a bishop's wife.

"Now, Barbara," Wilma said as she pointed to the plate of chocolate chip cookies. "You know that the little ones will want the cookies, so if you leave them on the edge of the table, they'll just take a cookie and run off."

Barbara pressed her lips together and gave Wilma a stern look. "I don't think parents are that lax with their *kinner*."

Wilma responded with a loud "Ha!"

"I've set up the table this way for the past five years, Wilma," Barbara sighed. "I'm not changing it now."

Clearly this response displeased Wilma, and she scoffed.

"Besides," Barbara said in a sharp tone of rebuke, "this is a charity fundraiser, not a business store, Wilma. It's supposed to raise money but also be fun. Let's not forget the purpose."

Verna emerged from behind the black buggy parked on the grass, her hands carrying more bundles of neatly wrapped baby blankets. "Oh Wilma, if the *kinner* want a cookie, let them have it. We have plenty, and I've no mind to go home with any extras."

Mary helped Verna lay out the remaining baby blankets. "At least the weather held off." She eyed the sky suspiciously. "Although that dark cloud over there sure looks ominous."

"It's not going to rain, Mary," Edna reassured her.

Wilma looked up. "It's going to rain?"

Edna sighed. "*Nee*, Wilma. I said it's *not* going to rain."

"Well, I sure do hope it holds off long enough for these blankets to sell."

Verna stopped short, her brow furrowed as she looked from Wilma to Edna, who merely shrugged. Verna hid a smile and continued unpacking the baby blankets.

Barbara joined Verna and Mary, helping to refold the blankets. "My word, you women made enough this year, don't you think?"

"They sold out last year," Edna observed. "Hopefully they'll do the same this year."

The crowds were light at this early hour of the day, but by the time eleven o'clock rolled around, Edna was pleased to see that more people seemed to have arrived, and plenty of *Englische* women stopped at their table to admire the baby blankets.

And, of course, plenty of children came for the cookies.

Barbara Brenneman returned to the table. "Such a big crowd here today. I was just over at the auction." She gestured toward the big white tent on the other side of the field. "There must be twice as many people there as last year." She scanned the table. "How has the traffic been through here?"

Edna shook her head. "Lighter than I'd hoped for. Mayhaps you should auction off some of the baby blankets."

"They'll sell. People will filter through after the auction."

Knowing better than to argue with her, Edna said nothing.

"I do have something I want to talk to you about, though." Barbara lowered her voice and stepped to the side.

Curious, Edna followed. What could Barbara possibly have to say that needed such privacy?

"I was speaking with Rebecca Yoder—"

Edna interrupted. "From Yoders' Store?"

"*Ja*, that's the one. Well, she agreed to sell your baked goods in her store to help raise money for Amish Aid." Barbara tilted her head and gave Edna a knowing look. "I told her I'd speak to you, to see if your cookie club would—"

"It's not a club," Edna mumbled.

"—be willing to bake more cookies each week. The cost of supplies would be taken from the profit, of course, but that could be a pretty penny toward helping a family or two in need each year."

Inwardly, Edna groaned.

She knew that the other women would agree. After all, it could be one of *their* families who needed help from the communal aid fund that each church district kept. But Verna, Wilma, and Mary weren't as busy as she was. Their only work was taking care of the house and family. Edna did that, too, but also would soon start cooking for the tourists. That was time-consuming, for she had to plan her meals, clean the house, and prepare the food. Baking *more* cookies each week would certainly be hard on her, timewise.

And yet, she knew that helping others was important. Wasn't this what Barbara's husband had been preaching about the other week?

Of course, Edna suspected that Barbara had made the request of her on purpose. While Edna might have suggested to Barbara that there were plenty of other women in the community who could use a prod in the direction of tending to the needs of other people, Edna also knew that Barbara wasn't stupid.

When you want something done, Edna's mother always used to say, *you ask a busy person, because they're the only ones who know how to get things done*.

"If you could start by baking twenty dozen cookies and bundle them in sets of five, that would be almost fifty packages." Barbara paused for a minute, her eyes looking upward. "That would bring in over two hundred fifty dollars a week."

Quickly Edna did the math. That would be a contribution of at least a thousand dollars a month. With tourist season being a good eight months, they could easily raise eight thousand dollars to help families in need.

"You discuss it with your friends and let me know," Barbara said.

Edna shook her head. "No need, Barbara. We'll happily do it."

"*Wunderbarr!*" She clapped her hands and grinned. "I knew I could count on you, Edna! A more giving person doesn't walk the earth."

At this unusual compliment, Edna laughed. "I highly doubt that."

It was just around noon when Edna felt a nudge at her arm. She'd been sitting in the shade of the buggy, crocheting a blanket and enjoying the happy atmosphere of the day. She'd almost forgotten that Mary was sitting beside her.

"Edna," she whispered.

When Edna looked up, she saw Mary staring down the grassy aisle between the neighboring vendors.

"What is it?"

Mary gestured with her head. "Look over there. Is that . . . ?"

Squinting, Edna looked in the direction that Mary had indicated. At first, she saw nothing unusual. People. Lots of people. Barbara had been right. The afternoon foot traffic had definitely picked up.

But surely that wasn't what Mary found so curious.

Suddenly, her eyes recognized a tall, willowy woman with a baby on her hip walking toward them. The red hair was a dead giveaway.

Catching her breath, Edna kept her gaze riveted on Myrna. "Well, I don't believe it." She glanced over her shoulder to see whether Verna and Wilma noticed that Myrna was approaching them, with a man and three small boys by her side. "If that don't beat all . . ."

Wilma must have noticed them staring into the distance, for she suddenly gasped. "Land's sake! Verna, isn't that your *dochder*?"

Edna watched Verna's reaction.

At first, she looked confused, as if she couldn't reconcile what she saw as being real. Then her expression changed to joy.

"I don't believe my eyes," she whispered.

An *Englische* woman stepped up to the table, gazing down at the different baby blankets. She ran her hands over a blue one before picking it up.

Reluctantly, Edna made her way over to the woman to assist her, all the while keeping one eye on Verna.

"Such beautiful work," the woman said. "But then, you Amish always make such lovely things."

Behind her, Edna heard Wilma scoff. *You Amish.* It was a cringeworthy expression, but one that Edna had gotten used to, especially in her business dealing with *Englische* tourists.

"We try," she managed to say.

One of the older Riehl boys must have broken free from Ezekiel and Myrna, for he suddenly appeared next to the *Englische* woman.

"Cookies!" He reached out and started to grab one.

"David!" Myrna quickened her pace and caught up to him. "You don't run off like that," she scolded in a soft voice.

The *Englische* woman watched with curiosity. "Such a handsome child," she said. And then her eyes noticed the baby. "And what an angel *she* is!"

Myrna rested her free hand on David's shoulder and pulled him toward her.

"You have a beautiful family," the woman said.

Edna's eyes widened, anticipating a response from Myrna. But she remained silent.

Ezekiel, however, did not. He appeared behind Myrna in time to overhear the woman's compliment. "*Danke.*"

"Well, I'll take this blanket," the woman said and reached inside her purse for her wallet. "A new grandson just arrived last month."

Here we go, Edna thought, keeping her smile plastered on her face.

"Such a handsome baby." She withdrew her phone and pressed a button on it. "See?" Flipping the phone around, she showed Edna a photo. "He's my fourth grandchild, but such a sweet angel." She turned the phone around again and stared at the photo.

Edna handed the woman her blanket. "Have a *gut* day now."

The woman walked away, the blanket stowed under her arm. Finally Edna could pay attention to what was happening with Myrna!

She stood by her mother, the smallest boy hanging on to her hand and swinging around her legs. Myrna, however, didn't appear to notice. Ezekiel held the baby in his arms and stood beside Myrna. To any observer, they appeared to be a small family. Edna, however, saw something much different, and it warmed her heart.

"*Ja*, so Ezekiel thought the *kinner* might like to see the fair," Myrna was saying. "Wanted to stop by and see how your baby blankets are selling."

Verna glanced at the table. "*Ach*, not so well yet. We still have more than half left."

Wilma walked behind Verna. "Don't want to be stuck with all of those, that's for sure. No babies on the way to give them to."

Edna choked back a laugh.

One of the older boys reached up and touched the edge of a pastel-colored baby blanket. His fingers stroked the soft yarn. "Daed?" He looked up at his father. "Do you think . . . ?" His voice trailed off but his eyes landed on his sister.

"I suspect I know what you're getting at," Ezekiel said. He shifted Katie in his arms and reached into his back pocket for his wallet. "If that's the one you like, you take it, David."

Myrna's eyes widened. "You needn't pay for that," she said. "I can surely make one for little Katie."

But Ezekiel insisted. "It's for Amish Aid, *ja*? It's a *gut* cause, and David seems to like this one here. Besides, Katie hasn't been the recipient of much spoiling."

Edna watched as he handed Verna a crisp ten and a five-dollar bill. Taking the money, Verna appeared speechless.

"*Danke*, Ezekiel," Edna finally said, stepping up beside Verna. "Much appreciated."

He nodded. "Amish Aid helps everyone," he said. "Mayhaps one day it'll help someone in my family."

Chapter Twenty-Three

Verna watched as Myrna left, chatting happily with Ezekiel and his boys, who were enjoying their cookies. Before they disappeared into the crowd, Ezekiel leaned over to speak to Myrna. And when Myrna tilted her head to listen to him, even from a distance, Verna could see her daughter's face light up.

"I . . . I scarce know what to say!" She could also hardly tear her eyes from the sight.

Wilma pursed her lips. "Best be planting celery, from the looks of it."

Both Mary and Edna laughed.

"Oh, Wilma!" Verna turned and gave her friend a playful swat on the arm. "Just because they're out in public like this—"

"Especially *because* they are out in public like this," Wilma retorted, not letting Verna finish her sentence.

"Well, if I have any need for extra celery to serve at a wedding," Verna said, directing her comment to Wilma, "I'll be buying it, thank you very much."

"And he bought that baby blanket without even batting an eye!" Wilma pointed at Verna. "Mark my words, you've got a wedding in your future, my friend."

Mary sighed. "Did you see how he looked at her?"

Verna felt light-headed. She *had* seen the way Ezekiel looked at Myrna. There was a possessive nature to his attention toward her daughter, one that came only with enormous fondness for another.

"He seems like a *gut* man," Mary said, turning to look at Verna. "And mayhaps not as conservative as you think."

Mary's comment caught Verna off guard. "Why would you think that?"

"Well, he mentioned that the money was going to Amish Aid and what a good cause it was." She raised an eyebrow. "And that one day his family might need it. Mayhaps he's not as opposed to medicine as you think."

Verna hadn't made that connection, but now that Mary pointed it out, she realized it *had* been a strange comment.

Mary sighed. "I think God meant for Myrna to lose all those jobs so that she could find her way to work for Ezekiel."

Wilma snorted.

"What?"

Wilma nudged her arm. "If that was His plan, God gave Myrna—and Verna!—a very long, winding road to get to the final destination."

"Sometimes God does that," Mary insisted. "Makes arriving at the journey's end more rewarding."

"*Ja*, well, I'm sure Verna could've used a little less stress along the way."

Verna appreciated Wilma's words. It *had* been stressful, dealing with Myrna and her constant issues at her jobs. But she also believed Mary might have spoken the truth. All of the trials and tribulations would be worth it if Myrna found happiness.

And she *did* look happy.

Verna stood near the display table and stared after the

retreating figure of her daughter next to Ezekiel. Try as she might, she couldn't reconcile her feelings. On the one hand, if Myrna had found love and companionship with Ezekiel Riehl, Verna was more than happy for her daughter.

But on the other hand, Verna had never imagined that Myrna would settle down as a second wife, marrying into a ready-made family. It was hard enough to get used to being newly married, what with the responsibilities of taking care of a man, house, and business, but to add four children into the equation?

Now that the possibility was real and staring Verna in the face, she had to take time to digest it.

An hour later, the bulk of the baby blankets had sold. As Barbara had predicted, once the auction ended, the crowds descended on the vendor tables, and the four women could barely keep up with the people wanting to buy their blankets.

Verna sat in the folding chair, trying to calculate how much money they'd earned for the communal aid.

"Land's sake!" Edna stared at the almost empty table. Only three blankets remained. "I've never seen such a mad rush!"

Wilma refilled the empty plate with the last of the cookies. "Clearly baby blankets are in hot demand," she joked.

Verna looked up. "Almost four hundred dollars." She set down her pencil. "Seems like an awful lot of work for not very much money, don't you think?"

Edna grimaced. "*Ja*, I agree."

Mary, however, did not. "Oh, I don't know about that. It's been a lovely day here, and I've enjoyed being with my friends. As far as the work, why! All those Wednesdays when we were together, that was more fun than labor." She smiled at Edna and Verna. "Besides, four hundred dollars is a lot of money. Someone will surely benefit from it."

Leave it to Mary, Verna thought. Always seeing the bright side of situations. "You're right. We should be happy that we've been able to raise so much money."

Edna cleared her throat. "I've got more news." She glanced at Mary. "Since you enjoy our company so much—"

Wilma laughed.

"—we can continue meeting on Wednesdays."

Verna squinted. "More blankets?"

"*Nee.*" Edna shook her head. "More cookies."

"Oh help!" Verna leaned back in the chair. "What for?"

"Not what, but who. Barbara pulled me aside earlier. Yoders' Store wants to sell our cookies. We could bake them on Wednesdays, and they'd have them on display Thursday, Friday, and Saturday each week. The money raised will go to Amish Aid. Minus the costs of supplies, of course."

For a moment, Verna sat there, speechless. Wilma and Mary remained silent, too.

"Are you saying that we're to go into business?" Verna said at last. "Baking and selling cookies?"

Edna made a face. "Hadn't looked at it that way. But I reckon you're right."

Mary spoke up. "Well, we do enjoy getting together—"

"Speak for yourself," Wilma teased.

"—and it is for a good cause."

"What will we call this little endeavor?" Verna asked.

"Call it?" Wilma crossed her arms over her chest. "Why would we need to call it something?"

"Verna's right," Edna said. "We'd have to name our cookies for the store display. We need a name."

"Oh, that's easy!" Mary gave a broad smile. "The Amish Cookie Club!"

Immediately, Edna groaned. But Verna liked the idea. It had a sweet ring to it, and after all, everyone seemed to call them that anyway.

"Well, I'll need to speak to Simon," Verna said. "But I can't imagine he'd deny such an opportunity to help our brothers and sisters in need."

Wilma agreed. "*Ja*, Jacob won't argue either, I'm sure."

Everyone turned to Mary, waiting for her response.

"Of course I'll help," she said. "But I think we should rotate where we bake each week. It'll be too much work for Edna to always host, especially since she'll be cooking for tourists again soon."

"I'd forgotten about that." Verna wondered how Edna would be able to handle baking the cookies *and* her business. "You really should get some help, Edna."

"My Rachel and Ella Mae are still available," Wilma sang.

"*Danke*, but not needed," Edna sang back.

Verna laughed. One of these days, she thought, Edna would need help and she'd have no choice but to reach out to Wilma and finally hire Rachel and Ella Mae. Just the thought of Wilma's two difficult daughters working alongside Edna gave her the giggles. She wasn't certain who would come out the survivor: Edna or the girls.

"We can start baking this next week," Edna said.

Verna raised her hand. "Let's start at my *haus* since it's central to everyone. I'll have Samuel and Timothy move the table so we have more room."

"And we'll need to make little note cards to tie onto the packages."

This time, Mary offered to help. "That would be perfect for Bethany to do. She's got quite a pretty hand."

"Well, seems like we've got everything in order," Verna said. "Great plans come together with great people working together, my *maem* always used to say."

"And God," Mary added quietly. "I think He had a little bit to do with this, too."

"Quite true." Verna smiled at the reminder. "Seems like He has quite a few great plans that are falling into place these days."

Chapter Twenty-Four

Despite the overcast skies, there were plenty of people who had poured into Shipshewana for MayFest. Ezekiel had had to park the horse and buggy almost half a mile away. Myrna didn't mind the walk so much, because Ezekiel had carried little Katie for the distance.

"Myrna!" David grabbed her hand. "Look! There's ice cream!"

Feeling his small, warm hand in hers, Myrna couldn't help but share his excitement. "Well, it's not particularly warm today, but I sure do like the idea of some vanilla ice cream."

Daniel turned his face to look up at his father. "Could we, Daed?"

Ezekiel nodded. "I don't see why not."

The boys cheered and even Myrna smiled. Their enthusiasm was contagious, that was for sure and certain.

Together, they walked toward the corner so they could cross the street to the block of buildings where the ice cream store was located.

They passed several people who smiled at them. Mostly the *Englischers*. It dawned on Myrna that the passersby must think that they were a happy little Amish family.

After all, Ezekiel still wore the mustache-less beard that married men grew. Strangers would have no idea that she was his employee and the little boy holding her hand was not her son.

As they waited at the traffic light in order to cross the street, several buggies drove by. As usual, Ezekiel lifted his hand in greeting to the drivers, a gesture that was usually returned.

Except by one driver.

Myrna saw Ezekiel raise his hand, but unlike the other times, he stopped and quickly dropped it again. His shoulders straightened and the muscles in his jaw tensed.

She stared at the buggy and only saw an older man with a long, white beard. His small, dark eyes glared at Ezekiel. She'd never seen such an open act of hostility from one Amish man to another.

"Do you know that man?" she whispered.

"Hm."

She wasn't certain how to translate that.

But it was David who gave her the answer she wanted.

Just as the light was about to change, David looked up and saw the buggy. "Look, Daed! It's the bishop!"

Myrna immediately looked at the man once again. The bishop? If that man was the leader of their church district, it also meant that he was Katie Ruth's father. The children's grandfather. Myrna watched as David waved, but the old man merely turned his head away and, as the light changed, slapped the leather reins on the horse's back. The buggy lurched forward and rolled down the road.

She stared after it, shocked that he hadn't even acknowledged his grandchildren. While she could understand his anger toward Ezekiel, she could not accept it toward the children. Besides, she thought, feeling her own anger rise, if he was the bishop, he should be practicing what he preached, which certainly included forgiveness.

As soon as the buggy moved away, Ezekiel seemed to relax a little.

"*Kum*," he said, shifting Katie in his arms and reaching for Henry's hand. "We can cross now." Without looking back, he walked across the street, and Myrna followed with only one glance in the direction of the buggy as it disappeared up the road ahead.

"Careful with those ice creams," Myrna said to the boys as they climbed into the buggy. "Don't let the sides drip."

The three boys sat on the back seat, each one holding an ice cream cone. Myrna handed them extra napkins.

"I reckon I could just take you home," Ezekiel said as they got situated in the buggy.

Myrna leaned over and adjusted Katie's dress to better cover the baby's legs. "Oh, that would be nice," she heard herself say before she quickly added, "but not very practical."

"Practical?"

Nodding, Myrna met his curious gaze. "My bicycle's at your *haus*, Ezekiel. How'd I get to work on Monday?"

"Hm." He took hold of the reins and urged the horse to back up so that he could turn the buggy toward the road. "I see your point."

And yet, as he approached the road, rather than turn south, the direction of his farm, he turned north.

"What are you doing?" She turned to face him. "Zeke?"

"I'm taking you home."

"But—"

He held up his hand. "No sense in driving back to my farm only to have you bicycle all the way right back here."

She started to ask how she'd get to work on Monday, but once again, Ezekiel interrupted her.

"I'll fetch you Monday."

Stunned, Myrna fell back into the seat cushion. While she appreciated his kind gesture, she knew that it would be a great inconvenience for him to drive all the way to her parents' house on Monday morning.

And yet, the thought of him not just fetching her but *wanting* to fetch her was touching. She couldn't deny that his consideration made her feel as if butterflies were fluttering in her stomach. But he was a kindhearted man. She'd learned that much about him in the four weeks she'd worked for him. And she didn't want to read too much into his gesture. After all, hadn't he been the one to seek her out at her father's store before she'd started taking care of his children to tell her that he had no intention of marrying again?

Still, despite his words over four weeks ago, she couldn't deny that his actions did not seem to mirror that sentiment.

"It's a long drive to come get me," she said at last. "And not very prudent with the *kinner*."

David jumped forward and leaned against the back of the seat. "I can watch my *bruders*."

Myrna raised an eyebrow. "And what about Katie?"

He peered over Myrna's shoulder at his sister. "Well, I can watch her, too. As long as she doesn't need a diaper change."

Hiding her laugh behind her hand, Myrna turned her head and stared out the window.

"Then it's settled," Ezekiel announced. "No more bicycle riding for you, Myrna. It's too far and too dangerous, especially near town. And *danke*, David, for offering to help out. I'm sure Myrna appreciates your thoughtfulness."

She sensed that he was looking at her as David settled

back into his seat next to Daniel and Henry. There was an intense energy in the buggy, and Myrna began to feel light-headed.

Surely Ezekiel had feelings for her if he intended to pick her up and take her home every day. And Myrna could not deny that she rather enjoyed the idea of spending time alone with him. There was something so soothing about being in his presence. The way he talked, the words he spoke, even that "hm" noise he always made as if deep in thought.

Suddenly, she remembered what her mother had said a few weeks earlier. *Ferhoodled*. Her mother had told her that she was *ferhoodled*.

Stunned, Myrna stopped looking out the window and turned her face toward him. While keeping one eye on the road, he was still watching her, his dark eyes searching hers.

She caught her breath and placed her hand on her chest. "Oh."

The corner of his mouth turned up, just the hint of a smile.

With her heart racing, Myrna felt as if the buggy walls were closing around her. She could only see one thing, and that was Ezekiel. She enjoyed his company. She adored his children. Those things she had known. But now, as she sat beside him in the buggy, she had learned something new: she loved him.

Dropping her hand from her chest, she stared straight ahead, her mind reeling. How could this have happened? Falling in love with Ezekiel Riehl!

She tried to slow her breathing, to calm down her nerves. But she felt as if every fiber in her being was on fire.

And then she felt something else.

His hand upon hers.

She glanced down at where her hand rested upon Katie's lap. His covered it. For a long moment, she studied his tanned skin against her pale flesh. And then she shut her eyes, feeling the warmth of his touch against her skin. She'd never held a man's hand, and she liked it, but only because it was Ezekiel.

Once again, she lifted her gaze to meet his. The hint of a smile was gone, replaced with a somber expression. She could only wonder what he was thinking at that moment.

Slowly, she withdrew her hand, tucking it around the baby. He, too, returned to holding the reins with both of his hands.

But the moment had occurred, and it had been enough.

"Your *daed* told me that Ezekiel brought you home today. Is that so?"

Myrna froze, her back to her mother. She'd been drying the plates from supper and hadn't anticipated the question. Not from her mother, and not now, in the kitchen, with her brothers lingering around the table while her father read the *Budget* in his chair.

"Oh, I—" She stumbled over her words.

Samuel gave a little laugh. "What's this? You stepping out with old man Ezekiel?"

Immediately, Myrna glared at him. "He's not an old man!"

He nudged his brother. "She's defending him."

"*Ferhoodled,*" Timothy said without looking up. "For sure."

Myrna pressed her lips together, angry at their teasing.

The sound of the newspaper crinkling directed her attention toward her father. "Leave your *schwester* alone, Samuel and Timothy."

"Sorry, Daed."

Myrna saw her father wink at her, and she gave him a small smile.

The last thing she wanted to do was give her family reason to speculate. If anything happened between her and Ezekiel, that was her business and she'd tell them in due time—when and if it was necessary.

But her mother did not drop the subject. "How'll you get to work on Monday morning, then?"

For a moment, no one spoke. The kitchen remained silent but for the ticking of the clock on the wall. Myrna felt her cheeks grow hot and knew that she was thirty shades of red. Her face probably matched her hair by now.

"Uh, well—" she stammered, her eyes shifting from her mother to her brothers to her father. "Well, Zeke said he'd come fetch me."

Samuel's mouth dropped. "Zeke? Now he's Zeke?"

"Told you," Timothy added. "*Ferhoodled.*"

"Oh, hush, you!" She threw a dish towel at Timothy, but it hit Samuel instead.

"That's a long way to come fetch you," Verna said in a slow and deliberate way. "But he's a grown man and knows his own business, I imagine."

This time, Simon put down the paper. "I'm sure it's not that much of a bother, Verna. It's only—what?—four or five miles or so?" He smiled at Myrna. "I reckon a farmer likes to get off his property every so often, especially if he's in good company."

She swallowed, wishing that everyone would stop paying attention to her. "Or mayhaps it's just more efficient. I won't be so tired when I get there."

Samuel chortled. "Efficient."

But her mother caught the unspoken truth. "You mean he intends to fetch you every day?" Her mouth opened and she looked at her husband. "And bring you back every afternoon?"

"Oh, I imagine it won't be for long," her father said. When Myrna shot a look at him, he lifted up his paper once again in an attempt to hide the smile that crossed his lips. "Come harvest time, that arrangement won't be practical, I'm sure."

Chapter Twenty-Five

On Monday morning, after washing the weekend's dirty clothes and hanging them on the clothesline to dry, Edna hitched the horse to the buggy so that she could drive to visit with Verna. Elmer and the boys were busy cutting the alfalfa and had no need of the buggy. And Edna knew that she'd never been able to wait until Wednesday to hear what Verna had learned about Myrna and Ezekiel.

Twenty minutes later, when she pulled into the Bontragers' driveway, she was hardly surprised to see that a bicycle was already parked there. She'd recognize that battered blue bike anywhere!

"Well, seems the party got started without me," she said when she entered Verna's kitchen. Sitting down at the table opposite Wilma, she raised an inquisitive eyebrow.

"Early bird catches the worm," Wilma quipped.

"What did I miss?"

"Jealous, are you?"

"With a lower-case *J* so it's not a sin."

Wilma laughed.

"Where's Mary?"

Wilma rolled her eyes. "I stopped by her place on the way over here. Apparently, she had to run errands in town."

She paused before adding, "Bethany refused to go for her. Again"

Edna knew that God had blessed Mary with extra patience or she'd never have survived raising such a shy daughter. "Something needs to be done to get that child out of her shell!"

"She's not a child, Edna," Verna said as she pushed a plate of fresh banana bread toward her. "She's as old as Myrna."

"Age is just a number in Bethany's case."

Wilma reached out and took two pieces of the banana bread. "Wonder what happened to that girl to make her so timid?"

For a moment, Edna almost wanted to respond, but her answer would not have been kind. Surely everyone knew that Mary overprotected and sheltered her daughter. Mary's own fears had been transferred to Bethany, doubling in size and scope.

"Well, I'm not here to talk about Bethany," Edna said sharply and turned her attention to Verna. "I want to hear about Myrna!" A broad smile covered her face. "What happened when she came home after MayFest?"

At this pointed question, Verna flushed.

Wilma nudged her arm. "Well? Tell her the news."

"There's news?" Edna's eyebrows shot up. "What news?"

Verna took her time responding. She sat there, primly tracing the outline of a flower on her teacup saucer. "Well, it seems Ezekiel brought Myrna home in the buggy after MayFest," Verna said in a slow and deliberate voice. "And he picked her up this morning. Apparently, he feels bicycling that far is too dangerous for her."

"Oh help!" Edna pressed her hand to her cheek. This was good news indeed. "He seems like such a conscientious man. I'm liking him more and more each day."

Verna tried not to smile. "I don't want to put the buggy before the horse, Edna. But I sense Wilma might be right. I just might have to plant a lot more celery for an autumn wedding."

Delighted, Edna clapped her hands together. "Oh, how *wunderbarr*! A wedding!"

"I said 'might,' Edna."

But Edna merely dismissed her with a feigned frown. "Oh, please, Verna. You saw how he was looking at her." She clucked her tongue. "He'd be a fool not to ask her. Why! Those *kinner* need a *maem*, and he surely needs a *fraa*."

"Well *that's* romantic!" Wilma rolled her eyes.

"Oh!" She swatted Wilma's arm. "You know what I mean!"

"Finally! One of our girls getting married!" Wilma grinned. "It's one thing to have sons marry, but I have a feeling that it'll be quite different when our *dochders* marry."

Edna kept her smile plastered on her face, but her heart dropped at Wilma's words. She was the only one of the four women who had no daughters. She'd lost several babies due to miscarriage and had one stillborn. *That* one had been a girl, and her loss had left a hole in her heart ever since.

Still, she begrudged no one the joy that she sensed in Verna. It was good that her friend was happy. She deserved it.

"Well, Maem, I found out some news about your Riehl fellow."

Edna looked up from where she sat by the window,

reading the Bible. "Oh help, John! Don't let it be bad news!"

Her son laughed and walked over to her. He sat down in the old recliner that Simon usually occupied after supper. "*Nee*, it's not bad." He scratched the side of his head. "Not good, either."

"Hmm. Not good *and* not bad?" Edna marked her place in the Bible with a crocheted bookmark and set the book aside. "That doesn't sound like it could be anything *but* bad news."

John smiled. "Daed sent me into town to get new traces for the harness. I ran into Nathanial Miller."

Edna furrowed her brow. "Our Nathanial Miller?"

"*Ja*, the very same."

"The one who married Katie Mae Kauffman last year?"

John leaned back in the chair and stretched out his legs. "Correct again."

"Oh." What on earth could Nathanial Miller know? He lived as far away from Ezekiel Riehl as they did! Besides, he had always been one to keep to himself, especially since *his* wife died.

"We got to talking, about crops and such, and I asked if he happened to know a farmer named Riehl."

Edna waited patiently for John to tell his story. He'd always been one to take his time elaborating when he shared details. She loved that about her son. Unlike many other Amish men, John wasn't one to get right to the point. He enjoyed storytelling.

"Well, he seemed right surprised that I asked."

"Oh?"

"Seems that Nathanial's first wife was cousins with Katie Ruth Riehl!"

Edna gasped. "You don't say!" Why hadn't she known this before? Probably because she'd never visited with his wife, Katie Mae Miller. Besides the fact that they lived on the far side of the *g'may*, Katie Mae was a young woman with her hands full, tending to Nathanial's children and a new baby of her own. And Simon certainly hadn't thought to ask any of the men at church. Not only wasn't he interested, but he'd never want to be tagged as a gossip.

But John? He was much more easygoing, even if he wasn't very social. Leave it to John to uncover a connection to Ezekiel Riehl within their church district.

"So, what did he tell you?"

John rubbed his chin. "That's the thing. Not much. He said he met the man a few times, at weddings and such, but since Martha passed away, he didn't have much opportunity for family gatherings like that."

She could only imagine. With four children and a farm to run, he wouldn't have time for socializing.

"But he did go to Katie Ruth's funeral."

Edna leaned forward. "Go on."

"Said that there was a lot of tension between Katie Ruth's father and Ezekiel. No one said much about it, but Nathanial sensed it. There was a comment, however, about Katie Ruth refusing to take treatment, though."

Clearly, John had heard the same thing that Edna already knew. She sighed and sat back in her chair. "Oh, I already heard that Ezekiel's rather conservative and doesn't approve of modern medicine. He forbade his wife to take it."

John frowned. "You sure about that?"

"Well, that's what I've heard." She paused. Who *had* told her that?

"According to Nathanial, Katie Ruth's *daed* is the bishop."

"So?"

John made a face at her. "Bishops aren't usually your

most liberal member of the community." He stood up. "Anyway, thought you should know." He winked. "Did my part, so no more scolding at the supper table."

For a moment, Edna mulled over her son's words. It was true that when preachers and bishops were nominated for the vote by the congregation, a vote that was conducted by lot, most districts did not choose liberal-thinking men but those who would uphold the standards of the community. Among the Amish, change was never evolution, but revolution.

If Katie Ruth's father was the bishop, he would've had sway over both Ezekiel *and* his daughter. And he could have convinced Katie Ruth to get cancer treatment— unless, of course, he didn't believe in it himself!

Was it possible that someone had gotten the story wrong?

Chapter Twenty-Six

"Oh, I just don't want to interfere," Verna said as she formed the round balls of dough to make drop cookies. The dough felt sticky against her skin, and she worried that it was too wet. She reached for some flour and sprinkled it onto the dough. "This question has already caused enough problems, and I'd hate to cause any more."

It was Wednesday and the four women had gathered to make their first batch of cookies for the store in town. Edna had just informed everyone of the news her son John had discovered. For starters, Verna wasn't certain what to make of it. The news that there was tension between Ezekiel and his former father-in-law wasn't startling. After all, she'd heard as much from Miriam already. And the news that the bishop had apparently supported his daughter's refusal of cancer treatment? Well, that wasn't uncommon.

"Don't you think Myrna should know?" Edna asked.

Mary chimed in. "I'd surely want Bethany to know."

Verna, however, shook her head. She might not understand everything about Ezekiel Riehl, but she did understand that sharing any information about the man with her daughter was not a good idea. "*Nee*, it doesn't make any difference now, does it? Bishops are known to be strict. They have to be in order to make decisions for their church members. Besides, it's in the past, isn't it?"

"But Verna," Edna said, "if Myrna *does* marry him, what if *she* gets sick?"

That thought had crossed her mind. But she knew that her daughter was an adult and had to make her own decisions. "I'll pray that she doesn't." She looked around the room at each of the friends staring at her. "Now, please, we really mustn't talk about this again. The only thing that matters is how Ezekiel treats my *dochder*, and from what I can see, there is no question of his good intentions in regard to her."

Edna held up her hands as if warding off an attack. "All right, then. I'll speak no more about it except for this: I think this whole nonsense should be addressed, openly talked about, before she decides whether or not to marry him."

Verna remained silent, focusing on the cookies. She didn't want to get into an argument with Edna. Everything else about the day had been wonderful so far. It was their first week making cookies for Yoders' Store. Mary had brought the little cards that Bethany had hand printed. They were, indeed, beautiful, with the words "Amish Cookie Club" on the label and a place for the women to indicate what kind of cookie was in the package.

No, Verna didn't want to continue this particular conversation, with Edna or anyone else. Sometimes least said *was* soonest mended.

When Simon came home early that afternoon, he greeted her with an unusually affectionate hug and kiss.

"My word!" Verna laughed as she steadied herself against the edge of the counter. "What was that for?"

He grinned. "Oh, nothing much, I suppose."

She didn't believe that for one minute. "Simon Bontrager! What are you hiding from me?"

Laughing, he walked over to the sink and flipped on the water, letting it run to warm up before he washed his hands. "Mayhaps I had a visit at the shop today from a certain person."

Verna narrowed her eyes. "A visit? From whom?"

Simon shrugged, pretending to hide his excitement.

"Simon!"

He reached for her hand and held it. "Ezekiel Riehl."

Verna caught her breath.

"He came to get some tools for the garden. Seems Myrna's been making his boys weed and water the garden every day after *schule*."

"What did he say?"

"He commented about how organized and hardworking she is," Simon told her. "'Industrious' was the word he used." He winked at his wife. "He asked if she'd always been such a tireless worker. When I said yes, he wondered why she wasn't working for me." He chuckled.

"Oh help!" She collapsed against the back of the chair. "What on earth did you tell him?"

"Why, the truth, of course. How she organized my stockroom and displays to the point that I couldn't find anything!"

"Simon!"

But his eyes were sparkling. She hadn't seen him look so joyous in a long time.

"Then he made a comment about how he looked forward to seeing more of us."

"Us?"

Simon nodded. "*Ja*, us. As in you and me."

Verna's mouth opened. "Oh, Simon! You don't think . . . ?"

He reached out and cupped her chin with his fingers. "I do think. Frankly, I have thought it. Remember I said that Ezekiel's picking up Myrna wouldn't be a problem come harvest time? What did you think I meant?"

"I . . . I guess I thought you meant he'd be busy in the fields."

He bent forward and kissed her forehead. "*Nee*, Verna. I meant that Myrna would be waking up each morning at his farm." He pulled back. "As his *fraa*."

Then, taking a step backward, he gave her one more wink before turning and walking to his chair. Verna barely noticed. Her mouth remained open and she put her hand onto her chest. If Simon thought it, surely it was bound to happen. He never speculated unless he felt it was a sure thing. Verna shut her eyes and took a deep breath, trying to realize that, at last, her daughter would be settled in and moving on with her life. She'd be marrying a good man and living on a prosperous farm. And she'd raise his four children alongside those that she bore Ezekiel. It would, indeed, be a fine life for her daughter.

She opened her eyes and swallowed, feeling as if a lump had formed in her throat. She had wanted nothing less for Myrna. But for a while, Verna had been too afraid that it would never come to pass. Now there was a light at the end of a long, dark tunnel. And that light came from one, and only one, place.

"Thank you, God," Verna whispered.

Chapter Twenty-Seven

Myrna was surprised when she looked at the clock and saw it was almost five o'clock. For a Wednesday, the day had surely flown by. Ezekiel should be coming in for supper soon, she presumed, and, at that time, she'd be able to leave. If Ezekiel didn't want to take her home before he ate, she'd just ride one of his bicycles home. She could bring it back the next day when he fetched her. There was no sense waiting around, especially since her chores were finished.

Realizing that the day was done felt bittersweet. To say she felt exhausted was an understatement. Her arm ached from having held Katie all afternoon. The baby had refused to sleep one wink! And she'd cried. A lot. Frankly, Myrna's brain felt like mush. With Katie fussing so much, it had been hard to entertain Henry, who got into everything: cabinets, shelves, the wood box.

Sleep.

Myrna smiled at the thought. She couldn't wait to go home, crawl into bed, and just sleep.

"You look peaceful."

At the sound of Ezekiel's voice, she started.

"Sorry." He held up both hands as if to apologize.

"You scared me." She took a deep breath and exhaled. "Again."

He leaned against the door frame and crossed his arms over his chest. He wore a peaceful expression as he watched her. "You were deep in thought." It wasn't a question, just a statement. "Was that smile about the *kinner*?"

She hesitated, just long enough that he didn't need her to answer.

Now it was her turn to apologize. "I'm sorry, Ezekiel—"

He raised an eyebrow.

"I mean, Zeke."

He nodded.

"It was a long day. Frankly, I was thinking about sleeping tonight." She pursed her lips. "Go home, forget about supper, and just crawl into bed. I just want sleep."

She noticed that he suddenly looked disappointed. "Speaking of supper—"

She interrupted him. "It's ready. I just need to call the boys. Katie's already fed and in bed sleeping."

He looked at her.

"I know, it's early, but she refused to nap at all. I'm not sure which one of us is more tired, her or me!" She almost laughed, but she couldn't find the energy. "So, if you don't mind, I'll head on home now. I can ride my bicycle so you don't have to be bothered."

At first, Ezekiel didn't respond. She waited for his dismissal, but it never came. Instead, he cleared his throat. "I . . . I was hoping you might sit a spell, mayhaps have supper with us."

The question caught her off guard. For the past four weeks, she had left every evening when Ezekiel sat down for supper with his children. While his farm was only four miles from her house, it took her almost an hour to bicycle there. She hadn't lingered past the time he needed her, as she certainly didn't want to ride home in the waning hours of daylight, especially because that was when the roads were busiest.

This week, now that he was insisting on picking her up and taking her home each evening, he usually packed all of the children into the buggy around four thirty to take her home. Despite the late hour, he said the children could wait to eat when they returned.

But tonight he was actually inviting her to stay for supper?

She stood there, her mouth agape. There was a hopeful look on his face, one that made her heart beat rapidly. Those dark chocolate eyes searched her face for an answer.

"Oh, that's a nice offer," she started slowly. "But I . . . I really should get home." The expression on his face changed and, for the briefest of moments, she thought he appeared genuinely disappointed. "I mean, I didn't tell my parents I'd be late. They'd worry."

"Hmm." He nodded. "Of course." He paused. "It's just that, well, I had something I wanted to ask you. And I thought the *kinner* might enjoy a livelier companion during supper." He raised his gaze to meet hers. "I'm afraid I've not been the best of company these days."

That surprised her. "Oh? I find you to be rather enjoyable company," she said without thinking. Immediately she bit her lower lip, wishing she could gobble up the words.

But Ezekiel didn't appear to think less of her for such a forward compliment. "Mayhaps because *you* are enjoyable company," he replied.

She felt the color flooding to her cheeks. Averting her eyes, she looked at the table, already set for the small family. What would it hurt, she thought, if she stayed? "I suppose I could stay a bit."

She heard him exhale as if he had been holding his breath the entire time.

"*Danke*, Myrna Bontrager."

Myrna Bontrager. The way he said her name made her stop. Had he ever said her full name? Or was that the first time? Either way, the manner in which he said it, the five syllables rolling off his tongue, gave her reason to pause. She looked at him, not entirely surprised to see that he was intently watching her.

"I . . . I'll go call the boys to the table, then," she said, softly.

It was dark when they left the house. She'd cleaned the dishes after everyone ate, and then, after ten minutes of pleading, she agreed to put the boys to bed with a story. She'd noticed Ezekiel smiling to himself as he watched her climb the stairs to the second-floor bedrooms. By the time she'd come back downstairs, Ezekiel was outside, and she was alone in the kitchen.

For a few minutes, she had stood there. She'd never been at the house this late, and the darkness mixed with the kerosene lanterns created strange shadows.

Funny how different things appeared in the evening, she'd thought.

She heard the screen door open. Rather than turn around, she stood there with her eyes shut. She wanted to see if she could feel Ezekiel's presence. Sure enough, she knew the exact moment when he stood in the doorway, most likely with those dark eyes fastened upon her.

"Supper was *gut*," he said, breaking the silence at last. "You're a right *gut* cook, Myrna."

She crossed her arms over her chest and smiled as she

turned toward him. "That's my *maem*'s doing. All that baking desserts and breads. Rubbed off on me."

"Hmm." He hesitated for the briefest of moments before he walked into the room. "Myrna, you wouldn't mind sitting for a spell, would you?" He gestured toward the sitting area. "I've something I want to talk to you about."

"Is everything okay?"

"Oh *ja*! It's just . . ."

"Myrna?" a soft voice called out from the darkness above.

At the sound of her name being called from the top of the stairs, they both looked in that direction.

"Henry?" Myrna got up and hurried over to where Henry was descending the steps. "What're you doing up?"

"I can't sleep."

"You need to try, Henry. That wasn't even ten minutes."

"Can you hold me?" He didn't wait for a response as he took hold of her dress, pressing his face into the folds of her apron.

She glanced at Ezekiel, who grunted and looked away.

"Come here, Henry," she had said, reaching down for his hand. "We can sit a spell."

Now, twenty minutes later, Ezekiel drove her home with Henry curled up on her lap. He'd refused to return to bed, insisting that he wanted to ride with his father when he took Myrna home. And, as much as Myrna wanted to resist his demands, she knew that they couldn't leave a three-year-old alone if he wasn't going to sleep next to his brothers.

They rode the rest of the way to her father's house in silence, Myrna finding a strange sense of peace sitting beside Ezekiel in the buggy. She shut her eyes and listened to the sound of the horse's hooves on the road and wondered at the secrets held in Ezekiel's heart. He appeared to be such a kind and loving man, observant and helpful in a way that she had never noticed in other Amish men. What a rare treasure he would be, she realized, for the right woman.

If only that woman could be me, she thought.

The next day, Katie wouldn't stop crying. No matter what Myrna did, the baby continued to cry. For over two hours, Myrna held the baby against her shoulder and paced the floors, rubbing the child's back and trying to soothe her with soft, whispered words. When she'd gone to fetch the boys from school, she had to carry Katie in her arms while Henry lagged behind, complaining every step of the way.

That hour had been the only break in Katie's tears.

Once they returned home, she began all over again.

Desperate, Myrna bathed the child, hoping that the warm water would make her sleepy. Instead, she fussed and whimpered during the entire bath.

Once she was dried and dressed again, Katie continued her wailed complaints that no one could understand.

"Make her stop, Myrna!" Daniel covered his ears with his hands. "She's so loud!"

Myrna frowned. "I'm trying, Daniel. But she just keeps crying."

David grabbed his brother's arm. "Let's go outside. Mayhaps Daed needs help."

For once, Daniel didn't argue.

Despite feeling bone weary, Myrna couldn't help but give a soft smile. "Seems there's a benefit to your tears, little one," she whispered to Katie. "They'd rather do chores than listen to you scream."

By four o'clock, Myrna gave up trying. Instead, she sat

in the rocking chair and, cradling the baby in her arms, just pushed her feet against the floor in the hope that the gliding movement might comfort one of them.

She'd been working for Ezekiel for five weeks, and she had to admit that she had grown to love the children. Each of the boys had a unique personality, but her heart swelled with extra love for Henry and Katie. David and Daniel had memories of their mother. They also had each other. But poor Henry remembered nothing, and Katie had not benefited from a mother's love.

So knowing that Katie was in distress upset Myrna to no end. If only she knew what was wrong with the child!

"What's this?"

Exhausted, Myrna could barely lift her head to look at Ezekiel. It was the first time she'd seen him since breakfast, for he'd been cutting hay in the back pasture, not even having stopped for a bite to eat. A week of rain was forecasted starting on Sunday. Ezekiel needed to finish the cutting in one day so that it could dry properly and he could bale it before the storms came.

Now, seeing him, Myrna felt a wave of relief.

"She's been crying all day."

He frowned and crossed the room to where she sat holding Katie. "And you didn't think to fetch me?"

She gave a little shrug. "I didn't want to interrupt your work."

"Hmm." He reached down and pressed his hand to Katie's cheeks. A dark cloud appeared to cover his face. He moved his hand to touch her forehead and then the back of her neck. "She's burning with fever."

"What?" Myrna shifted Katie in her arms and freed her hand so that she, too, could feel the child's face. "I . . . I didn't notice."

"You didn't notice that she's feverish?"

"I . . . I thought she was just warm from all the fussing and crying." Saying those words made her feel foolish. How could she have been so stupid that she didn't realize the child had a fever?

Ezekiel didn't respond. Instead, he walked over to the kitchen sink and turned on the faucet so that he could soak a clean cloth in cold water.

Myrna watched from where she sat, wondering what he was thinking. Was he angry that she hadn't fetched him from the fields? What did it matter anyway? It wasn't as if he would give the *boppli* medicine to bring down the fever.

Still, she felt terrible for having ignored the obvious warning sign.

Returning to where she sat, Ezekiel handed her the washcloth. "Cool her down with this."

Obediently, Myrna took the washcloth and gently pressed it to Katie's flesh.

Ezekiel stood by the rocking chair, his presence causing Myrna to feel nervous, and not just about the baby's temperature. Twice she felt him brush against her arm.

"She's probably just teething," Myrna said. "Babies often cry in church when that's happening, and it's around this age."

"Hmm." He nodded and reached for the cloth to run it under fresh water. When he handed it to her, he gave her a half smile. "I'll keep the boys busy outside so you don't have to worry about them."

Myrna sighed. "Well, I'll have to let her cry a bit while I cook your supper."

She felt his hand on her shoulder, a gentle but firm touch at the same time. "*Nee*, Myrna. I can cook for the boys. You take care of little Katie."

When he didn't remove his hand right away, Myrna looked up, surprised at how worried his eyes looked. She wished she could recommend ibuprofen, but another argument would linger far longer than any pain from teething.

"I'll check back in a little bit."

She felt his fingers give her shoulder a soft squeeze before he withdrew his hand and left the kitchen. Long after he retreated outside, she could still feel the lingering warmth of his touch. Holding the baby, Myrna shut her eyes and wondered about Ezekiel and the conflicting emotions that arose within her whenever he was around.

Chapter Twenty-Eight

"Crying and a slight fever, you say?" Edna sat at the table in Verna's kitchen, watching as Wilma washed and Mary dried the bowls. "Sounds like teething," she said.

Even though it was not a worship Sunday, they'd gathered again at Verna's house on Friday to make a second batch of cookies for Yoders' Store. The first batch had almost sold out already.

As the cookies baked in the oven, the sweet smell of warm sugar filled the room. Six baking sheets were waiting on the counter to go into the oven as soon as the first batch cooked.

They'd been making cookies for so many years that everything came second nature to them. No one had to instruct the others as to who did what. They just innately knew and went to work.

But now, as the cookies baked, it was time to relax and get caught up. And, as usual, everyone had turned to Verna for an update about Myrna and Ezekiel.

Verna leaned against the counter near the sink. "It worries me," she admitted. "Myrna looked exhausted when Ezekiel brought her home last evening."

"What ho!" Wilma turned off the kitchen faucet. "He brought her home? Again?"

Mary set the last bowl into the drying rack and hung the towel over the counter. "Well, that certainly progressed quickly, didn't it, now?"

"It normally does," Edna said, "when two people realize they are meant for each other."

"No sense dragging it out like the *Englischers* do!" Wilma added.

"I never thought of it that way," Edna said. "But you're right. They do drag things out, don't they?"

"And it doesn't seem to make their marriages any stronger."

Edna raised her eyebrows. "Another good point. Why, Wilma, when did you become so wise?"

"Always have been." Wilma laid her hand on Edna's arm. "It's about time you realized it."

They laughed—all of them except Verna.

"I'm really concerned about her," she said. "She practically fell right into her bed. Said the baby just cried all day."

Wilma put her hand to the side of her mouth and whispered none too softly, "Better get the ear candle."

"Oh hush!" Verna took the towel from the counter and threw it at Wilma. "This is serious."

"I'm sorry, Verna." She glanced at Edna and winked.

Ignoring Wilma's theatrics, Verna continued. "I told Myrna to keep an eye on the child. I thought she was teething, too, but that fever . . ." She shook her head and clucked her tongue. "Don't like the sound of that one bit."

"Me, neither." Edna could hardly remember when her own children had teethed. It felt like a lifetime ago. But she did remember that it was a horrible phase, especially when they were as young as little Katie Riehl. "Myrna really should take the *boppli* to see a doctor."

Verna sighed. "You know Ezekiel would *never* agree to that."

"Give her some beaten egg whites mixed with sugar and water," Wilma offered.

Edna cringed. "That sounds terrible!"

"My *maem* swore by that remedy."

"It still sounds terrible."

"Well, it might have tasted terrible, but it sure cured our fevers."

The other ladies laughed.

"Well, terrible-tasting or not, she might have to try it," Verna said. "Neither one of them can continue at this rate. And I'm sure Ezekiel's exhausted, too. He works all day and then has a crying baby all night."

"It just doesn't make any sense," Wilma said. She moved over to the table and sat down across from Edna. "Why wouldn't he take the *boppli* to a doctor?"

Verna shrugged. "Just his principles, I suppose."

"Well that's just plain ignorant." She crossed her arms over her chest. "Mayhaps you don't want him courting your *dochder* anyway, Verna."

Mary gasped. "Don't say that! Not with everything so close for Myrna!"

Edna raised her hands into the air, a gesture to shut down the inevitable bickering that would eventually arise if the conversation continued. "Might I suggest we change the direction of dialogue here? We've a beautiful day before us, and there's no sense ruining it with escalating arguments." She scanned their faces. "Wouldn't you agree?"

A silence ensued, and Edna took advantage of it to pass around the little white cards that Bethany had made. "Now, we should each take ten of these and neatly write *oatmeal cookies* on them. That should keep our hands from being idle as well as our tongues." She looked at Wilma and widened her eyes. "Right?"

"Hmph."

"And just think of all the money we'll be raising to help families in need within our community," Edna continued. "If we have to be known as the Amish Cookie Club, then at least the name will be associated with charitable works."

Chapter Twenty-Nine

"How was the baby today?" Verna asked when Myrna walked into the house.

"Fussy. Very fussy," she said as she kicked off her black sneakers. "It's exhausting taking care of children." She plopped herself into the recliner and shut her eyes. "But she did nap a little better today than yesterday. And she was sleeping soundly when I left. I sure hope she stayed asleep while David was watching her. She's terribly cranky when she's awake."

Her heart broke for her daughter. Verna knew all too well the pain of watching a sick child suffering. And yet, as their mother, Verna had been able to make decisions about her children and their care. How painful it must be for Myrna not to be able to do the same for Katie.

"And Ezekiel?" she asked, hoping that her voice didn't sound overly curious.

Myrna sighed, opening her eyes and peering at her mother. "He spent a good deal of time checking in on us. I don't know how he'd manage if I wasn't there. Even so, he surely got nothing done."

"Well, little ones do get fevers, especially this time of year when the seasons change."

Myrna gave a half-hearted smile. "I know that, Maem. But I just wish he . . ." She stopped midsentence.

"He what?" Verna prodded.

"Oh, I don't know." She rubbed her cheeks with her hands. "He was so quiet when he drove me back home. Something was bothering him, I could tell."

Verna could understand that. Whenever one of her children took ill, she'd always withdrawn into herself. Focusing all of her energy on their well-being was just as exhausting as tending to them when they weren't sick.

"He's concerned. I'm sure that's all."

Myrna took a deep breath and exhaled slowly. "I suppose that's it. I just wish I understood him better."

"How so?"

She sat up and straightened her apron on her lap. "Well, things were going so well, you know?"

Verna nodded but didn't dare speak. She didn't want to interrupt her daughter. This was the first time Myrna had opened up about Ezekiel. While she had a dozen questions that she'd have loved to ask, Verna knew that it was better to just let her speak and remain silent.

"I . . . I guess I had hoped that, well, something might have happened." She glanced at her mother but then quickly averted her eyes. "I can't deny that I have feelings for him."

"Feelings?"

Myrna nodded. "I do, Maem. Just like you told me before. I didn't *want* to have feelings for him, especially with his strange conservative beliefs. But I reckon I just forgot about that." She frowned. "I mean, he doesn't seem so conservative otherwise. He's good with the boys and truly concerned about Katie. A man who is so tender-hearted and considerate cannot be anything other than a *gut* man, *ja*?"

Verna wasn't certain how to answer that.

"But when I see the *boppli* crying and there's nothing in the house to make her feel better, I feel different about him." She paused as if seeking the right word. "Torn. *Ja*, that's better. I feel torn. How can I want to spend my life with someone who wouldn't call the doctor or fetch medicine to take away the child's pain?"

The hurt in her daughter's face tugged at Verna's heart. She shared Myrna's sentiments. After seeing Ezekiel with Myrna at MayFest, she, too, had become hopeful. Everything else about the man was just right for her daughter. His attentiveness and thoughtfulness were clear indicators of how he felt for Myrna. And an older Amish man would never lead on a young woman. Clearly a marriage proposal was imminent.

But Verna wasn't certain how her daughter could agree to marry Ezekiel with this one thing coming between them.

"Mayhaps you could talk to him, Myrna?" It made the most sense. There was no time to beat around the bush on this issue. "You seem to have a strong enough friendship. You should just ask him straight out."

Myrna gasped, a horrified look covering her face. "I couldn't do that!"

Verna gave her an exasperated look. "Oh, Myrna. Don't say that. Why! You've always been the one who spoke up and did what you thought was best."

"And it always got me into trouble!" Myrna reminded her.

She couldn't help but give a little laugh. "That's true, *ja*. I'm quite familiar with your history in that regard." She took a second to become sober once again. "But you always knew in your heart that your intentions were *gut* and followed your righteous beliefs. And, frankly, I've never seen you happier than when you started working for Ezekiel."

Myrna nodded. "I do enjoy being there and taking care of his family and house."

"So, speak with Ezekiel. Share your mind on this matter."

"What if he gets angry again? Like how he reacted when I tried to treat Henry?"

Verna had suspected that incident had been weighing heavily on her daughter's mind. But fear was clouding Myrna's judgment. Verna longed to share what she'd learned about Ezekiel's father-in-law, but it would be even better if Myrna learned the truth directly from the man she loved. "I won't deny that speaking your mind might upset him. It even might end your chances of marrying him, true. But would you want to marry the man if you held back?" She leaned forward and touched Myrna's knee. "And this is very important. It's not something to keep inside, don't you agree?"

She could see Myrna reflecting on her words. For a few long moments, she remained silent, her finger tapping against the arm of the chair. Finally, she nodded. "You're right, Maem. If we cannot right this between us, then there is no future, no matter how much I feel for him. But if I speak up and he gets angry, at least I have spoken my mind."

Verna patted her leg. "There you go. That's my *dochder*."

Myrna gave her a half smile. "*Ja*, I'm still in here, I suppose."

"Indeed you are," Verna said. "I never doubted that for a moment. It's just that when you feel so strongly for someone, your emotions can cloud your thinking. Let's have no more mistakes like we had with Henry. Confront him in a kind and respectful way, but don't let another day go by. You need to know, one way or the other."

Nodding, Myrna stood up. "One way or the other," she repeated. "I just hope it's my way and not the highway."

Verna watched as her daughter headed toward the stairs. *Me, too,* she thought. *Me, too.*

Chapter Thirty

On Saturday morning, Myrna waited inside the kitchen, hovering near the window so that she could see when Ezekiel's buggy pulled into the driveway. She had made it a habit to always be ready so that he didn't have to wait for her. He was already going out of his way, driving across town to fetch her.

"Waiting for your beau?"

Myrna cast a stern look of reproach in the direction of Samuel. "Oh hush!"

He laughed as he walked over to the coffeepot. "I'm just teasing you, Myrna," he said, pouring himself a mug of black coffee. "Don't be so sensitive."

"I'm not sensitive," she snapped back. "I've just a lot on my mind."

"All girls are sensitive when they're *ferhoodled*!"

"Samuel Bontrager!"

They both snapped their attention toward their parents' bedroom door. Verna stood there, her hands on her hips.

"Now you just leave your *schwester* alone, you hear?" She marched into the room and stood before him. "Or I'll have her tease you mercilessly when *you* find yourself courting."

He gave her a lopsided grin. "As if either of you would ever know."

Verna swatted at his arm, but he darted away, still laughing, and carried his coffee toward the door.

"Never you mind him," Verna said, listening for the screen door to shut behind him. "He's just—"

"—being a *bruder*." Myrna nodded. She had more important things to think about than Samuel teasing her.

"You sleep all right last night?" her mother asked, picking up the coffeepot to replenish Myrna's mug.

"*Nee*, not really."

"I'm sure. You've a lot on your mind."

Myrna couldn't have agreed more. It wasn't the first sleepless night she'd had in the past few weeks. But last night had been the worst. All she could think about was how she would bring up the subject with Ezekiel, to find out why he hadn't wanted his wife to get medical treatment. She knew that the answers might disappoint her. But she'd spent a long part of the early morning hours praying that *that* wouldn't be the case.

Verna glanced toward the window. "*Ach*, he's here. You best get out there before Samuel says something foolish to him."

Myrna hurried outside and climbed into the buggy. As she sat down, she caught a glimpse of Ezekiel. To her surprise, he looked completely disheveled. His hair was tousled and his shirt wrinkled. And he had big, dark circles under his eyes.

"Zeke?"

When he looked at her, she noticed how completely exhausted he looked.

"What's wrong?" she asked.

"The *boppli*," he managed to say, his voice cracking. "She cried all night long."

"All night?" No wonder he appeared so depleted. "My *maem* suggested she's teething."

Under his breath, he grunted, and he focused on guiding the horse down the road. In the mornings, there was always more traffic, even on Saturdays.

The silence in the buggy felt deafening, and Myrna stared out the window. She wanted to broach the subject about calling a doctor or stopping for medicine. But his mood was so dark and dour that she knew it wasn't the right time.

But there was something else lingering in the air. He might have been tired, but he also seemed indignant.

No, she thought, this was not the right time to speak to him about what weighed so heavily on her heart.

As soon as she arrived at the house, she hurried to the bedroom where Katie lay on her back, crying. Her arms reached upward and her legs kicked as tears fell down her red cheeks.

"Oh, Ezekiel!" she fumed. "How could you have left her alone like this?"

She reached into the crib and picked up the baby. Almost a year old, Katie was heavy for her age. But again today she was too hot. Immediately, Myrna sat down on the edge of the bed and rested Katie on her lap. Her hands felt the child's head and neck. She was absolutely burning up. Much worse than before.

"Ezekiel!" she called out. "Ezekiel!"

He appeared in the doorway, his eyes widening when he saw her sitting on his unmade bed.

She didn't care about propriety. Not now. "She's sick with fever again!"

He frowned and approached her. Reaching down, he touched the baby's face. "She wasn't earlier."

Somehow Myrna doubted that.

"I'll run some cool water," he said and hurried back into the kitchen.

Myrna quickly removed the baby's dress and carried her to the changing table to clean her. "You poor little thing," she cooed to Katie, who, as soon as the air hit her bare skin, began to whimper instead of cry. "We'll cool you down." Behind her, she could hear Ezekiel approach. From the sounds of the sloshing water, she knew that he carried a basin.

"Here." He set it on the changing table. "And use these cloths."

Carefully, Myrna dipped the cloth into the water and wrung it out before dabbing at the baby's hot skin. Ezekiel lingered behind her, watching her every move.

"I really don't know what else to do for her," Myrna said, hoping that he would suggest taking the baby to a doctor.

But Ezekiel stood there, staring at Katie, who now slept in Myrna's arms. "Seems a bit better, don't you think?"

Myrna frowned. "I suppose."

"Well, she's sleeping anyway."

"I'm sure she's exhausted, too."

He nodded. "I imagine so."

Above their heads, the sounds of feet on the floorboards indicated that the boys were starting to awaken.

"You stay with Katie," he said. "I'll tend to the boys."

For the next two hours, Myrna held the baby, rocking her in the chair in the kitchen. Ezekiel had fed the three boys and taken David and Daniel outside, leaving Henry with strict instructions not to disturb Myrna or his sister.

Now it was almost ten o'clock, and Myrna could feel that the fever was back.

The baby needed to see a doctor.

She waited until Henry took his nap before she bundled up Katie and put her into the stroller. She knew that she couldn't take Katie to the doctor—not only because she had no way to get there, but because she didn't want to upset Ezekiel. But if she could walk to the neighbors' home and borrow their phone, she could call her father's store and have Samuel or Timothy fetch her mother.

With her mother as support, perhaps they could convince Ezekiel that proper medical care for little Katie was necessary.

Chapter Thirty-One

Edna stood in the aisle of Yoders' Store and stared at the shelving that held the packages of homemade cookies. She could hardly believe that those were *their* cookies in the clear cellophane wrappers, tied with pretty blue yarn and Bethany's handwritten cards attached.

She couldn't believe that more than half of the shelf was empty. And it was the second batch she'd brought to Yoders'. The drop cookies they'd baked the previous week had sold out by midday on Friday. One of the Yoder children had bicycled to Edna's house and told her about it. Immediately, Edna had gathered the Cookie Club on Friday to bake more cookies and sent them with John to drop off at Yoders' on Saturday morning before he went to the auction house.

"Edna? Is that you?"

She turned around and smiled as Barbara bustled down the aisle. "I can't believe how pretty the display looks," she said to the bishop's wife. She pointed to the large sign overhead. "Who made that?"

Barbara craned her neck to look at the sign. "Oh, I reckon Steve Yoder had one of his boys make it." She returned her attention to Edna. "It matches the cards that you made."

"Actually, Mary's Bethany made those," Edna admitted. "She's got a prettier hand than the rest of us combined."

Barbara laughed. "*Ja*, my own hand is a bit shaky anymore."

Edna stepped aside as a young woman and her two children walked toward them. She watched as the children immediately saw the cookies and asked their mother if they could have a package. To her surprise, the mother acquiesced and picked up not just one package but two!

When they were out of hearing, Barbara shook her head and whispered, "That's the problem with the *Englische*. They don't teach their *kinner* restraint."

"One of many problems, I think," Edna replied in a low voice.

"Well, anyway, I'm glad you could stop in today to see the display." She pointed to a large, open gap. "It's nearly empty already."

Edna had noticed that. "Well, we're gathering Wednesday at Verna's *haus* to bake cookies to drop off to replace them."

"Oh?" Barbara frowned. "I thought you all usually met at your *haus* to bake."

Edna nodded. "*Ja*, we usually do, because my kitchen is bigger and set up for baking larger batches. But it's *gut* to rotate houses. Besides, Myrna's run into some problems, and Verna didn't want to leave her alone."

She noticed that Barbara immediately appeared concerned. "Oh bother! I hope it had nothing to do with Daniel Gingerich."

That wasn't a name Edna was familiar with. "I don't know who that is," she said. "But I'm sure it has nothing to do with whoever he is. Seems she's had a falling-out with Ezekiel Riehl."

Barbara clucked her tongue. "Oh, that poor man. I hope nothing is wrong."

Immediately, Edna froze. "You know Ezekiel?"

"Of course."

If Edna had been alone, she'd have slapped her own forehead. Why hadn't she thought of speaking to Barbara before? With Barbara's husband being the bishop, it made sense that she'd know of other happenings in nearby districts. And she'd certainly remember the death of Katie Ruth, the bishop's daughter. Quite often, bishops preached at neighboring church districts and attended weddings and funerals.

"I'd heard that Myrna Bontrager was helping Ezekiel," Barbara said. "He needed someone like Myrna to step in. I was glad to hear it. But you say they've had a falling-out?"

Edna gave a little shrug. "I'd hate to speculate . . ." She certainly didn't want the bishop's wife to think she was a gossip.

"I'll pray for them," Barbara said with a sigh. "I'd like nothing more than to see him married again, only this time to a kind woman from a good family."

Edna frowned. "This time?"

Barbara pursed her lips. "Let's just say that Katie Ruth's father, Daniel Gingerich, is quite a difficult man, and Ezekiel never did get on well with the Gingerich family. Things only deteriorated after Katie Ruth fell ill." She shook her head. "Such a shame, too. Ezekiel's a truly kind man. He deserved better."

Cocking her head to one side, Edna repeated Barbara's words in her mind. "I'm not sure I understand what you mean."

Sighing, Barbara stepped closer to her and lowered her

voice. "Katie Ruth listened to her father over her husband. Why, Ezekiel all but cried to her, begging her to get treated for her cancer. But that bishop had her convinced that prayer alone would cure her." She gave a soft *tsk, tsk, tsk.* "Nothing wrong with taking some medicine. God gave us the intelligence to make it. But in Katie Ruth's case, she didn't have the common sense to take it."

Stunned, Edna tried to wrap her head around what Barbara had just told her. "Are you saying that it was Katie Ruth's father who talked her out of treatment, and not Ezekiel?"

"That's exactly what I'm saying."

But that didn't make any sense, not to Edna. "Everyone claims it's the other way around," she said, more to herself than to Barbara.

"Hmph. I'm hardly surprised. And Ezekiel's too righteous a man to speak up for himself, while the bishop refuses to speak about it at all." Barbara shook her head, a look of disgust etched upon her face. "I only know because my husband was called there to help just before Katie Ruth died."

Edna hardly heard another word from Barbara's mouth. She'd switched topics and begun talking about the success of the MayFest table.

But Edna wasn't listening. Instead, she thought about this new bit of news she had just learned. If what Barbara was saying was true, perhaps everyone had gotten the story wrong from the beginning! She could hardly wait to get to Verna's. Even if she didn't *want* to discuss this anymore, Verna had to learn that what they originally thought about Ezekiel might have been one big terrible lie after all.

Chapter Thirty-Two

Verna was outside in the garden, pulling at the newly sprouted weeds, when she heard the buggy pull up. Wiping her hands on her apron, she struggled to get to her feet. Her knees ached and her ankles were sore from having spent almost two hours weeding the garden.

When she realized that it was Edna, Verna gave a satisfied sigh. The perfect excuse to take a break from one of her least favorite chores, she thought as she walked over to greet her friend.

Raising her hand to shield her eyes from the noon sun, Verna met Edna just as she stopped the horse and buggy near the barn. "What brings you here again so soon?"

"I was at Yoders'," she explained. "Picking up some things for next week's dinner guests."

"Oh! Is that all starting again next week?" How time flew, she thought. It felt as if the season had just ended a few weeks ago.

Edna nodded. "But that's not important right now. While I was there, I ran into Barbara Brenneman. She just told me something that I simply have to share with you."

Verna made a face and rolled her eyes, feeling a bit

indignant. Hadn't she made it clear that she didn't want to hear anything else about Ezekiel? "Oh, Edna. Not something more about Ezekiel. Please."

"But this is different," Edna urged. "It's *important*."

"Oh, fine then." She knew that she had no choice but to relent—otherwise her own curiosity would get the best of her. Besides, she needed to know Edna's news, just in case it impacted Myrna. "Tie up and come inside. I'll warm some water for tea."

No sooner had she walked into the kitchen and headed toward the cabinet where she kept her teakettle than she heard horse hooves yet again.

"Oh help! It's a busy *haus* today, I suppose," she said to herself. She glanced out the window and, to her surprise, saw it was her husband's buggy. But it wasn't Simon driving. It was Timothy.

In all the years that Samuel and Timothy had worked at the store, not once had either one come home in the middle of the day. Surely, something terrible must have happened.

Panic-stricken, she hurried outside and practically bumped into her son as he bounded up the stairs.

"What's wrong, Timothy? Has something happened?"

"It's Myrna. She needs you at Ezekiel's."

Verna gasped. "Myrna? What's wrong?"

Timothy put his hands on his mother's arms and peered into her face. "She's fine, Maem. Don't panic. But the little one—"

"Katie?"

He nodded. "*Ja*, that's the one. Her fever hasn't broken, and Myrna asks that you come. She told me that you should stop for medicine to help the *boppli*'s fever."

"Oh help," she muttered. The last thing she wanted was

to interfere again between Ezekiel and Myrna. But she also knew that if Myrna had reached out for help, she couldn't say no.

"You can drop me off at the store and take the buggy, if you want."

But Edna appeared behind Timothy. "*Nee*, that's okay. I'll take you, Verna." She motioned toward her buggy. "It's already hitched, and we can stop at the pharmacy on the way to buy fever reducer."

"I could use the company," Verna admitted. "And the support. I have a feeling that both will be needed when we arrive."

"You called your *maem*?"

Ezekiel stood in the doorway, his hands on his hips as he assessed the scene before him. He'd walked in, probably after seeing the buggy parked in the driveway. When he stood in the doorway, he stared first at Verna, holding the baby against her chest, and then at Myrna. Verna's heart pounded.

Clearly, he wasn't happy.

Myrna took a deep breath and faced him. Verna knew that her daughter had never been one to shirk her responsibilities, nor to deny her own transgressions. She knew that Myrna would take ownership of what she had done.

"*Ja*, I did, Ezekiel."

"When?"

"An hour ago." Myrna pressed her lips together and lifted her chin. "I took Katie for a walk to the neighbors and borrowed their phone."

He reached up and removed his hat. Setting it on the

counter next to him, he ran his fingers through his hair. "Oh, Myrna."

"She brought medicine for the *boppli*." Myrna straightened her shoulders. "She *needs* medicine, Ezekiel." Myrna swallowed. "She probably needs a doctor, too."

"A doctor?"

Myrna nodded. "*Ja*."

"A doctor?" he repeated slowly, as if tasting the word.

"I know you won't approve, but . . ."

Ezekiel held up his hand, cutting her off midsentence. "I wouldn't approve?"

Verna moved forward, hoping to avoid a scene. Clearly this was not going well, but the focus needed to be on the baby, not on their differences.

"Ezekiel," she said. "I brought her some medicine to take down her fever. She's so hot. She needs something while her body fights whatever ailment she has. Please, may I give her the medicine?"

He met her gaze, a questioning look in his eyes. "May you give her the medicine?" Just as he had before, he repeated her words slowly before he answered with a soft, "*Ja*, of course."

Verna didn't wait another second. She nodded toward Edna, who withdrew the medicine from her purse. Carefully she opened the medicine and, using an eyedropper, measured out the correct dosage.

The sound of car tires on the gravel driveway could be heard. Verna didn't look up. She put the eyedropper to the baby's lips and gave her the medicine.

"Ezekiel?" a voice called.

"In here," he answered.

A man walked into the kitchen. He wore khaki pants

and a white button-down shirt. In his hand, he carried a brown leather bag.

Myrna looked at Ezekiel. "Who's this?"

But it was Edna who answered Myrna's question. "Dr. Graham!"

Verna held the baby in her arms, staring at the man, her mouth agape. "You know him?" she whispered to Edna. The last person she'd expected to see show up at Ezekiel's was a doctor

"*Ja*, he's the doctor who treated Elmer." Edna smiled and walked over to shake his hand.

He smiled at her. "I trust Elmer is doing well? Staying away from sweets?"

"Only when I'm watching him," she said. "He thinks I don't know he sneaks cookies when I'm not looking."

The doctor laughed. "Sounds like Elmer for sure!" After setting down his bag, the man moved toward Myrna, extending his hand. "You must be Myrna. Ezekiel called me to come see the baby. Said she's been feverish and crying." He approached Verna. "May I examine her, please?"

"Doctor?" Myrna's mouth opened and her eyes widened. She turned toward Ezekiel. "You called a doctor?"

The doctor took the baby from Verna and held her gently in his arms. "Oh, Katie. How big you've grown since I last saw you!" He ran his finger along her cheek and rested his hand on her small forehead. Then he gestured toward his bag. "If you don't mind?"

Verna picked it up and took it to him. "We didn't know he'd called you. We just gave her some pain reliever, to fight the fever."

The doctor nodded. "I'd have done the same."

Carefully, the doctor carried the baby and his bag to the sofa. He sat down and laid Katie beside him. "I'm sure it's nothing major, but one can never be too careful."

Verna watched as the doctor examined the baby, keenly aware that Myrna was staring at Ezekiel. Too many unanswered questions lingered unspoken in the room. There would be time for asking them later. For now, the most important thing was that Katie get the medical treatment she needed.

Chapter Thirty-Three

An hour later, after the doctor left and Katie had been put to bed, Ezekiel stood in the kitchen, his eyes darting back and forth between the two older women and Myrna. No one spoke, and she felt surrounded, not just by people but by her emotions. She didn't understand what had just happened.

She'd never heard of hand, foot and mouth disease. But the doctor had told them it was very common, especially since babies didn't have immunity to the virus. Chances were that she'd caught it from one of her older brothers, who might have picked it up from school.

But she'd be fine, the doctor had reassured Ezekiel. "Just keep giving her pain reliever and lots of fluids." He had clapped Ezekiel on the arm as he started to leave. "I'll check back on her in a few days, but this illness should just run its course." And then he had left.

Now Myrna stood there, unable to process the conflicting emotions that coursed through her body.

Had Ezekiel called the doctor because he knew it would make her feel better? Or had he done it because it was the right thing to do?

Her thoughts were interrupted when Ezekiel shuffled

his feet, his boots making a scraping noise against the hardwood floor. "Might I have a word with you, Myrna?" He glanced at her mother and Edna. "Uh . . . in private?" He gestured to the door. "Outside?"

Swallowing, Myrna nodded. She avoided looking at her mother and Edna, but she had to walk past them. Myrna knew that her cheeks burned red. She took a deep breath and walked toward Ezekiel.

He held the door open for her, and she brushed past him.

Outside on the porch, Myrna moved as far away from the door as possible. The last thing she wanted was for her mother or Edna to overhear their conversation. She was embarrassed enough as it was. She breathed in the fresh air, hoping that it would help to loosen her tight chest. Why was her heart pounding so rapidly?

"You want to talk here?" he asked, a confused look on his face. "We could walk a spell, if you'd prefer."

But Myrna saw no point in that. "I don't understand, Ezekiel. What just happened in there?"

"The doctor said she'd be fine," he responded in a flat tone.

"I know *that*. I was standing right there!" She took a deep breath, trying to calm herself. "I meant *why* did you call the doctor?"

He answered her question by avoiding it altogether. "You seem upset."

She felt her throat constrict and knew that she was close to tears. "I am upset. I mean I was. Before." She didn't know what she was saying. She'd been so angry at Ezekiel for not taking care of Katie. And she'd been ready to stand up to him in the kitchen when her mother had arrived. But all of the fight had vanished from her when the doctor had come.

"Why were you upset?" he asked. "Before."

"Because of Katie," she said, not able to stop the tear spilling from her eye. She swiped at it. "I've grown rather fond of those boys and little Katie. And the thought of anything happening to one of them upset me."

"Hm. I see."

Another tear fell. "Do you? Do you see, Ezekiel?" She started to reach up to brush the tear away but, to her surprise, felt his hand on her wrist. He kept hold of her arm and reached up with his free hand to gently wipe the tear. Her eyes met his, and she saw a deep sorrow in his dark chocolate gaze. "I wasn't supposed to care so much," she whispered. "That wasn't my plan."

"Care about the children?"

Her heart felt as if it would pound its way right out of her chest. She didn't want to confess how she really felt to him. What if he didn't feel the same way? But the intensity of his gaze made the last of her resolve to be strong fade away.

"*Nee*, Ezekiel," she conceded. "About you."

His grip on her wrist loosened, and she heard him exhale.

"I didn't *want* to care about you," she continued, knowing that if she stopped, she'd lose her one opportunity to speak so candidly to him. "And I fought it, Ezekiel. I truly tried to fight it. I mean, you made it clear from the beginning that you weren't looking for a . . ."

She hesitated, not wanting to use the word "replacement."

"Well, anyway, after all that you've been through, I didn't blame you. Besides, I just wanted a job where I would be appreciated and helpful."

The hint of a smile turned up the corner of his lips. "So what changed?"

"I don't know," she admitted. "I fought caring for

you. I truly did. The whole situation with Henry and his earache . . . well, I should've known better, given that you don't care for medicine and all. I should've let—"

"What did you just say?" His eyes narrowed. "About medicine?"

Her eyes widened. "Well, everyone knows you didn't want Katie Ruth to get treated for her—"

He held up his hand, stopping her in midsentence. "Hold on there, Myrna. Wherever did you get that idea?"

Stunned, she responded with an incoherent stammer of sounds.

He released her wrist and turned his back to her as he walked the length of the porch. His boots made loud clunking noises on the floorboards, and she could tell that he was tugging at his beard. Finally, he turned around and faced her. "Mayhaps it's time for us to take that walk, or—better yet—a buggy ride. We've a lot to talk about, Myrna. You see, you've got things backward. It wasn't that I didn't want Katie Ruth to be treated; it was that *she* didn't want it."

For the first ten minutes, they sat in silence as the horse trotted along the road, pulling Ezekiel's buggy behind it.

Myrna couldn't speak to the reasons behind his silence, but she certainly knew the reason for her own: shock. If what Ezekiel had said was true, there was a lot of explaining to be done. The only problem was that Myrna wasn't certain *who* needed to do the explaining in the first place.

Up ahead was a small park. Ezekiel guided the horse into the parking lot and quickly tied it to the hitching post near the far end of the gravel lot. Then he walked around to help Myrna get down. Only, when her feet hit the ground, he did not loosen his hold upon her hand. Instead, he held it.

"Let's walk over to that picnic table, *ja*?" He didn't wait for an answer as he began walking toward it. Myrna's feet followed him practically without her even thinking about it.

Only after she was seated did Ezekiel begin to pace along a small patch of grass, his head dipped down as if he was deep in thought.

"Myrna, I'm not the type of person who would speak poorly about anyone, especially Katie Ruth. After all, I really couldn't blame her." He glanced at her as if to make certain that she was paying attention. He needn't have bothered, because Myrna was hanging on his every word.

In the five weeks she'd been working for him, Ezekiel had never talked about Katie Ruth. That realization reinforced the seriousness of their discussion, and she remained riveted on Ezekiel and what he was about to say.

"You once asked me why her family never visited the *kinner*." He swallowed, his eyes drifting to look at the sky as if deep in thought, or perhaps memory. "We had disagreements about Katie Ruth's treatment, you see."

He took a deep breath and exhaled. For a moment, he remained silent. She could tell that discussing Katie Ruth was difficult for him, and she would give him as much time as he needed to say what was on his mind.

"When I met her, I didn't know her family. Her family's *haus* was in a neighboring church district at the time."

Myrna nodded. She knew that church districts often redrew the lines as communities expanded. It wasn't uncommon for families to be reassigned to another district.

"It wasn't until after I asked her to marry me that I learned her father had been raised in a Swartzentruber family." He glanced at her, clearly waiting for her reaction.

Try as she might, Myrna couldn't help but catch her breath. Swartzentruber Amish? They were renowned for being the most conservative of the different Amish communities. They followed the commandment of avoiding pride so strictly that, in some cases, they didn't mow their yards, remove their garbage, or even clean their houses for fear of being considered prideful.

She'd never met a Swartzentruber family, but she had known there were small pockets of them living in LaGrange County.

"Was she raised the same way?" Myrna asked, unable to mask her genuine curiosity.

He shook his head. "*Nee*, she was not. But her *daed* was very strict." He exhaled. "You just can't shake that type of upbringing, I reckon."

Myrna could only imagine.

"Katie Ruth didn't appear to be so conservative, but after we married, I noticed little things. The *haus* wasn't very clean. The garden was poorly maintained." He rubbed his face with his hands. "I didn't say anything, Myrna. She was my *fraa*, after all. And she was right *gut* with the little ones. When she began to show signs of not being well, we thought it was because of the *boppli*. It wasn't until her first trimester ended that we found out about the cancer."

"Breast cancer?"

He nodded. "*Ja*, breast cancer. But it had spread."

"That must've been frightening."

"For me? *Ja*, it was." Something shifted in his eyes, a darkness that spread as he spoke. "But it was God's will, Myrna. That's what her *daed* said. And Katie Ruth listened to him. Even though I begged her and pleaded with her, she would not relent. She said that if God wanted to take her, who was she to question Him." He laughed, but it was a bitter laugh. "That's when I realized that no amount of arguing would get through to her. I spoke with her family, but they supported her decision. In fact, her *daed* accused me of being prideful and threatened to have me shunned."

Myrna gasped. "Shunned for wanting your *fraa* to heal?" That made no sense to Myrna, but then again, she knew that a lot of things about Swartzentruber Amish didn't make sense. "And you have to see him every other Sunday at worship? Listen to him preach?"

He grunted.

"Oh help," she muttered. She wasn't certain how he could sit there, listening to this man preach to the congregation. But church leadership was divinely appointed, even if not all of the members favored the man leading.

"No one knew, you see," he continued. "They all presumed that I was the one who didn't want her getting treatment. And I knew that I couldn't defend myself, Myrna, or I would risk being accused of gossiping. Besides, it's not my way to accuse others. They have to answer to a much higher authority, *ja*?"

She let all of this sink in, realizing that everything people had thought about Ezekiel was backward. If she'd had any doubts before, she had none now.

But she did have some questions.

"If all of this is true—and I don't doubt you, Ezekiel— why did you get upset when I used that ear candle on Henry?"

He gave her a sideways glance. "Oh, Myrna, if you'd only talked to me, I'd have taken him to a doctor. When I left the farm that afternoon, after our words, I went to town and spoke to my doctor. He gave me amoxicillin for the *buwe*."

Once again, his confession caught her off guard. "Why didn't you tell me?"

He gave a little laugh. "When I saw that ear candle—silly thing, that!—I thought that *you* were against medicine, like Katie Ruth and her family." He shrugged. "I gave Henry the medicine before you arrived in the mornings and after you left in the evenings."

Her eyes widened.

As if sensing her astonishment at his confession, he quickly explained, "I didn't want to offend you."

Suddenly, she understood what had happened with Katie. Just as she hadn't wanted to upset Ezekiel by suggesting the doctor should see her, Ezekiel had feared the same reaction from her. And yet, when he became concerned, he had done the one thing that he knew might upset her, just as she had called her mother.

"But they are your children," she said in a matter-of-fact voice. "Why would it matter if I was offended?"

"Because I had fallen in love with you."

She caught her breath.

"*Ja*, Myrna. Mayhaps from the very first day you showed up here, I knew that you were special. But I hadn't wanted to marry again, just as I told you at your *daed*'s store that Saturday. I never wanted to go through again what Katie Ruth and her family put me through. I never wanted to realize that someone I loved was a complete stranger to me. But then you happened."

You happened. Those two words struck her heart, and she caught her breath. It wasn't that she hadn't suspected he cared for her, but hearing the words made her heart flutter.

"What are you saying, Ezekiel?"

He took a few steps toward her and stopped just inches from where she sat. He crouched down and took her hands in his. "Myrna, I'm telling you that I want a second chance at happiness. That I feel ready to commit to another woman. But not just any woman. You see, I want to have more than just a second *fraa*. I want *you*."

She could hardly believe what she'd heard. "Are you asking me . . . ?"

"To marry me, *ja*, Myrna Bontrager." He squeezed her hands and gazed upward, into her face. "I want us to marry, Myrna, and for you to be my *fraa* and my friend. My best friend, Myrna. And mother to my children. They love you so much."

And there it was. The children loved her. But Myrna needed to make certain that, despite his protest otherwise, she was not just a replacement wife.

"And you, Ezekiel?" she asked. "What about you?"

He paused, his eyes searching her face. She held her breath as she waited.

"Well," he started in a measured tone, "if you remembered to call me Zeke, I'd love you even more than I already do."

It took her a second to understand what he'd said, and she found herself laughing.

"So, Myrna, will you? Will you marry me?"

She wrapped her arms around his neck, laughing and crying at the same time. "*Ja*, Zeke, I will happily marry you!"

Epilogue

Myrna sat on the porch of Ezekiel's house and stared across the field at the cows as they meandered through the pasture, their heads dipped down as they grazed. Behind them to the west, the sun began to sink into the sky, casting a soft glow on their flanks.

"Myrna?"

She turned at the sound of David's voice.

"I mean, Maem," he said shyly as he pushed open the screen door and joined her on the porch. "That sounds funny," he said as he sat next to her on the bench.

She laughed. "I agree." Leaning over, she nudged his arm. "But I like hearing it anyway. We'll get used to it, don't you think?"

He nodded.

It had been two days since the wedding. Being that it was a spring wedding—and Ezekiel's second marriage—it had been smaller than usual. But Myrna hadn't minded. In fact, she felt that the intimacy of the service and celebration had been better than a large, all-day gathering with four hundred people coming and going.

Everything had been perfect. From the worship service given by Bishop Brenneman to the meal prepared by the women in her church district, Myrna wouldn't have changed one thing about her wedding day.

Still, she found it hard to reconcile the fact that she was no longer Myrna Bontrager but Myrna Riehl. That her home was Ezekiel's home. And that his children were now her children.

That, too, would take some getting used to.

"I'm glad you're our new *maem*," David said.

"Because of the cookies?"

"Well, I like those, *ja*." He gave her a sheepish grin. "But I like having a *maem* around to take care of me."

She put her arm around his shoulders and hugged him. All of the children had been thrilled when Ezekiel and Myrna told them the news just three weeks ago. Their excitement made the transition much easier for her, and for that she was thankful.

"Maem," David said, interrupting her thoughts. "Remember how you told me about your *maem* and her cookie club?"

Myrna nodded. "*Ja*, I do."

"Do you think we could start our own club and make cookies for worship Sundays? So that everyone could enjoy them?"

Her heart swelled at his question. David was learning to be like his father, generous to others. "I think that's a *wunderbarr* idea, David."

"What's this?"

Both David and Myrna looked up, surprised to see Ezekiel leaning against the side of the house, watching them.

Myrna flushed and pressed her lips together, a surge of energy coursing through her veins, and she had to look away. She heard him chuckle and knew that he must've caught her. He walked to the steps and joined them on the porch.

"Go on inside, David," Ezekiel said, his voice soft but stern. "It's time to be getting to bed, *ja*? We've worship service tomorrow."

Obediently, David did as he was told, sliding off the bench, which left an opening for Ezekiel to occupy next to Myrna.

Once the boy disappeared, Ezekiel reached out and took Myrna's hand in his. He lifted it to his lips and pressed a soft kiss on her knuckles.

"How is Myrna this evening?" he asked.

"Myrna is fine," she teased back. "Especially now that you are here, Zeke."

"Hmm." His leg brushed against hers, and Myrna leaned against him.

"What did you do today? I didn't ask earlier," he said in an apologetic way.

"Oh!" Myrna sat up straight and turned enough so that she faced him. "I started organizing that basement."

He laughed.

"It's a mess, you know! Why, the shelves haven't been dusted in years, I believe!"

"I believe so, too."

"And I organized those boxes down there. Some of them need to be thrown out, I hate to say. But I have everything spick-and-span, ready for all of the wonderful food I'll can this August." She beamed. "And Daniel and Henry helped me while David watched little Katie!"

"Did they, now?"

"It was truly a family effort."

Ezekiel chuckled. "It's right *gut* to teach them to be organized."

Those words were music to her ears. She sat back again,

resuming her position next to him, her arm pressed against his. "You like that, *ja*? When I organize things?"

He nodded. "I do, indeed, Myrna. It makes you happy, and that's all I want. For you to be happy." He paused as he entwined his fingers through hers. "A happy *muder* makes for a happy *haus*." Once again, he lifted her hand and kissed her skin. "And a happy *fraa* makes for a happy husband."

She smiled and leaned her head against his shoulder. "I *am* happy."

"*Gut*." His fingers brushed her skin.

"And you?" She lowered her voice. "Are *you* happy?"

She felt him take a long, deep breath. "Oh, Myrna, I'm happier than I've ever been in my life."

That was exactly how she felt. But she was too shy to admit it.

He gave her hand a gentle squeeze as he looked across the field, his eyes following the cows as they wandered. "It's a beautiful evening, don't you think?"

"I do."

"I like sitting here next to you."

She smiled, even though he couldn't see it. "Me, too. Sitting here with you."

She felt him relax beside her. "It just feels so right, Myrna. As if this is what was meant to be."

Oh, how she understood that feeling. She felt exactly the same way.

"Now, let's see about putting those little ones to bed, shall we?" He stood up, and, reluctantly, she followed. "I know they much prefer having their new *maem* do it, but I think I'll help you tonight."

"Nothing would please me more," she said as he opened the screen door for her to pass through the opening. As she did, he reached for her arm, took hold of it, and gently stopped her. Turning, she peered up at him, wondering what was wrong.

But nothing was wrong.

He reached out his hand and brushed his fingers along her cheek. "Hmm." Slowly, he lowered his head until his lips caressed hers in a soft, loving kiss. "I love you, Myrna Riehl," he whispered as he pulled back.

Behind him, the sun dipped farther beneath the horizon, the sky aflame with reds and oranges. In the distance, the last of the cows lingered on top of the hill, still grazing as they slowly wandered beyond the crest as if melting into the sunset.

The day might be over, but for Myrna, it seemed to be just beginning. "And I love you, Ezekiel Riehl," she replied.

Recipes

Why not gather your friends
and start your own cookie club?
To help you get started,
here are some of the recipes mentioned in

The Amish Cookie Club.

EDNA'S CINNAMON ROLLS

1 teaspoon white sugar
1 package active dry yeast
½ cup warm water
½ cup milk
¼ cup white sugar
1¼ cup butter
pinch of salt
2 eggs, beaten
4 cups all-purpose flour
vegetable or corn oil
1½ cups brown sugar
1 tablespoon ground cinnamon
OPTIONAL: 1 cup chopped pecans, divided

Dissolve 1 teaspoon sugar and yeast in warm water and set aside for ten minutes.

Warm the milk in a small saucepan until it bubbles, then remove from heat.

Mix in ¼ cup sugar, ¼ cup butter, and a pinch of salt; stir until melted. Let cool until lukewarm.

In a large bowl, stir together the yeast and milk mixtures, eggs, and 1½ cups flour. Add the remaining flour, a little bit at a time and mixing well before adding more.

Turn out the dough onto a lightly floured surface and knead until smooth and elastic.

Set the dough in a lightly oiled bowl and turn to coat with oil. Cover with a damp cloth and place in a warm spot, letting it rise until doubled in size.

Melt ¾ cup butter over medium heat and add ¾ cup brown sugar, whisking until smooth. Pour the sugar mixture into greased baking pan and set aside.

Combine remaining brown sugar, ½ cup pecans, and cinnamon and set aside.

Melt remaining butter and set aside.

Turn dough out onto a lightly floured surface, roll into a 20 x 14 inch rectangle.

Brush with half of the melted butter and then sprinkle the top with the brown sugar mixture.

Starting at long side, tightly roll up, pinching seam to seal.

Brush with remaining 2 tablespoons butter.

With serrated knife, cut into 12 to 14 pieces and carefully set them, cut side down, in the baking pan. Set aside, covered, and let rise for 1 hour or until doubled in volume.

Bake in preheated oven at 375 degrees for 25 to 30 minutes.

Let cool in pan for 4 to 5 minutes before inverting them onto a serving platter.

Best served warm.

MYRNA'S SUGAR COOKIES

2¾ cups all-purpose flour
1 teaspoon baking soda
½ teaspoon baking powder
1½ cups white sugar
1 cup butter, room temperature
1 large egg
1 teaspoon vanilla extract

Mix together the flour, baking soda, and baking powder and set the mixture aside.

Cream the sugar and butter together until smooth.

Beat in egg and vanilla.

Mix in the dry ingredients.

Roll teaspoonfuls of dough into small one-inch round balls.

Spread out the dough balls onto ungreased cookie sheets.

Bake 10 minutes in a preheated oven at 375 degrees.

Let stand on cookie sheet for a few minutes before removing them to cool on wire racks.

VERNA'S CHOCOLATE CHIP COOKIES

2 cups all-purpose flour
1 teaspoon baking soda
¼ teaspoon salt

½ cup butter
½ cup shortening
½ cup white sugar
¾ cup packed brown sugar
1 teaspoon vanilla extract
1 egg
1½ cups semisweet chocolate chips

Preheat oven to 350 degrees F (175 degrees C).

Combine flour, baking soda, and salt and set aside.

Combine softened butter with shortening, sugar, brown sugar, and vanilla and beat until creamy.

Beat in the egg.

Slowly add the flour mixture and mix well.

Stir in chocolate chips.

In a preheated oven at 350 degrees, bake on ungreased cookie sheet for 8 to 10 minutes.

VERNA'S EASY BREAD RECIPE

2 cups warm water
⅔ cup white sugar
1 package of active dry yeast
1½ teaspoons salt
¼ cup vegetable oil
6 cups flour
vegetable or corn oil

Dissolve the sugar in warm water and then stir in yeast. Set aside until creamy.

Add the salt and oil into the yeast. Mix well.

Slowly add the flour one cup at a time, mixing well.

Knead dough on a lightly floured surface until smooth.

Place in a well-oiled bowl, and turn dough to coat.

Cover with a damp cloth and set in a warm place, allowing it to rise until doubled in size.

Punch down the dough and then knead again for a few minutes.

Divide the dough into two equal amounts and shape into loaves. Place each one into oiled 9 x 5 inch loaf pans.

Set aside and allow it to rise until dough has risen above the pan.

Bake in preheated oven at 350 degrees for 30 minutes.

Want to read more about the Cookie Club?
Watch for
AN AMISH COOKIE CLUB CHRISTMAS,
available this holiday season!

Sugar and spice make love extra nice . . .

**Baking cookies every other Friday for their respective
church districts gives Edna Esh and three of her
closest friends a chance to give to the Plain
community and strengthen their bond with one
another. Now, with the blessings of Christmas in the
air, they may even whip up a recipe for love . . .**

With the holidays around the corner,
Edna is busier than ever, juggling her baking with her
business serving meals to *Englische* tourists.
Thank goodness for Mary Ropp's help—
until she breaks her leg. Mary's daughter, Bethany, is
available to fill in, but Edna isn't so certain. She knows
Bethany is so painfully shy that she's never even courted,
never mind interacting with *Englische* tourists!
How will she be able to interact with her customers?
But the remedy may be closer than they think . . .

When Bethany gets into a scrape with her bicycle,
a personable, talkative young man comes to her rescue,
and even accompanies her home. And he's none other
than John Esh—Edna's oldest son. When he stops by
again the next day, Mary gets an idea. Soon, with the
encouragement of the Cookie Club, Bethany is indeed
helping Edna, and spending more time around the
Esh household—and John. As Bethany slowly comes
out of her shell, it seems she and John have much in
common—maybe enough to inspire a winter wedding—
and the club's sweetest creation yet . . .

Connect with Us

Visit us online at
KensingtonBooks.com
to read more from your favorite authors, see books
by series, view reading group guides, and more.

Join us on social media

for sneak peeks, chances to win books and prize packs,
and to share your thoughts with other readers.

facebook.com/kensingtonpublishing
twitter.com/kensingtonbooks

Tell us what you think!

To share your thoughts, submit a review,
or sign up for our eNewsletters, please visit:
KensingtonBooks.com/TellUs.